THOMPSON ROAD

By Scott Wyatt

Beyond the Sand Creek Bridge

Dimension M

Thompson Road

THOMPSON ROAD

SCOTT WYATT

Booktrope Editions
Seattle, WA 2015

Cover Design by Laura Hidalgo
Edited by Vicki Sly

PRINT ISBN 978-1-62015-955-2
EPUB ISBN 978-1-62015-986-6
Library of Congress Control Number: 2015913730

For

Aaron W., Todd, Aaron D., and Teija

CHAPTER ONE

1937

OUTSIDE YELM, WASHINGTON

BRIGHT FLAMES CONVULSED behind the curtain of trees. Raleigh Starr held his breath. He pictured the Garrison farmhouse ablaze, its white clapboard sides streaked with smoke.

They made the clearing. The Model A pickup flew past rows of bushy, juvenile filberts. "Look," said Raleigh's father, pointing.

An outbuilding was on fire; it wasn't the house. Raleigh exhaled. A man—tall, big-bellied—staggered free of the barn leading a panicked, sidling horse as two other men sprinted toward the barn. Raleigh glanced at his father. Was the barn on fire, too?

* * *

Raleigh ran in step with his father across a stubble field toward the crackling flames and the shouts of men. Simon Garrison, the farm's owner, emerged from the barn leading a black yearling toward a secondary corral. Another neighbor grabbed the halter and Garrison rushed back into the barn. The outbuilding was a car length or two from the side of the barn. Two buckets in the scorched grass showed where efforts to douse the flames had been abandoned.

From inside the barn came shouts.

"Take the mare!"

"We've got smoke! Why not let them all go?"

"Take the mare, Cliff! Get her out! We've got time."

Raleigh and his father jumped clear of a small irrigation ditch onto the bare dirt of the barnyard. Raleigh felt his father's hand on his arm. "Wait here!"

"But—" The long fingers squeezed his forearm.

"Do what I tell you!"

His father raced into the barn. "George!" someone shouted. "Over here! Take the sorrel."

Mr. Garrison materialized out of the shadows, this time half-running a gray horse. Garrison's ashen face shone with perspiration.

Raleigh stepped forward to help. He was about to call out when Mr. Garrison waved a thick hand. "Out of the way, dammit!" Raleigh's breath caught and blood rushed to his face.

A high-pitched scream pierced the air. A girl of ten or eleven scrambled down the steps of the house's front porch. She ran toward Raleigh, arms flailing. She cried out, but it was impossible to understand her over the roar of the flames, the pounding and whickering of the horses in the stalls, and the shouts of men. What did she want?

His father's voice thundered inside the barn. "Why don't we let 'em go?"

"Garrison wants 'em taken one at a time, George," came a reply.

"You gotta...help me," the girl said.

Raleigh knew every kid on Thompson Road, but he'd never seen this girl before. "What do you mean?"

A collapsing rafter inside the toolshed cracked and thudded to the ground. Raleigh's father ran from the barn with a bay on a rope lead.

"Here, Raleigh. Take it."

Raleigh dashed to the horse. His father ducked back into the barn beneath ribbons of white smoke.

Forgetting the girl, Raleigh trotted the animal to the secondary corral. It was less than he wanted to do, running horses without going inside the barn, without taking a risk. At almost fourteen, wasn't he old enough to do what the others were doing?

A roan stallion checked at the barn doors. It neighed loudly, kicking up dust while another of the Garrisons' neighbors, Mr. Stedden, tripped forward at the end of a long lead. The animal forced its head around, dipped its muzzle and snapped its hind legs high in the air. "Easy, boy," said Raleigh, stepping tentatively in front of the animal and holding his arms out. "Eas-sy."

Mr. Stedden regained his balance. Red-faced and smelling of whiskey, he shouted, "Get out of here, kid!"

Raleigh stepped out of the way, stunned by a second reproach.

"The barn's caught!" someone shouted from inside.

"I see it! Simon! The barn's caught. Over there!"

"All right. Get them all out. We've only got a minute!"

Raleigh gaped at the men, ghostlike figures crisscrossing the smoky gloom. A hand touched his arm—a light touch, but as urgent as the men's shouts.

It was the girl. Her face was pale save for a few freckles and her blue eyes shone with pooled tears. She spoke without looking up from his chest.

"My cat...my kittens..." She seemed to struggle to speak and swallow at the same time. Her eyes shot up to his chin, but no higher. A tear slid down her cheek. Her face darkened and she tightened trembling lips. "Candy...my cat...is in there." She pointed with her chin.

"In the barn, you mean?" asked Raleigh. "You have a cat in the barn?"

The girl nodded. "A box...kittens."

Raleigh narrowed his eyes. *Why are you talking that way?*

He looked away and rubbed a hand through his hair. "Wait here," his father had said. That's what he aimed to do.

But something nagged at him, made him want to look at the girl. "Look, I'd like to, but my dad told me—"

Her sideways glance toward the barn stopped him. What did that look mean? "If you won't go in there, I will?" Frowning, he forced a deep breath.

I'll be darned if I'll go in there for a couple of cats.

A lone mule trotted out of the burning barn. *Focus on other things: that's the answer. No, don't look back at her! Don't—*

"Where are they?" he heard himself demand. He swiped the back of his hand over his mouth nervously.

"The loft," she answered. "In the loft."

A second column of smoke, this one much whiter and cloud-like, inward-turning, rose from the side of the barn. Small, scarcely visible tongues of flame explored the air above the eaves.

Am I really doing this?

"Which side?" If it was on the far side, it was already too late. But the side she pointed to was the east side, nearer the road.

Low, gruff shouts from inside the barn—"Yee-ah!" "Get on, there!" "Git!"—preceded a turbulent drumming. The last of the horses trotted out and veered off in three directions, tails high. The men emerged, each carrying a harness. Raleigh's father angled past the burning toolshed and jogged into the woods after a young colt. Raleigh closed his eyes for a moment, then turned to face the girl.

"Is there another door?"

She nodded.

"Come on," he said. He heard the girl running through the grass behind him. "Nothing burns quite like a barn," he remembered his grandmother telling him once..

Nothing burns quite like a barn.

CHAPTER TWO

THE BARN'S DILAPIDATED BACK DOOR was scratched white by canes of fall-spoiled blackberry. "Wait here," shouted Raleigh. The door thudded against a barrel. He set his shoulder and pushed. The obstacle gave way. Inside: a tack room, two dark saddles hanging on the wall, a long, workbench—nails and screws in a neat line of bright red Golden West Coffee tins—lit by four small windows thick with dust and cobwebs. As he stepped toward the tack room door, his nostrils filled with the pungent odor of hay, leather and dust.

Roaring flames had spread across the north side of the barn and ghostly spheres of black smoke summersaulted into the cavernous apex. Beyond the ladder to the loft, a charred beam fell from the ceiling and disappeared into one of the stalls. Raleigh's heart flailed. Stepping back to the outer door, he shouted. "You're sure they're in there?"

The girl pointed. "Up there."

Raleigh hesitated. He didn't want to say it, but saying it was easier, and safer, than venturing up that ladder. "The smoke will have killed them."

The girl's hands flew to the sides of her head, and she opened her mouth wide, as if trying to breathe. Or scream. But out came an unexpected sound. Not a scream, but a song-like "Ahhhhhhhhhhh! Ahhhhhhhhhhh!" It so unnerved Raleigh that he wanted only to end it.

"Don't do that. I'll go—okay?"

She didn't seem to hear him over her own voice or the roar of the fire. Raleigh pulled a handkerchief from his back pocket, covered his nose and mouth, and tied it behind his head. He took a deep breath and ran toward the loft ladder. He climbed as fast as he could. His eyes burned, and halfway up, blinking desperately, he could no longer force them open. He hesitated, pushed back against a creeping panic. *There's time. Just get up there, grab the cats, and get back.*

He pulled himself up. Three more rungs. Two. At last, the edge. He scrambled onto his knees. Eyes closed, he raised an arm to shield his face from the intense heat. He patted the straw-covered floor. *Where's the box? I don't feel anything.*

A spasm of fear sent him reaching back for the ladder and its side rails. His hand found nothing.

He turned and waved both hands frantically. He twisted side to side, patting the floor.

Where is it? I've got to find it!

His right foot struck something. He reached over. One of the rails. His pulse thudded in his ears. He had his bearings again.

With his foot hooked on the rail, he extended his hand into a hill of straw and swung his arm to the right to feel for the edge of the loft. There was the edge all right, but no box of cats.

A thunderous cracking erupted above his head. He drew back instinctively. With a loud *whoosh,* a burning timber crashed close to him sending sparks against his face and arms.

Time to go.

He swung onto the ladder. *No cats today.* The sturdiness of the rungs reassured him. He climbed down two steps, then stopped, arrested by the thought of the strange girl. Of the look she'd given him.

To the left! Was it her voice he heard, or his own? *Left of the ladder. What if—?*

She'd pinned every hope on him. He had to be able to tell her he'd looked everywhere. Groaning softly to himself, he scrambled back up and lunged to the left.

There it was! The edge of a wooden box under his fingers. The softness of kittens. Tiny bodies moved against his skin.

Hardly believing his luck, he dragged the box toward him, cradled it beneath his arm, and started down as fast as he could go. The complaint of collapsing timbers erupted in his ears again. The loft was giving way, and with it, the ladder. Raleigh managed one more step, and then there was no time—all he could do was jump.

He landed awkwardly with the box under his arm. Which way was the door? He forced his eyes open for a split second. Smoke covered the ground. Pitch dark now.

The snapping and moaning of burning timbers surrounded him. He reached for a wall, a post—anything. The need to breathe tore at his insides. He was out of time. Five seconds ago. *Choose a direction.*

He tripped twice but managed to make the wooden floor of the tack room. At last, through watery lashes, a filmy rectangle of light: the door. He fell into the arms of the blackberry vines, cutting his face and hands. But he was out. He rolled on his back, jerked down the handkerchief, coughed, gulped a deep breath of air.

Never had blackberry prickles crisscrossing his back felt so good. The kittens stirred and mewled from their box. He blinked his eyes open. His right hand was gashed, blood pouring down his arm. He must have hit a nail while reaching out and running for the door. It didn't hurt—not yet, anyway—but it was deep.

As he examined the wound, his throat and eyes stinging, he felt the wooden box being lifted clear of his left arm. The girl ran a few steps carrying the box in front of her. She stopped and turned. It was the first time she had looked into his eyes. She didn't speak. His mind reeled from lack of oxygen. What did she want? Why was she staring?

"Mama cat," she said in a plaintive tone.

He understood: The box held kittens. There was no mama cat. She'd expected a mama cat. "I don't know," Raleigh said between coughs, exhausted. "I don't know."

The girl stood a moment longer, spun, and ran toward the house.

* * *

"Time out! Time out!"

Coach Hancock paced the sideline like a caged lion. Staring at the ill-kept gridiron, making eye contact with no one, tearing off his black and red Yelm High baseball cap, and throwing his arms in the air, he screamed, "Are you kidding me?" His voice broke into a high soprano.

The reserve players on the freshman football team, thick with shoulder, thigh, and knee pads, moved back from the sideline to get out of the line of fire. Coach Hancock rolled a fist on each hip. "You call that a block, Lamont? You let that man waltz right by you! And Johansson, if you're going to get tackled behind the line of scrimmage, throw the damn ball out of bounds like I taught you."

Stanley Johansson, second-string quarterback, trotted off the field, eyes downcast. His face, smeared with dirt, blood, and sweat, was not unlike those of several of the linemen who were used to close combat. A knot above his left eye showed angry blue and yellowish streaks. The players formed a circle. The reserves joined them on the field.

"Kessler was wide open, Johansson," the coach bellowed, storming into the center of the circle. "Didn't you see him over here? And Smith, you..."

Raleigh hadn't dressed for the Orting game. He joined the others and stood at the outermost ring of players, looking in on a company of shell-shocked faces. Boys a year older—some fifty pounds heavier—on the verge of tears. He felt a new distance between himself and them. Maybe it was natural, a way to make the impending loss theirs, not his.

I could have scored. Kessler was open. I could have hit him with my eyes closed.

Raleigh stepped to the side to get a better look at Johansson, the boy taking the brunt of the tirade. He felt a strange mixture of emotions. On one hand, he was sorry for Johansson. The lanky freshman hadn't taken a snap in a game all season, and with an undefeated season on the line and his parents and half the town looking on, he had to perform—and, against Orting, perform well. On the other hand, Johansson's poor play was proof that Raleigh was indispensable, that he was the team's best offensive player. And an eighth grader, to boot.

They need me. With me out there, we would have our undefeated season.

"I hope it was worth it."

Raleigh turned to the boy next to him, a reserve lineman. His fleshy face was pinched into his leather helmet, giving his eyes a comical turn. "What's that, Jim?" Raleigh asked.

"I hope it was worth it, is all—whatever you did to your hand yesterday."

* * *

Lying on his bed, staring up at the ceiling, Raleigh wanted to escape the memory of that afternoon's football game. He rolled on his side and stared at the framed photograph of his mother on the nightstand. She smiled back from the deck of a sailboat on Puget Sound, with

Mount Rainier in the background. He wished he could talk to her. He wished he could explain about the kittens and all. He closed his eyes.

"You'd do the same," his father had shouted over the squeal of the leaf springs and the rumble of the Model A's engine. The words were directed at Mr. Garrison, who stood in his field with his hat off, wiping his forehead with a handkerchief. The truck lurched forward. Raleigh's father punched through the progression of gears, and "you'd do the same" seemed to claim a semi-permanent place in the air eddying past his father's open window. But there was something else. When Raleigh glanced at his father, waiting for the reprimand, or for questions about the blood streaking down Raleigh's arm, Raleigh had seen it: the posture of bereavement, stooped shoulders, loose elbows, a faraway look, as though Raleigh's deceased mother—Elise Starr, dead these two years—had appeared to her husband and had whispered into his ear "You're responsible for him, George. He's our only son."

Raleigh had never gotten used to the feeling that overtook him when he sensed that his father, in words or in the act of shaping silence, spoke for two. It didn't happen often, but when it did, it took something from his father, and he felt something missing within himself, too. As though his mother, who had succumbed to cancer, had taken part of them with her without permission; that they grieved not altogether for her, but for something lost within themselves, as well.

Raleigh rolled over on the bed onto his other side, being careful not to compress his injured hand. He remembered his mother's face melting into tears three years earlier, in the fall of 1934, when his father had come home from the lumber mill for the last time. He'd set his lunch pail down on the dining room table and stood in filthy jeans and a thick red and black plaid shirt covered in fine sawdust, biting his lip. She'd cried, "Oh, George! What are we going to do?" Raleigh, reading *Robinson Crusoe* at the table, had raised his head to see his mother looking around the dining room helplessly. "How are we going to get by?"

* * *

"Raleigh, come on down here."

Raleigh rolled off his bed and went to the door, cradling his throbbing hand. "What is it, Dad?"

"Just come down. Make sure you're dressed."

Make sure I'm dressed?

He knit his brow. Was someone here? He hadn't heard the door open.

He made his way back to the bed and used his good left hand to slip on his brown leather shoes without tying them. He picked up the green cotton shirt he'd worn to school, and to the football game afterwards, and shook it on, buttoning it with difficulty. He was tucking it in as he passed his sister's open door.

"You're in for it," sixteen-year-old Lauren said lightheartedly.

He retreated a step and leaned into her room. "Who is it, do you know?"

His sister sat at her desk with her bare forearms bathed in the glow of a table lamp. She brushed back a curtain of long dark hair and looked up from her secretarial studies correspondence course book. "I have no idea." She seemed pleased that her off-hand comment might have been taken seriously, but her amused expression changed the moment she saw his bandaged hand. "How is it, by the way?"

He held it up. "I'll be all right."

"Keep it dry. We'll change the dressing in the morning."

Raleigh frowned and nodded. Since their mother's death, Lauren had quit school and added cook, nurse, confessor, and homemaker to her repertoire.

Raleigh paused at the top of the stairs. Hushed voices came from the parlor, a man's and a woman's—middle-aged by the sound of it—but neither seemed familiar. His father's voice said, "You didn't have to do that. That's kind of you."

"Not at all," said the woman.

Raleigh jumped off the last step, traversed the hall, and rounded the corner into the parlor. He was met by four sets of eyes: his father's, Mr. Garrison's, Mrs. Garrison's, and the brown-haired girl's—the one who had sent him into the burning barn. His father held a lattice crust apple pie wrapped in a blue-and-white checkered dish towel.

"Raleigh, you know Mrs. Garrison," George said.

"Sure."

"And Mr. Garrison."

The boy stepped toward the large, silver-haired man and extended his injured hand. "Oh, sorry," he said, withdrawing his right hand and turning his left over to grasp the visitor's hand. "Yes, sir."

"Son," Mr. Garrison said.

Raleigh had lived on Thompson Road his whole life, had passed the Garrisons' farm hundreds of times. He didn't know either of them well, the old man or his wife—had no reason to get to know them, although his father had traded vegetables and eggs with Mr. Garrison for blackcaps and filberts, and Raleigh had seen them from time to time at Wolf's grocery store or Patterson's pharmacy in Yelm. Their own farm was six miles farther past the Garrison place, so it was not unusual to see the Garrisons' dusty green Pontiac leading a slanting dust cloud, coming or going. But Raleigh knew the Garrison farmhouse well enough, and the outbuildings and the lay of the land, the way you'd know the features of a landscape hanging above your grandmother's couch.

Raleigh wondered if Mr. Garrison remembered shooing him away when he'd offered to help with the horses. A hint of smoke still clung to the man's clothing.

Mrs. Garrison cleared her throat. "This is Mona," she said, tilting her head in the girl's direction.

Unused to being introduced to children, Raleigh wasn't sure how to respond. He glanced at his father. Three and a half hours earlier, the man had wasted no time excoriating Raleigh after picking him up from the football game: "It was a damn fool thing you did yesterday. Some girl you don't know asks you to go into a burning building to chase after a couple of cats, and you *do* it? You hurt your hand for no good reason, and then you let the team down today. It makes me wonder what you have between your ears."

Raleigh had tried to explain. "I thought she was going to—"

"I don't want to hear it, son. There's no reason for putting yourself in that kind of danger. When we get home, you get yourself upstairs. You just plan on staying put until morning."

But now Raleigh was in the parlor. The longcase clock ticked loudly behind him. Seeking to avoid eye contact with Mr. Garrison, he studied the girl. She kept her head bent and her eyes downcast, with no reaction to the sound of her name. Her hands were buried in the pockets of an ill-fitting orange winter coat. A handful of freckles rode the crests of her high cheekbones, and these, with the ridge of her petite nose and strands of unruly hair, as though she were fresh from sleep, were the only features visible to Raleigh.

"Mona," said Mrs. Garrison, "please say hello to Raleigh. This is the boy whose life you endangered yesterday." The chubby-faced woman with wavy black hair touched her frameless glasses. "Raise your head, child." With a wintry smile, Mrs. Garrison turned to George. "She has something she wants to say to you and your boy."

"I see," said George gently. "Well, that's all right."

"No, it most certainly isn't," said Mrs. Garrison. She looked down on Mona. "Well?"

The girl showed no sign of hearing any of it.

"Hello," said Raleigh. When the girl didn't respond, he added, "I'm Raleigh."

On top of ten seconds of silence, Mrs. Garrison added, "Mona is Simon's niece from Portland. She's feebleminded, aren't you, dear? We're not sure what caused it, probably a birth defect of some kind. Her mother's been institutionalized, and—well, with no kids of our own, we told them we'd take her. She's been with us about a month."

Raleigh felt a stab of pity. The girl stood impassively, as though she were used to being referred to in the third person. Or being powerless to do anything about it.

"Go ahead, Mona," said Mrs. Garrison. "We practiced this. Say it."

Mona wetted and rolled her lips, but it seemed to have nothing to do with the prompting.

"I'll tell you what," said George. "Let me go put this pie in the kitchen." He disappeared and returned a few seconds later. Mrs. Garrison had moved a step closer to the girl and put a guiding hand on her shoulder. "It's not worth the fuss, Grace," George said, forcing a smile. "No need to apologize—or, better yet, apology accepted. How's that? I suspect she's doing the best she can any—"

Mona uttered something unintelligible. Raleigh thought he heard the word "kitten."

"What's that, Mona?" said Mr. Garrison. "Speak up."

"Going…to name…a kitten," she managed, blinking but not looking up.

"You're going to—good grief, girl," said Mrs. Garrison. She removed her hand from Mona's shoulder. "That's not what we practiced. Where in the world do you get these ideas?" Mrs. Garrison laughed. "You don't know what's going to come out of her mouth one minute to the next. I swear, that's one thing you never get used to with this kind of mental...defective."

Mona momentarily lifted her face and wiped her mouth with the back of her hand. Raleigh had seen something. What was it? A twitch? The start of a smile?

George seemed to respond to something in his son's expression. "This escapade is not something we're celebrating around here," he said, directing his comment to the silver-haired man.

"I don't imagine," said Mr. Garrison.

The two men began talking about the condition and sheltering of Garrison's horses and plans to rebuild the barn next spring. Mrs. Garrison folded her arms in front of her. A black purse hung from her left forearm. "When this one ran into the house with that box of kittens," she said, "I thought she'd gone into the barn herself. I about had a heart attack."

Mr. Garrison took the hint. Adopting a peremptory tone, he said, "We came over here so Mona could apologize. Young lady, why don't you go ahead, and we can leave these people alone."

"I want to teach her cooking and cleaning, that sort of thing," said Mrs. Garrison, ignoring her husband. "It was Simon's idea, this business of letting her take care of one of the cats, although I think she was fixing to do it behind our backs anyway."

As Raleigh looked at Mrs. Garrison, he thought he saw Mona's bright blue eyes flash up, lighting her pale face. By the time he looked, she was staring down in the vicinity of his shoes again—so intently, in fact, that Raleigh looked down himself. He remembered his shoes were untied. Had she noticed his threadbare sock showing through the ripped welt of his left shoe?

Mona said, "Raleigh. The gray one."

Raleigh looked up. He felt a sudden, unexpected surge of pride.

Mrs. Garrison's face clouded over. She seemed unable to speak.

"What about the mama cat?" asked Raleigh. "Did she show up?"

Mona looked up, smiled, and nodded. She gazed at Raleigh, and her smile grew wide.

"And now I want you to apologize," demanded Mrs. Garrison.

Mona lowered her head again and fell silent.

"It's all right, Grace," said Mr. Garrison. "It's no use anyway."

"Well, I never!" Mrs. Garrison said at last.

But Mona wasn't done. She glanced in the direction of George's feet. "I...helped make...the pie."

"What did she say?" asked Mr. Garrison.

"That she helped me make the pie this afternoon," said Mrs. Garrison, rolling her eyes to the ceiling.

George looked at Raleigh and Mona. "Which was done by way of apology. Yes, yes, that's wonderful. Thank you, Mona."

CHAPTER THREE

1941

THE LATIN TEACHER wrote on the blackboard—TOMORROW: PP. 219-232—then made a show of tapping on the hard surface with her fingernail to emphasize the assignment, but Raleigh's mind was elsewhere. Two rows over. The instant the second bell rang, chairs screeched over the worn, wooden floor and thirty-one juniors—most of them, like Raleigh, seventeen years old—erupted in a cacophony of chatter and commotion. Raleigh closed his notebook and screwed the cap on his fountain pen. He commanded his heart to slow. Twice in the last ten minutes he had reminded himself to breathe. The commitment he'd made to himself was upon him—to talk to Sally Springs after fourth-period Latin.

He pretended to yawn and stole a glance in Sally's direction. She rose just then, twisting free of her chair's tablet arm. Bonnie Draper spoke to her. Sally smiled wryly. Her green eyes met Bonnie's as smooth, tan arms floated down to pick up her book and notebook. Her voice rose—a word or two—in the crescendo of voices and laughter. But mostly, it was Bonnie's voice he heard. She faced him, while Sally, hugging her book and notebook to her chest, had turned away, waiting for the aisle to clear.

Sally had a strong, angular, but not overly long nose, auburn hair, eyes that could topple an empire. The prettiest girl at Yelm High School or anywhere else, Raleigh thought. He'd fallen for her the minute he'd laid eyes on her at the start of their sophomore year.

But Ted Ellington had claimed her on the first day of school. "She's mine," he'd said, looking across the gymnasium at the clump of girls eating lunch. "In the red dress, with the white collar. The rest of you, forget it."

Ted had spoken. It was done—just like that. Almost two years later, nothing had changed. Including Raleigh's feelings. He had hardly spoken two words to her, except to say hello. It was always his "Hello," with "Hi, Raleigh" in return. And her smile was magnificent.

As soon as she was at the door, Raleigh jumped up. He followed her down the crowded hallway, waiting for Bonnie to say good-bye. He had five minutes before the next bell.

Sally was headed for fifth-period chemistry, and he was due at American lit. If he didn't have time to get to his locker and retrieve his book, it didn't matter. Nothing mattered like this. He weaved around knots of chattering and laughing students. Sally's involuntary movements—the bob and sway of her hair, the slight rise and fall of her shoulders as she walked—were as mesmerizing to Raleigh as her most practiced dance steps. And wasn't she the best dancer around? Hadn't she and Ted placed third at last year's swing dance contest at the Western Washington State Fair? At last, Sally stopped. He stopped ten feet behind her. Bonnie said her farewell and trotted up the stairs.

"Sally!" Raleigh called.

Sally spun around. Raleigh, at five feet eleven, was tall enough to be visible in the crowd. "Oh hi, Raleigh."

"I was, um, wanting to talk to you for a minute." Was he shouting? He hoped not, but he knew he had to speak up to be heard. In this racket, he could hardly hear himself think. "I would like to—I was wondering..."

Sally made a face, grabbed his forearm, and led him to the side of the hallway. He couldn't believe how wonderful, how electric, her hand felt against his skin.

"I can't hear you," she said, letting his arm go and smiling up at him. "Here, this is better. Sorry, what did you say?"

He was struck yet again by how beautiful she was and how alive he felt with his face inches from hers. For a split second, he was the center of her universe—wasn't that it?

This is how it's meant to be. Forever. This feeling.

"Sally, I—there's something I want you to know. Maybe you…maybe you do already. It's just that, well, you're very beautiful, and—"

The color drained from her cheeks. Her eyes shifted to the side as though she wondered if others could hear.

The icy wave of uncertainty returned, but it was too late. This was his chance. He'd waited almost two years. She was here. They had this moment together. Once she knew how he felt, surely she would…

Words poured from his mouth. Unbelievably, at one point he leaned over and whispered into her ear, "I think about you constantly." As his wits returned, he babbled about a motion picture, something about Fred Astaire and Ginger Rogers, and how much Sally liked to dance, and what a great dancer she was, and then after the motion picture they could go to the Green Lantern for french fries, that is if it wasn't too late, and if…

Her expression and slight backwards movement said it all. Her smile was perfunctory, compensating. "I'm sorry, Raleigh. I can't. I'm flattered, but Ted wouldn't like that."

Had she said that? *Ted* wouldn't—?

"I've got to get going," she added. "I'm going to be late for class."

Raleigh searched her eyes for an ounce of understanding. It wasn't there. Hadn't he just told her that that he was crazy about her?

She wanted none of it. She turned.

"Look," said Raleigh. Sally stopped, still pressing her Latin book and notebook to her chest. "I'm sorry I said that. I hope I didn't embarrass you."

"It's all right," she answered. "I…I'll see you tomorrow though, okay?"

"Can I ask you something?" Raleigh's heart stumbled forward like a mortally wounded man, a man whose last shadow reveals the ends of a dozen arrows. He threw caution to the wind.

Sally looked up reluctantly. "What?"

He leaned close. Out of breath, he asked, "Do you love Ted?"

She nodded. "Of course I do. I'll see you, okay?"

She disappeared down the crowded hallway. Raleigh sank back against the wall, raised his face to the ceiling, and closed his eyes.

How...? Why in the world...? Did this...did this just happen? I've made a fool of myself. An utter fool.

"Hey, Starr! What are you doing over there?"

Raleigh opened his eyes. Leonard "Wheels" Henderson shouldered through the crowd. Raleigh was relieved that his best friend hadn't seen his undoing at the hands of Sally Springs.

Wheels was dressed in his black and red letterman's sweater, loose-fitting tan slacks, and brown leather oxfords. The wiry second baseman wore his stiff chestnut hair in a crew cut. Both of his front teeth were shunted to the side—the thing you noticed the instant he opened his mouth. "You look like you're taking a nap." His humorous brown eyes turned it into a question. "Hey, where's your letterman's sweater? It's Friday."

"I decided not to wear it today."

"You decided...?" Wheels gave him an inscrutable look. "Never mind. Have you seen Rollins? He's got an angle on some booze for tomorrow night. White Horse, if you can believe it."

"Tomorrow night?"

Wheels looked at him cockeyed. "Yeah, the party. Lake Lawrence? You with me?"

"Oh, sure. No, I haven't seen him."

"Hey, what's wrong with you?" said Wheels. "You look like crud."

The hallway had thinned out. Raleigh walked toward his locker. Wheels kept pace. "You sick or something?"

"Or something."

"You're coming tomorrow night, aren't you? Clarice Austen is going to be there, and she's bringing her cousin from Seattle. It's going to be a clambake."

"I wasn't planning on it," Raleigh said, keeping his eyes pointing forward.

"You weren't *planning* on it? What the hell? This is going to be the best party ever. We're juniors, man. There's a war going on. Hitler's on the march. Naomi Scheck is raring to go—I can feel it."

Raleigh chuckled in spite of himself. He glanced behind Wheels.

"Oh hi, Naomi," he said cheerfully.

Wheels scooted three steps forward, ducking the expected and well-deserved blow. When he saw that Naomi Scheck was not behind him, he grinned at Raleigh. "Funny." He touched his heart. "You're a regular Will Rogers."

The first bell rang as Raleigh arrived at his locker. He checked his watch. "I gotta get going."

"Yeah, yeah. All right, so are you going to the party or not?"

"I wasn't going to. I don't feel much like it. I asked someone out. I was going to go to a motion picture, but she wasn't—she's not interested."

"Who'd you ask out?"

Raleigh looked closely at Wheels. If he could trust anyone to say, and do, right by him, he knew it was Wheels. They'd been friends since Boy Scout days. They played football and baseball together, traveled together on the team bus, drank together, shared opinions about the war in Europe—and girls. But never about Sally Springs. Raleigh uttered her name under his breath.

"What?" Wheels leaned in close. "You asked Sally Springs out?" He looked left and right to make sure no one was within earshot. "Tell me you're kidding. What's gotten into you?"

"He doesn't own her, you know."

"Yeah, but do you think Sally knows that?" Wheels looked closely at his friend. "So that's what's going on. Just now?"

"Yeah."

Wheels bit his lip and nodded, evidently considering possibilities Raleigh knew to be nonexistent. "Well," Wheels began at last, slamming Raleigh's locker shut for him, "that tells me you *need* this party. That's all there is to it. I'll drag you there myself if I have to." Raleigh set off for American lit, and Wheels was right beside him for the first few steps, slapping Raleigh's back good-naturedly. To the rhythm of four sharp blows, he said, "Par-tee, par-tee."

Wheels stopped, content to let Raleigh go. But not to stop chanting. With each step, it was "Par-tee! Par-tee!" echoing down the hall. A few strides from the end of the long hallway, Raleigh looked back over his shoulder. His friend hadn't moved—except to raise both fists high in the air. "Par-tee! Par-tee!"

* * *

No sooner had the bus rounded the corner at Solberg Street and fallen in line with five other buses arriving at the front of Yelm High School, than Mona, sitting in the second seat on the right, began to scour the milling crowd for some sign of Raleigh. When she spotted him at last, she was surprised to find him standing alone, leaning against a bicycle rack, with his head down and arms folded, a sad and distracted look in his eyes. Had something happened to him? Was he ill?

Twisting her brown hair in her fingers, she watched him walk slowly to the bus. She glanced the other way just as he lifted his gaze to mount the steps. Soon he would brush by her as he walked down the aisle. Most days she would look up at him, and he would smile or nod as he passed. She would listen to his footsteps—to the extent she could make them out—and to his banter as he made his way to the back of the bus with the rest of the high school students. Today, she only glanced up for the briefest instant, for there was something wrong.

If only I knew what happened. Why he's so miserable.

She stole a second glance over her shoulder. Raleigh tossed his book bag onto a seat, leaned over it and opened the window. He sank slowly into his seat, staring into space then closed his eyes and leaned his head back. When he lifted his head again, their eyes met. His were distant and pained. Mona spun away quickly, jostling the fourth grade girl sitting beside her. "I'm sorry," Mona said.

"He's sick or something, isn't he?" said the girl.

"I don't know."

The girl waited several seconds then turned to spy on Raleigh herself. She was much shorter than Mona and had to get up on her knees to see to the back of the bus. When she sat again, she whispered into Mona's shoulder. "He's reading now."

Mona couldn't blame the girl for looking, but she worried that Raleigh might think she had put the girl up to it. She was glad her friend was back in her seat, facing forward.

Fifteen minutes later, with the bus pounding and shaking over potholes, Mona had resigned herself to the fact that she would probably never know what had happened to Raleigh. She was bent over, rounding her nails with an emery board when she felt something land in her hair. As she reached back, something else struck her hand. Her heart froze at an eruption of giggles from the seventh grade boys four rows back. What were they doing?

When she turned to see, a third spitball struck her in the face below the left eye. "*Ow!*" She spun back and ducked, covering her head with her hands.

It's Steve Abbott. Why won't he leave me alone?

A wave of catcalls and whistles rolled toward the front of the bus. Another boy midway back shouted, "She's an idiot! Look at her!"

The girl beside Mona popped to her knees again and faced the back of the bus. She yelled, "Takes one to know one, Steven!"

On the heels of more laughter, a barrage of spitballs and wadded paper struck Mona and her seatmate over the next half minute.

"Get Garrison! She's a freak!" shouted Abbott.

Crying out for help, with her hands still clasped around her head, Mona looked up into the driver's mirror. She saw the driver's bald head and forward-looking eyes. That he didn't look up, or lift a finger to help Mona, was no surprise. He was famous for ignoring the antics of the gaggle behind him, the students who called Thompson Road home.

"Get her!" cried Abbott. Mona stole a quick glance back, covering her face. Abbott was standing up in the aisle wearing a broad grin, his cheeks and forehead red with excitement. "Get the freak!" What he couldn't see—although Mona glimpsed it before turning back—was Raleigh rising slowly from his seat at the back of the bus, setting his book down, and starting up the aisle.

She could tell from the series of sounds what happened next. One by one, the junior high and grade school boys noticed Raleigh's approach and scrambled into their seats. By the time he arrived at the sixth row only Abbott was throwing wadded papers at Mona as fast as he could tear them from his notebook. When he saw Raleigh standing there, he stopped. He would have looked into the high school letterman's eyes. His grin would have melted. She knew there was nothing—no part of a grin—left when Raleigh's fist struck him in the face, knocking him backwards. You could hear the blow from every seat on the bus—no mistaking it.

With tears in her eyes, Mona dropped her hands and looked back once more. Raleigh faced forward in the aisle, his fists clenched. He stared into the driver's mirror as though daring the driver to look up. She turned with the rest of the students to watch in the mirror as the driver averted his eyes and idly scratched the back of his head.

"I'm sorry that happened," said the girl sitting beside Mona. Mona's tears had dried. Steve Abbott lay across his seat covering his right eye. He was no longer crying.

Mona looked down and tried to smile. "Thank you."

The girl quickly glanced back at Raleigh. "He's reading now," she said. Her flaxen braid swung over her left shoulder as she looked up at Mona. "Are you all right?"

Mona nodded.

"How old are you? My friend says you're eighteen, but I say you're sixteen."

Mona smiled. "I'm fifteen."

The girl's mouth fell open. "You are? Oh my gosh, my cousin is fifteen. She lives in Spokane."

The bus stopped a half mile before the Thompson Road turn to let four students off. Three had to contort themselves to stretch over Abbott's sprawled legs. They did so without a word. "Why are you in the fourth grade then?" the girl asked when the doors had closed and the idling engine rumbled to life again.

"I don't know. Words—letters and words go backwards, I guess. I can't do arithmetic."

"You can't?"

Mona shook her head. "Not very well. I try." Two high school boys in the back of the bus erupted into deep gales of laughter at something one of them was reading aloud from a first aid manual. Mona looked over the girl's head in the direction of the passing fields, listening.

"They're not laughing at you," said the girl. "No one is. Not after that."

CHAPTER FOUR

IT WAS A PARTY all right, but Raleigh sat alone on top of an immense outcrop, rooted to the spot. High above the silver-blue surface of the Lake Lawrence, upward-straining clouds with orange, rose, and purple tops drifted eastward. Where were the clouds headed, he wondered, and how far would they get before they lost their color and melted into darkness?

He thought of his grandfather—how he used to sit with Raleigh and his sister on the porch of his home in Bellevue and wait for the "supreme moment," the exact time when the sunset, and therefore the world, was at its most spectacular and grand. "There it is," he would say. "Breathe deep, Lauren. Breathe it in, Raleigh." And they would.

Raleigh scanned the horizon somberly.

Is this the supreme moment? I don't doubt it is—somewhere, for someone.

He leaned back, hands splayed over the smooth flat surface of stone, beside him a half-full bottle of White Horse whiskey. He shuddered at the first fingers of cold night air ruffling his hair and the back of his shirt. Everything was just right for some people.

A sudden eruption of laughter coming from the classmates grouped around a snapping bonfire high on the bank seemed to prove it. He thought not of them but of Sally.

If you and I were here together, all this would be perfect—even the chill in the air, which would bring us closer. I would feel your warmth next to me, feel you squeeze my arm. I would turn to you and see your smile. You would be my supreme moment—always.

"Hey, old man." Wheels's voice was thick with drink. Raleigh turned his head, nodded. "What are you doing out here?" Wheels groaned like an old man as he lowered himself to the rock and leaned back. "Nice, huh?"

"It is nice."

"You out here for a reason?" Wheels asked.

Raleigh turned a crooked smile on his friend. "Feeling sorry for myself is all."

Wheels took a long drink of beer and belched. Raleigh waited, but apparently the belch was meant to stand alone.

After a few beats, Raleigh asked, "What are you doing out here?"

When Wheels didn't answer, Raleigh turned. Wheels was gazing, trance-like, at the picturesque sky. His head bounced with the utterance of a deep-chested "huh," and, after a while, he said, as if to himself, "You know, I thought of something last year that's gonna make me a million bucks some day." He took another drink of beer. "Most people see a sunset like that and think they're seeing it all. I mean, that's the sunset, right? There it is. Well, that's not it. That's the thing. What we're seeing there is a tiny fraction of a continuous ribbon of color stretching clear across the earth right this minute—everywhere the sun's going down or coming up. Do you follow me? The sunset doesn't have a 'here' or a 'now.'"

"Yeah, I guess." Raleigh looked for a clue in the ever-mounting clouds overhead, two of them boasting bright pink tops. "But how's that going to make you a million bucks?"

"Oh, it—" Wheels stopped, sniffed. "Well, I don't know yet. That's part of the beauty of it, I guess."

Raleigh nodded. Wheels was being Wheels.

"Here's another one," Wheels continued. "You know how Mr. Robbins talked about light? Photons and rods and cones in our eyes that let us see?"

His enthusiasm had a hint of religious zeal about it. Raleigh reached for the whiskey. He examined the distinctive white horse emblazoned on the bottle before taking a swig.

"Anyway, you know what that means? Everything except us, and the animals, is in the dark. No eyes, no light. This lake here, those clouds, the trees—they're surrounded in pitch black twenty-four hours a day. Is that weird, or what? This place is solid black as far as everything out here is concerned, except for us and the animals. When we play baseball, we're playing in the pitch dark—except in our brains."

Raleigh took a second swallow. He examined the liquid swishing back and forth at the bottom of the bottle. "Is that another million, or is that part of the first million?"

Wheels ignored the remark. "That means not only can we not see our backsides, but our backsides are encased in darkness. Those old cottonwoods over there have never seen a second of light. From a star's point of view, it's as black as obsidian."

Behind them, Ted Ellington's laughter was followed by a quick rejoinder and more laughter, accompanied by the sighs and sparks of the bonfire. Raleigh started to look but then thought better of it. Sally would be with him. Raleigh didn't want to see her.

"Oh, yeah," said Wheels. "That's why I came down here. To tell you *they* showed up."

"Hmm. Okay. Thanks."

Wheels seemed surprised by the silence that followed. "You coming up, or what?"

"I don't think so. Not for a while, anyway." Raleigh wasn't aware of Wheels's leaving to join the others. *If it's all black, there are no supreme moments, no brilliant-colored skies, no dramatic cloud formations. It's all in our minds.*

* * *

Raleigh held the brown bottle by the neck and pressed it into the seat of his father's pickup—the only way he knew to keep it from spilling. Minutes before, he'd spilled whiskey over his leg—a good amount—while downshifting to turn onto Thompson Road, and he was too busy wondering if it would dry or leave an odor to think about shifting back. For more than three miles, he crossed the dark landscape in second gear.

The engine roared and complained, and the vehicle weaved, at one with the tenor and direction of his thoughts. "Big congratulations to you. You won her heart—fair and square...and square. I don't understand square. You did whatever you did...what did you—?" Raleigh took a deep drink, and jammed the bottle down again. The headlamps—first the left, then both—picked up the tall grass on the side of the road. The grass, he noticed with satisfaction, was no match for the Model A. By the dozens the blades dipped down and out of view. But there were more of them—a great deal more—and now the truck was at an odd angle. "She's listing, sir!" a sailor on watch might have said.

Too late, Raleigh realized that a sharp turn to the right might have rectified the situation. The truck lurched to a stop. In a ditch. A dust cloud rose in the headlights. Something didn't look right.

Raleigh took another drink and squeezed the bottle of White Horse between his legs. With difficulty, he shifted into reverse and gave it gas. Nothing happened, save the spinning of the rear tires. He shifted into first. Nothing.

He let the door swing open and stepped into the tall grass. With the bed of the truck for support, he climbed onto the starlit road. He stood outside the vehicle, pacing up and down to stay warm. He checked his watch: 9:40. "Somebody's bound to come by," he muttered, kicking gravel into the ditch.

Jake Stedden. He'll be soused and on his way home any minute.

Why in the hell had he left his coat on that damn log? It was cold now, but it had been too hot by the fire. He'd forgotten it when he left the party early. He was too distracted and drunk and befuddled by Sally Springs. He had to get out of there. He was just glad to get to his dad's truck and get it started. He hadn't thought about the coat 'till now. Where was Mr. Stedden anyway?

Forget it, I'll walk home. He reached head and shoulders through the passenger window and felt for the bottle.

He walked along the road, cursing at first, and then singing "Ninety-nine bottles of beer on the road, ninety-nine bottles of beer..." Turning back to see the Model A ghostlike under the stars a few hundred yards away, he raised the bottle high over his head. "I shall return, dear friend!" he shouted. He tipped the White Horse back and took a deep drink, closing his eyes. He felt dizzy. The crickets in the fields stopped for—one thousand one, one thousand two, one thousand three, one thousand four.

Raleigh had made the woods above the rise when he became aware of the strange sensation that he was walking to a banjo and bass rhythm—to the distant sound of music. It faded and a moment later died away. Raleigh wrote it off to the booze. There was nothing—and then there were trumpets.

A trombone solo...and a saxophone riff. Jazz. Fast. Clear. Music.

Raleigh waved the bottle and shook his head to the pleasing sounds of Mills' Merry Makers, happy for the company the music provided. Head down, sidestepping, he danced his way more or less forward for several minutes. The music stopped, but he continued with something like a dance that slowed, drew itself in, and became a stumbling walk again. The music had to be coming from the Garrisons' place. But it wasn't like them to play loud music.

A few seconds later, static poured through the trees followed by Gene Krupa's opening tom-tom licks in Benny Goodman's unmistakable cover of *Sing, Sing, Sing*. When the brass section opened up, Raleigh smiled. He felt a quickening in his chest, a sudden upwelling of ecstatic energy. He raised his arms in the air, and circling in the road he shouted, "Yeah! Benny! Woo-hoo!" He ran closer—or half-ran, as the liquor would allow. Were the Garrisons having a party? You never knew with people.

Waves of irrepressible sound, the band in full swing, animated his strides. When he reached the turn in the road, he stopped. The drive was empty—no cars, front or back. The Garrisons' Pontiac was missing from the carport. Lights glowed in the house, and over the front yard fell the shadow of someone moving inside, a shadow stretching to the road.

A body, dancing wildly, dramatically. Raleigh moved to the far side of the road. With the fast, driving rhythm flowing from the open upstairs window, he inched forward into the light and stopped. Visible through the small sash window above the porch roof was Mona Garrison, moving back and forth, in and out of view, her bare arms swinging, her lithe body twisting. She wore a sleeveless pale pink nightgown. With her dark brown hair flying from one side to the other, she kept the rhythm fully at her command. Raleigh was mesmerized. Her shoulders dipped, first one way, then another, and with her head held high—her chin high—she moved like nothing or no one he had ever seen before. She leaned forward and spun a complete circle, not once but twice, and came back to center, driving her bare shoulders down with the beat—left, right, left, right. Her thin nightgown could not hide the shadowy points of her hips and her breasts, stretching tight the loose-fitting material one moment, disappearing the next.

Raleigh found himself hoping the music would never stop. His breathing was shallow. Nothing mattered so much as this rhythm—hers. Whenever she moved in either direction and became partially cut off from view by the window frame, he felt a spike of yearning.

Come back. Don't disappear.

A bright yellow light from an unseen lamp revealed a sheen of perspiration over her face, and strands of hair clung to her forehead and cheeks. She pouted, deep in thought. Her blue eyes seemed to avoid the window for the most part, and held no obvious joy. And yet her dancing was frenetic, full bore, tireless, driven. She consumed the pulsing sensations as much as danced to them. The instruments were alive in her limbs, in her hips. She was theirs; they were hers.

When the music stopped, the figure disappeared.

No!

A few seconds later, a scratched recording started. Raleigh's heart rose with expectant joy, to be dashed again when the needle was lifted off the record and all was silent.

"Let's try that again, folks," came a deep male voice. Raleigh recognized Warren Ames, the Friday night master of ceremonies on KMO radio. In the full embrace of more papery static came Pee Wee Hunt's *High Society*.

The sharp, unrelenting drumbeat gave Raleigh reason to hope. What he saw first was Mona's dancing shadow on the opposite wall. He struggled to make out her form, but even this, he thought, was a vision. She drifted partially into view. Here she was, not her shadow. Those serious eyes. The body in fluid motion. She moved slowly out of view—arms straight down one moment, akimbo the next, shoulders rolling in perfect time to the beat.

Raleigh stepped to the right, hoping to regain the vision, but had to content himself with the bobbing shadow that crawled across the golden-papered wall at the back of the room. "Good God," he muttered. "How did she learn to dance like that?"

He felt warmth spreading through him, and a clarity as certain as the trumpet section's blaring notes.

What if Sally could dance like that?

He pictured Sally, her smooth, angelic face moist with sweat, eyes fixed on his, inviting him closer, to join him. With the shadow of Mona Garrison undulating and twirling in the background, Raleigh imagined Sally at the window wearing the same flimsy pink nightgown, waving him in. Her green eyes held the question, "Can't you see I want you? Come here!"

He imagined Sally's languid body moving close, parts visible through the thin nightgown that he had only dreamt of. He could taste her lips. His knees weakening, he spotted a tall Salmonberry bush beyond the reach of the window light. He set the bottle on the edge of the road and went behind the bush. He had to—and wanted to. The vision—Sally, her eyes, her rotating hips—deepened his intoxication. He could feel her body rising to his. The music played on.

* * *

Raleigh was within two miles of home when he took the last swallow of whiskey and tossed the empty bottle into the ditch. He relived the moment he first saw Mona Garrison's body in the window above the porch roof. He'd never seen a body move like that. Never.

The last trailing edge of pleasure he'd felt behind the Salmonberry bush was gone. He'd banished shame and guilt, and over the dark, stepping miles he had set store in the certitude that what felt good—what was remarkable—was remarkable.

A car horn blared. As he squinted into the headlights, he made out Wheels's voice above the crunching and scattering of gravel. The car skidded to a stop. "There you are, old man. When we saw your dad's truck back there, we figured you'd be up here somewhere."

Raleigh found himself staring into the smiling eyes of Naomi Scheck.

"Hi, Raleigh," she said, giggling at the look of confusion on his face.

"Naomi." Raleigh sought the bleary eyes of his friend and teammate. *So it's your lucky night.*

Wheels said, "Get in. Let's go back and get your truck. I've got a rope in the back. We can pull it out."

Raleigh had all but forgotten about the truck. He nodded and moved toward the back door of the Chrysler Coupe. Better not to have to explain to his father about the truck anyway. As he crawled in, he said, "What are you two doing up here anyway?"

As if I don't know.

He looked from Wheels to Naomi and back again.

Wheels smiled. "You left your coat at the party, old man. We thought we'd bring it to you." Raleigh detected a wink in the dark. Naomi had been using the coat to cover her legs. She lifted it off her lap and handed it to Raleigh in the back seat.

"Thanks," he said. He was glad to have the coat back, even if Wheels's real intention had been to return it on Monday.

"Mission accomplished," said Wheels. He pulled forward a short distance, angled into a turnout, and hollering "Hold on!" swung the car around without stopping. Five minutes later, they drove back past the Garrison house. Wheels was describing—his eyes flitting up to the rearview mirror—the antics of one of their classmates. "So Harris lost the bet, right? He had to strip down and dive in." Wheels laughed uproariously. Naomi laughed, too.

Raleigh smiled, but his thoughts had drifted out the open side window. Above the Garrisons' misaligned porch roof the window was black, and the Garrisons' Pontiac was snug in its carport. Raleigh set his head against the cushion and closed his eyes. *What an amazing sight!*

And in his mind: the music again, the bright tones and rolling rhythms that an hour and a half earlier had filled the chilled, country air that he could feel against his face.

CHAPTER FIVE

NOW THAT SCHOOL WAS OUT, what were the chances that she would be spending even a minute with Raleigh Starr? It had all happened so fast. Mona reached into the back of the pickup and lifted out the mop and bucket. *But what if I can't do this? I'm sloppy. Aunt Grace says—*

"What's wrong?" Raleigh said, stepping around the back of the truck. He gently took the mop and bucket from her. "You're going to do great."

Mona examined her bangs in the reflection of the passenger window, and straightened and smoothed the front of her tan, threadbare dress. "Aunt Grace says God made me and the mud puddle on the same day."

Raleigh was retrieving brushes and cleansers scattered across the bed of the pickup and putting them back in the bucket. When he didn't respond, Mona turned to him.

"Aunt Grace says God made me and the mud puddle on the same day."

Raleigh stopped. She stared into his blue eyes, at golden flecks lit by the sun. He let a smile form. "That's funny," he said. "Your aunt's funny."

I'm not sure she was trying to be funny.

"Are you ready?" he said, waving with his head toward the two-story house. "My Aunt Edith is nice. You'll see." He started up the walk, but Mona didn't move. He retraced his steps. "Are you all right? You're going to clean her house is all. And I'm going to help you. It'll be fine."

"I've never cleaned her house before."

"No, I know you haven't—and I'm going to help."

"I'd rather clean my house."

"Yes, I understand. But this is a job. You're going to get paid for this. Remember we talked about it?"

Mona trained her eyes on his face so intently and at such close quarters that she didn't know which of his eyes to look into. Eventually she let her gaze rise up to the tips of his dark blond hair vibrating in the morning breeze. People didn't like it when she stared too intently, she reminded herself.

But I don't mind him being this close. Not at all.

Raleigh looked away in the direction of the gray-green water tower in the distance. "Do you remember, I told your aunt and uncle that my mom's sister lost her housecleaner? That she was looking for a new one, and I recommended you?" He looked back at her. "This is a chance for you to get paid, and, like I said, I'll help you for as long as it takes."

"Why?" she heard herself ask, once again staring deep into his eyes.

"Why what?"

"Why did you recommend me?" *Why did you think of me at all? Since school's been out, I haven't... Your truck goes by, and I want to wave, but I can't tell if it's you or your dad or even your sister...and by the time I see it, it's too late anyway. It's disappearing.*

Raleigh ran his hand through his hair. He seemed to be having difficulty with the question.

Maybe I've embarrassed him. I shouldn't have asked this. Sometimes Mona felt as defective as people said she was. Other times, she felt like herself. *I spend so much time by myself I don't know how to act around a boy my age.* She averted her eyes and tried to think of something else.

"Uncle Simon trusts you," said Mona. "He says not to worry."

Raleigh was still lost in his own thoughts.

"Did you hear me?" asked Mona.

"What?"

"Uncle Simon trusts you. He told Aunt Grace, 'Don't worry.' She said I shouldn't go with you—a boy."

"She did?"

"She says I can't be trusted either—" Mona interrupted herself with trickling laughter. "Any more than someone who's common."

"*Common*? She said that?"

Mona squinted in the morning sun. "Like my mother. She said Mama is common...with men and all. Uncle Simon told her, 'No, you worry too much.'"

Raleigh looked at her compassionately. "Was this in front of you? I mean—"

"I could hear them in the kitchen. Aunt Grace said it's too risky, but Uncle Simon said, 'You worry too much.'"

"Raleigh?" came a quiet, birdlike voice from the porch. Fifty-two-year-old Edith Moore stood with the screen door half-open, her sightless eyes angled away from the voices at the roadside. The hem of her blue-and-white floral print dress waved gently in the breeze. "Is that you?"

"Hi, Aunt Edith. It's us." Raleigh leaned close to Mona and whispered, "There's something I have to tell you. We need to talk—later, okay?" Mona opened her mouth, but Raleigh broke in. "It's about this job, and you and I being together on Tuesdays." He stood up and said, "Good morning! Here, come along, Mona."

With her head down and fingers locked in front of her, Mona followed Raleigh's long strides up the walk. She climbed the porch steps and stopped next to him. Raleigh hugged his aunt with his free arm and accepted a peck on the cheek. "Aunt Edith, this is the neighbor I told you about." Setting the mop and bucket aside, he steered Mona's hand into Edith's palm.

Mona pulled herself away from the sight of her slender fingers lost in the warm, dry embrace of the other woman's *two* hands—no one had ever shaken her hand this way before. She stared up at two bright red, freshly painted lips, at heavily rouged cheeks, and the source, she knew, of an overpowering scent. "This is Mona Garrison."

"Hello, dear," said Aunt Edith.

Mona observed her a moment longer and said, "You can't see, can you...you're blinded?"

"That's right, dear." Aunt Edith blinked.

Raleigh cleared his throat. "Should we—?"

"Well, you're right on time," said Aunt Edith. "Come in, come in. Let me show you what needs doing."

Raleigh held the screen door open for Mona. They were assailed at once by the warmth of the room and a crippling combination of fragrances. Mona imagined bottles upon bottles of perfume having spilled in that room alone.

Aunt Edith tried to face the girl, missing the mark by an inch or two. "So you're Mona Garrison. Raleigh has told me about you—and, do you know what?"

Mona stood on one foot, looking around the ornate living room. After a few seconds, she shook her head and said, "No."

"Give me your hand, dear, and walk with me into the kitchen. I've known your aunt and uncle for better than twenty years." She stopped by the stove and turned to Mona with confidence. "I may have met your mother once or twice, too, when she visited from Portland. You sound a lot like her. Let's see, what was her name? It's on the tip of my tongue... Oh, darn it. What was it, dear?"

Mona slumped. She didn't answer.

Raleigh looked down at his feet. At last he blurted, "She's shy, isn't she? Especially where family's concerned." Some color came into his face. He added, "She's a hard worker. Mrs. Garrison trained her to do housecleaning. And honest, too. I can vouch for that."

"Well, it doesn't matter one whit," said Aunt Edith, patting Mona's hand. "She was a lovely woman, your mother. I didn't know she'd gotten married, but—well, here you are." She reached for the kitchen sink and felt around for dishes. "Grace never mentioned you that I recall. But, welcome. Welcome."

Raleigh rolled his eyes, made a face for Mona, and then squeezed his nose. She saw it, tried unsuccessfully to suppress a smile, and looked down at once. "Thank you," she whispered to Aunt Edith with difficulty. Aunt Grace had never said a kind word about her mother. It confused Mona to hear Raleigh's aunt speak so highly of her.

Obviously pleased with himself for having forced a smile from Mona, and impressed with her self-control, Raleigh said, "So, shall we get started? What should we do in here?"

But Mona was already in motion. "Let's start with these dishes," she said, carrying plates from the draining board to the sink. "They can dry in the rack while we're sweeping the stairs."

Raleigh looked at Mona, nonplussed. Her eyes flashed up at his only briefly as she stepped past him and deposited the dishes in the sink. Aunt Edith's red lips parted in a wide smile.

"Why, yes, that would be wonderful," she said. "My, you're a self-starter. I like that. I like that very much."

Mona thought of the commands her aunt had drilled into her. "Start at once. Don't lollygag." She heard Aunt Grace's tone as surely as if she were there, and in the process she paid scant attention to what Raleigh said next.

"I told you she'd be great."

* * *

Raleigh had forgotten how exhausting tedious housework could be and was surprised at how efficient Mona was prioritizing the work and getting things done. She'd been the one who was patient with him, when he'd expected it to be the other way around.

"Fumble fingers," Mona said, smiling at Raleigh's inability to hold on to one corner of a sheet they held stretched above Aunt Edith's bed. It was the last room of the house.

"I didn't know you were going to try to pull me over."

His answer tickled Mona more than he could have imagined. Her smile grew wide, and he realized he had never seen this look, this smile, before. He had to force himself to look away, but at the same time he resolved to draw it out again.

Be smart about it. It doesn't hurt that she's attractive. It'll make things easier for the judges. And, who knows, Sally might be doubly jealous.

They leaned over at the corners of the bed, tucked in the top sheet, and then swung into action on the opposite corners like a practiced pair. "See, I know what I'm doing," said Raleigh.

"All right."

Raleigh feigned shock. "What's that supposed to mean?"

Mona stared at the corner he'd made, pressed her lips together, and looked up as though unsure he could handle bad news.

"What is it?" he said.

She moved to his corner of the bed and tried to smooth the fold with her hand. "It's just...if you..." She gave up, pulled the sheet out, and completed a hospital corner, tucking the sheet in with a burst of sudden energy. "If you fold it this way first, you don't end up with a bump, and the sheet will stay tucked in." She stood back and her face turned pale.

"Good heavens," said Raleigh. "That's fantastic." He looked at her admiringly. "That's so much better."

Mona smiled, and the color returned to her cheeks.

"Here, let me try it up here."

She lunged after him with an arm extended. "No! You don't—" She withdrew her hand self-consciously. "You don't do it at the top. Just at the bottom."

Raleigh realized his mistake. "Of course not. What was I thinking?" She tried but could not avoid laughing with him.

* * *

"This will take longer when you're working by yourself," said Raleigh, chewing on one of the peanut butter and honey sandwiches Aunt Edith had made for them. He nodded to himself.

I've talked myself into this. Talked her and her aunt and uncle into it, too. They think she'll learn from working for Aunt Edith, but they don't know the real reason. Neither does Mona. None of them know about Sally.

They sat half in and half out of the sun on the back porch steps. Five minutes earlier, Raleigh had insisted they move from the front porch to the back. "It's more comfortable to eat back there," he'd said, leading Mona around the corner of the house, past a leggy blue hydrangea. Truth was, he didn't want to be seen sitting with Mona on the front porch.

She picked small pieces of crust from her sandwich and put them in her mouth. Two untouched glasses of milk stood between them.

"I would guess three hours each time," said Raleigh. "That's a dollar twenty. That can't hurt, right?"

Mona stared dully at the riot of flowers in Aunt Edith's back garden, her thoughts, who knew where. Her lips rolled with chewing. Not the sumptuous, sublime shape of her guileless smile, but something new.

He cleared his throat. "I guess I better get you home."

Mona nodded and looked at the sandwich in her hands.

Now! Tell her. You've given her a job, something she wouldn't have a chance to do otherwise. Why did I recommend you? I need your help. If this works you're going to make me the happiest senior at Yelm High School.

He looked around to make sure the back door was closed. "You know, Mona, you asked me why I recommended you. The truth is I have a favor to ask you."

Mona turned toward him. She froze with a small wedge of crust inches from her mouth.

"There's a dance contest coming up at the Western Washington State Fair in Puyallup. In September." Mona eased the morsel into her mouth. "The first-place dancers get one hundred dollars. I want you to teach me to dance the way you do—and I want you to dance with me so we can win a hundred dollars."

Raleigh picked up a glass of milk. There was no reason to mention Sally or Ted. Mona wouldn't understand any of it anyway, would she?

That Raleigh had insisted on fleeing the front porch to avoid being seen with Mona in public and was now proposing they dance together in one of the most public places in all of Western Washington generated not a ripple of concern in him.

"You want me to...

"To teach me." He set the glass down and wiped his top lip with the back of his wrist. "And then—see?—you and I'll dance at the fair. I think we'd win. I know *you* would. I'm sure you would. But since it's a couples' competition, I need you to teach me how to hold my own with you. I mean, I know how to dance, but not good enough to—"

"You want to dance...with me?"

Raleigh frowned. Mona seemed to be missing several pieces. "To *teach* me. First, you'd have to teach me to dance like you, see, and—yes, to dance together. Yes, that's right. We'd have to practice a lot beforehand, though."

"Practice?"

"Yes, practice. Again, that's for me. You already know how. But it's essential..."

Raleigh stopped. Not only was he using words he was sure she didn't understand, but he was in danger of botching the whole thing.

I shouldn't have brought it up this way. I should have asked her if she likes dancing or something like that. Do you like music? What do you like about it? Do you ever dance to music? What's your favorite song?

Unsure what to say next, he looked into her inquisitive eyes. It was too late to go back.

The cat's out of the bag.

Raleigh looked over his left shoulder again to make sure Aunt Edith wasn't listening. He began again, this time looking into her eyes. "I would like to practice dancing with you…because I know you are a very, very good dancer. The best, in fact. There's a contest coming up in a couple of months, you see, and the best dancers are going to win a lot of money. I would like to enter this contest with you."

Mona looked down. She whispered, "I don't know how to dance."

Raleigh swung back and laughed into the sky. "I knew you were going to say that. I must be a mind reader."

"I don't know how to dance," she repeated.

"Sure you do. You're an amazing dancer."

Mona looked at him doubtfully.

"Let me worry about your aunt and uncle," Raleigh said. "I'll figure that out. Look, I don't want to force you to do something you don't want to do. But I'm asking as a favor because…well, I think you're the kind of person dancing was invented for. I think your dancing is sublime—which means perfect. You see, I saw you dancing once through your bedroom window. I wasn't spying on you or anything. My car had broken down, and I happened to be walking by. I was walking home. You were wonderful, Mona."

Her mouth fell open. "You…saw me?"

"It was nothing. I happened to be…It was late."

I was drunk.

Mona swung her whole body, including her knees, partway to him, as if trying to understand. "In the window?"

His mouth went dry; his heart thudded in his chest. A wave of heat like a blast from a furnace struck his face. At least she didn't know the rest of it. He pushed the words out to force them free of his guilt. "Yeah. You were upstairs. I don't think anybody else was home. You had the window open, and you were listening to KMO. I wasn't spying on you or anything. I happened to be on the road walking by."

Mona's face turned multiple shades of red. Raleigh began to throw tiny pieces of concrete from the porch into the backyard. His best bet was to switch back to the dance contest and talk like it was no big deal.

"We'd have to keep it secret, of course—I'd tell your aunt and uncle eventually, but here's what I've come up with. Every week after you clean Aunt Edith's house, I'll come by to pick you up. I know a place where we can practice. There's a jukebox, and no one's there except maybe a couple of drunks. It's the Osprey Club on Pine Street. No one goes there before two o'clock anyway. Do you know it?"

Mona shook her head.

"Well, it doesn't matter. I've arranged things with the manager, Ed Becker. We can park in the alley every Tuesday at twelve thirty and go in the back way. Just you and me—and whoever's drinking in there, you know, but believe me, it won't matter. You can give me dancing lessons for an hour or so, and I'll get you home by two thirty at the latest."

Mona remained silent, still blushing.

"You can't tell your aunt and uncle. You can't tell anybody. That's the key."

Embarrassed, and with nothing else to say, he took another quick bite of sandwich. He imagined for the hundredth time the look of utter disbelief on Sally's face as he and Mona were awarded the grand prize. Utter disbelief yielding to the realization that he had done all this for her, that he cared for her that much.

Mona continued to pick at the crust of her sandwich. Her eyes held a faraway look. After several seconds, Raleigh wondered if she had understood him at all. What was he doing? This was crazy! She was feebleminded. So what if she could dance? Did she even know what a contest was?

"Is this bothering you? Me talking about this?" he asked. "Have I made you uncomfortable?"

Mona brought him into focus. "No."

"You seem to be thinking of something else."

"I'm thinking of you."

CHAPTER SIX

THE PICKUP LURCHED to a stop between a beat-up Ford Cabriolet and a black box truck with Archie's Taxidermy written in faded gold and red Gothic lettering on the side. Raleigh glanced at a vacant second-story window above the unmarked back door of the Osprey Club.

This is perfect. No one'll see us here.

He allowed himself a moment of wishing it were Sally next to him, not Mona. He pushed the spark control lever. Mona seemed to occupy only the far third of the seat. Not uncharacteristically, her head was bowed. "What is it?" he asked. "You scared?"

"I don't know."

Her tone told him she was, a little. "It's crazy, all right," he said with a smile. "I'm sort of scared, too. But hey, it's only dancing." He made as if to dance behind the steering wheel, from the hips up, his head rocking back and forth.

Mona glanced up and smiled at his antics.

Raleigh felt a sudden surge in his heart. He wasn't ready for the smooth evolution of her features, the symmetry of nose, eyes, forehead, and chin framing the perfect smile. It caught him off guard. He squinted at the absurdity of his reaction and pushed it away. "You trust me?" he asked. "I'm here for you. I just want to dance—learn to dance—and I promise I'll have you home by two thirty."

Mona nodded reluctantly.

"Is that all right?"

Mona nodded again. For the first time, Raleigh detected a hint of perfume on Mona, a light jasmine scent.

"Our secret. Don't tell your aunt or uncle or anyone else, okay? Can you promise me?"

She nodded a third time.

"You have to say it."

"Okay."

Raleigh put a foot out, stopped, and looked back over his shoulder. "And if this is no fun—if you decide you don't want to—you tell me, okay?"

Again, he wouldn't accept a nod. He waited until Mona said the word before getting out.

When Mona walked around the front of the truck, he noticed she wore hard-soled buckle shoes, not the dilapidated lace-up shoes she'd worn to Aunt Edith's the week before. Raleigh held out his right foot to show her that he too had worn shoes suitable for dancing. She grinned. From her smile, he felt the joy of the week before when she'd torn the bedsheet from his hand.

Not a bad bonus. She's no Sally Springs, but in a way, her smile is just as pretty.

"Let's do this," Raleigh said, reaching for the scarred door and holding it open for Mona. When she passed, he exhaled a deep, nervous breath that he wasn't aware he had been holding.

I've thought about this so many times—but here it is, and it doesn't seem real. I hope it's worth it. It's going to be. When Sally sees us, she'll realize what I've done, that I'd do anything for her.

The smell of tobacco and whiskey was strong at the threshold. A bare bulb hung from a cord opposite the stairs leading upstairs to the vacant apartment. The bulb was covered in blotches of rust-colored paint, staining the walls with shadows.

"This is it," he told Mona, guiding her in. She inched forward and stopped. Raleigh sidestepped past her as the door closed, leaving them diminished in the thin light. He walked past the lavatory doors and the strong odor of disinfectant to a darkened main room that began to take shape in muted, yellowish tones. He looked both ways, called: "Mr. Becker? Ed? You here?" He turned and waved Mona forward. "It's all right."

The barroom was empty. Ed Becker was nowhere to be seen. To their left, the mahogany bar stretched thirty-five feet to the opposite wall. On three sides, the room shone dimly with varnished oak wainscoting. Behind the dance floor waited a dozen empty black tables, each with a clear glass ashtray and a menu standing snug in a silver holder. Advertisements for Coca-Cola, Schlitz Beer, homemade pies, and french fries dotted the peeling golden walls. To the right of the bar stood the jukebox, a Wurlitzer, the brightest object in the room with its backlit panel and pulsing red, green, and blue light diffusers—a rainbow visible on the polished parquet dance floor.

"Let's see if this works." Raleigh reached into his pocket and made his way to the jukebox. Halfway across the dance floor, with his hard-soled shoes shattering the room's silence, he was assailed by pinpricks of doubt all over again.

I'm in a bar with a fifteen-year-old girl—a feeb at that. What would Dad say? Ed said it was all right—didn't mind if we practiced for the dance contest—but that's hardly going to save me if Dad finds out.

Raleigh dropped the nickel in the slot and pushed lever seventeen.

This is the craziest thing I've ever done.

He'd had this all worked out in his head, but being here was different. He rested an elbow on the glass and leaned over, watching the 78 settle on the rising turntable. A scant two seconds after the tone arm touched the record, the bar filled with the driving rhythm and full-throated instrumentations of Benny Goodman and his band. The room, strangely lighter, held no secret corners. It was alive with sound—alive and throbbing. He looked around again for the bartender, closed his eyes and bobbed his head, trying to dispel the image of his father, trying to resurrect the belief that everything would be fine. He had to stick to the plan.

He became aware of something else. Behind him was a presence beyond the music—the tentative scraping and sliding of Mona's shoes as she tested the dance floor. The soft rhythmic shuffling lasted less than thirty seconds.

If Dad finds out, I'll tell him that—

She started over. With every beat, her steps grew louder and more self-assured. Within ten seconds, she was fully involved. He spun around to watch her. Mona was in thrall to the music. Moving side to side, her arms floated out like an ice dancer's. With her head down, she seemed to watch her feet as though she, too, were amazed at the sight: her shoes—on a parquet floor, a real dance floor! Raleigh, too, was mesmerized. Her feet twisted and fanned out, shoe buckles shimmering in the colored light. Mona thrust her pale arms out and went forward and back, fast. None of it made sense to Raleigh, and yet it made perfect sense.

The music swelled, offered more. Goodman's clarinet solo seemed like a rising breeze to a feather already floating. The soft scuff-scuffing of her soles, the slight bouncing of her body. Raleigh dared not look up, and yet he found himself beginning to—to take in her narrow ankles rising above rolled white socks and the bottoms of her calves visible below the hem of her yellow cotton skirt.

Stop, he told himself, while his brain insisted that the higher he looked, the more he'd enjoy.

Yes, I know that. But this is Mona Garrison. There's no pretending this is Sally.

He tried to bypass Mona's breasts, to ignore them altogether, which he could do by pretending they weren't there and that she was not wearing a white blouse with faded blue pinstripes. But it was all folly. Her face in this light, in this music, above that dancing figure—with those large, blue eyes downcast—was not the face of a knobby-kneed fifteen-year-old girl but of a desirable woman.

Contradictory and insistent feelings began to stir within Raleigh. He looked around the strange room and got a sour taste in his throat. Without knowing what he was doing or why, he stepped past Mona and gently took her arm, turning her. "Let's get out of here," he said.

"What?"

"Come on." Raleigh charged for the door, and within seconds he could hear the scuffing of Mona's shoes as she ran in short, quick steps to catch up. The music, which had set Mona to soaring with the grace of a feather, seemed to be chasing them out the door.

* * *

Raleigh drove her down side streets, three lefts and a right—images of the water tower south of the center of town swinging right and left in the rearview mirror—until they hit Clark Road north of the Yelm Ditch. He spun the wheel at 109th, which was outside the city limits and, more importantly, removed from that part of town where his friends were likely to be. He looked on either side of the road for a driveway or turnout that would give them a few minutes of privacy before he had to get Mona home by two thirty. He knew he had some explaining to do. At last he spotted a little-used access road. He swung to the right, bounced over a few potholes, and nosed the truck under the outstretched branches of an apple tree less than one hundred feet from the county road. After shutting off the engine, he leaned back and exhaled a loud breath through pursed lips.

"Give me a minute," Raleigh said at last, not looking in Mona's direction. Mona didn't speak. She sat hunched with her hands in her lap. Three minutes later, with his head thrown back against the rear window and his eyes closed, he whispered, "Where'd you learn to dance?"

Mona snapped one thumbnail with the other. "My mom."

Raleigh rolled his head sideways. "Your mom taught you to dance like that?"

Mona nodded.

Raleigh snickered mirthlessly. "Wow. That's some mom."

"Before."

"Before what?"

"They took her. They let her take me to a movie first."

"What do you mean, 'they took her'?"

"That was the last day I saw her."

Raleigh raised his head. "Who took her?"

Mona hesitated. "I don't know."

"So you—"

Mona leaned over farther like she was trying to hide her hands from him all of a sudden. Raleigh felt a surge of pity. He sat up. "Are you okay?"

She didn't answer, but when he started to speak again, she said, "She was a dancer for men. But they said, 'No, you can't live here. You have to move.'"

"Where was she living?"

"In a building downtown, with nobody in it. It was just me and her, and they said that's too bad."

Raleigh waited for her to say more, but Mona fell quiet. "And you say she danced for men. You mean, like a burlesque dancer or something?'

Mona didn't look up. "I don't know. She was sick a lot. She would put herself to sleep."

He fell back again, still impressed. "Nobody dances like you, Mona. I mean *nobody*. I've seen a lot of dancing in the movies and all, and, by God, no one can do it as good as you." He turned and opened the driver's side window and stared at the dried gray and black leaves blanketing the ground. That way, he could let his compliment float out, as well, for it had made him uncomfortable.

He welcomed Mona's silence. Breathed in the fresh air. Thought of Sally Springs again. Wasn't this *her* town? He reimagined Sally's shocked expression as he and Mona danced under the moving spotlights at the Western Washington State Fair. He could hear the applause building all around them from the gallery. It would all be for Mona—the applause, that is—but that didn't matter. It was a couples' competition. He would win, too.

He would win, and Sally would see a different Raleigh Starr. Someone who helped a kid, who let a neighbor girl blossom. She'd like that, Sally would. Raleigh felt a chill run up his spine as he imagined Sally finding the opportunity to slide her hand into his before that night at the fair was over.

Mona shifted in her seat and tucked her skirt under her legs.

"You cold?" asked Raleigh.

"Nah."

A flock of starlings landed in the branches beyond the truck's window and, with a sudden fluttering of wings, took off again. Raleigh licked his thumb, rubbed a smudge on the speedometer glass, and said, "Sorry I got cold feet back there. It was just that..."

Just that what? That you're two years younger than me and you look like a grown-up dancing that way? That I can't keep my eyes off your hips and your... When in reality you're, what? A fourth grader? Not all there? Am I going to say that to you?

"The contest is a couples' competition," he heard himself say. "You're a great dancer, but people don't dance that way—the way your mom taught you to. It's going to be the Lindy Hop, you know? The jitterbug."

When Mona didn't answer, he turned to her. "I mean, I thought you could teach me, that we could develop our own dance, but when I saw you dancing I realized…" Mona lifted her eyes to him. "I don't know what I realized. I don't think I'm being fair to you."

She sat back and closed her eyes.

She doesn't owe me any words, anyway.

He gripped the steering wheel with both hands. "Look, Mona, here's the deal. I was drunk when I saw you that—"

"We could couples dance," Mona interrupted.

"What?"

"I could teach you. It isn't the jitterbug, though. Or Lindy's Hop." Mona's large, intense eyes were open again, staring out the front window of the truck. "She showed me. But we can—" Mona's eyes grew wide with imagining, and a slight smile touched the corners of her mouth. "I can change it, so we can dance together." She turned to Raleigh. "Do you want to?"

Raleigh drank in the sight of her.

"Do you want to?" she said, not in a woman's voice—but a squeak. "Do you want to?" She's a girl. She loves to dance. What's the harm?

* * *

The note on the Garrisons' front door read BACK AT 2:30. Raleigh checked his watch. "They'll be here in a minute." He pointed to the steps. "Let's wait here."

Mona looked at him, confused. "Don't you want to come in?" She stepped past him and opened the door.

"No. Go on in. I'll wait here till your aunt and uncle come home."

Raleigh sat on the top step. Mona entered the house and came back a minute or two later wearing a worn wool cardigan and carrying a small plate with two large sugar cookies. Raleigh took the plate; Mona stepped down and sat next to him.

"Tell me about your mom," Raleigh said, picking up one of the cookies.

"I miss her."

"You said they took her away. Is she in prison?"

Mona brought her knees up, wrapped her arms around her legs, and lowered her chin to her knees. "No. She's in a home. In Oregon. For women."

"A home?"

"She didn't have a home, and they told her if you have a kid you have to have one. You can't live in the buildings downtown. So they made her go there, and Aunt Grace and Uncle Simon came and got me."

Raleigh wondered if Mona's mother ran around, but he wasn't going to ask. He chewed the cookie and stared past the hood of his father's Model A to the road and the field and the woods beyond. "What about your father?" he ventured. "These are good, by the way."

Mona smiled. "I'm glad you like them. Mom said my dad was a teamster. That's all I know, and she said I'm better off not knowing. She told me once I should dream up my own dad if it meant that much to me."

Raleigh turned to her, surprised. "She did?" The matter seemed to rest easily with Mona. He added a quiet "Huh."

"What about *your* mom?" Mona asked, breaking off a small piece of the remaining cookie and raising it to her lips. "Is she dead?"

Raleigh glanced at Mona, then looked away. He hated talking about his mother. *Why'd I even bring this up?*

He remembered that night, the weakness in his father's voice: "We have to prepare ourselves for the worst, kids. The doctor says anytime now." His mother's coughing and choking for air in the next room. His father's unshaven, tear-streaked face. The way the kitchen looked: its stark shadows, its sudden foreignness. Lauren crying into her hands.

He'd avoided talking about his mom, or what it was like to lose her, all these years. He had tried to talk to his father once, about six months after her death, but he was frightened into silence by the sight of his father breaking down, doubling over and crying, something Raleigh could never have imagined, something he had never seen before or since. He couldn't talk to Lauren about it either. Instead of listening, she would tell him how he should feel.

On top of everything else, he realized he didn't have a clear picture of his mother, hadn't sorted the dying, emaciated woman from the living one, the one who smiled, and danced with his father in the kitchen, and could pull Raleigh's T-shirts over his head without hurting him. Which one would he describe if he had to? Which one would he remember?

I could tell Mona. She'd listen. She wouldn't tell me how to feel. Without turning back to her he nodded. Some other time though.

"Well, aren't we a pair?" said Mona quietly.

The comment startled Raleigh. This didn't sound like a mental defective. He sensed Mona's long body sitting beside him anew and wondered what to say next.

Maybe she was wondering the same thing.

"Do you have any dreams?" he said at last. "You know, things you'd like to do some day?"

Mona took another piece off the cookie. She seemed to ponder the question until she put the cookie in her mouth and began chewing. When Raleigh turned to her, she shook her head. "No."

He cleared his throat and sat up. He was brushing crumbs off his thighs when the Garrisons' Pontiac appeared at the edge of the forest and made its way along the rows of filbert trees. "There they are," said Mona. They watched the car slow and angle into the drive.

This is where we have to be careful. Should I remind her not to talk? No, it's too late. Besides, it might fluster her and make things worse.

Mr. Garrison pulled next to the Model A and backed into the carport. Raleigh jumped to his feet when Mrs. Garrison emerged from around the corner of the house, followed by Mr. Garrison carrying a bag of groceries.

"Sit," said Mrs. Garrison, waving him back down.

"Can I help with the groceries?" he asked.

She waved her hand again. "He only has the one bag."

"I got it," said Mr. Garrison. He winked. "Thanks, though."

Mrs. Garrison touched her glasses with a gloved hand. "Sorry we're late. How long have you two been sitting here?"

"A few minutes is all," said Raleigh. He and Mona both scooted forward to give Mr. Garrison room to pass and enter the house behind them.

Mr. Garrison spoke through the screen door. "You could have waited in the living room."

"Simon!" snapped Mrs. Garrison, eyeing her husband severely. "Were you raised in a barn? No, they're fine out here."

"Oh, I know," said Raleigh. "She offered. But this is fine."

Mona was silent. She had cupped the cookie remnant in her hands as though hiding it from her aunt.

"How did she do today?" Mrs. Garrison asked Raleigh.

"Oh, she did swell," he said. "Aunt Edith is pleased. I'm sure she'll tell you next time you see her."

Mrs. Garrison hesitated. She dipped her chin, and a skeptical glint entered her eyes. "Well, it's good of you to help her find work." She glanced over at the Model A as though an idea were striking her. "Tell me, how is it you're not helping your pa on Tuesdays? It seems mighty strange, you driving Mona into town and back every week."

Raleigh stood and brushed the remaining cookie crumbs from his pants. He used the time to collect himself. "He doesn't want me going into farming, for one thing. He told me a couple of weeks ago to take Tuesdays off this summer and look for work in town. Dad says I need to get my foot in the door somewhere, start looking. Plus, I do some shopping for Aunt Edith on Tuesdays." None of which explained his getting Mona involved, he realized. "When Mrs. Corning left Aunt Edith, I knew Mona—or I guess it was you who said once that you were training Mona for cleaning work and such... So I thought of her...since we live on the same road."

"Well, I may have—"

"And I'm happy to do it." Raleigh jumped to the ground and walked toward the pickup. He pulled out the bucket and mop and handed them to a surprised Mrs. Garrison. "See you next week, Mona," he said, sliding into the driver's seat. "Same time." Raleigh made eye contact with Mrs. Garrison and glanced at Mona.

Don't say anything, Mona. I'm counting on you. If you talk, the whole thing's going to blow up.

Raleigh felt the need to address Mrs. Garrison again. "And I'll have her home again by two thirty—sharp."

CHAPTER SEVEN

"I CAN'T DO THAT."

"Sure you can. Here, watch." Mona demonstrated, waiting a half beat to catch the rhythm from the solo sax in Woody Herman's *Woodchopper's Ball*. She stepped forward and back, her elbows high. Raleigh stood with his hands on his hips in the empty bar, gazing at Mona's face. "Watch my feet," said Mona, still in motion. "Up and back, up and back."

Raleigh shook his head. He lined up next to her to try again. Their bodies bounced out of synchronization. "One-two-three-four, one-two-three-four," encouraged Mona, almost out of breath. As she bounced forward and back, a rosy sheen covered her cheeks and forehead.

This is hard for him. Oh, but he's so handsome! What's he doing? Now he's trying too hard.

"That's it. Don't worry about your arms, just the feet."

Forward, back, one-two-three-four, one-two-three-four. He fell into the rhythm. His body kept it up. Mona began to inch away. She swung around to face him, changing her steps. She moved back as he stepped forward, forward when he stepped back.

"There you go!" Ed Becker called out from behind the bar. Becker, a wiry, diminutive man with silver-gray hair and brown eyes, spoke through a wide mouth that, when arched into a smile, creased his face, temple to jaw. He was famous in town for his unique, high-pitched cackle that every child in Yelm, at one time or another, had tried to imitate.

Raleigh looked at Mona. She bit her lip, suppressing a smile.

Oh, God, I can't believe this. How lucky can a girl be?

She drew closer.

Raleigh took her hand and spun her, first one way and then the other. The music ended with a syncopated point-counterpoint of brass section and full ensemble.

"Hot damn!" shouted Becker.

She didn't want the tune to end. As if Becker could read her thoughts, he shouted, "Hey, don't move, you two. I've got this." Becker threw down his rag and hurried to the jukebox. Raleigh and Mona froze in place when the music stopped, each smiling. While they waited for the next record, Mona looked up, as if drawn by the force of Raleigh's stare. "You're doing great," she said.

Raleigh laughed. "I know how I'm doing. All I have to do is look at you."

She slapped his forearm playfully. "You goose."

* * *

By the end of July, Raleigh was no longer looking at his feet. Much of their dancing involved one or two hands touching. Her soft hands were in his or brushing across his back as he turned. He could spin Mona on a dime and they had the "Mona Garrison base step" down pat. Mona seldom looked up, but it didn't matter. Her dancing was so unique, so loose-jointed, so smooth—it lacked nothing and seemed to contain everything. She had a style all her own. Which had been Raleigh's point all along.

In mid-August, he hit upon something: a simple motion that would free Mona to dance alone for long periods while he maintained a simple jitterbug four-step at her side. The first time he did it, it was by accident. She had completed a turn at the end of his outstretched arm and was coming back to join him, to take his other hand, when he pulled away and raised both hands, palms out, as if to say, "Okay, okay, I won't touch you." As he did this, Mona backed away and began to move to the music as only she could. He, in turn, pivoted on his left foot to take a position out of the way. The result was like clouds opening for the harvest moon. It occurred seamlessly, as though they'd practiced it for months. Raleigh was surprised to have come up with the move and delighted that he could carry off his part so neatly. He included it every time they danced.

* * *

On the way home, Raleigh spotted the forest green Chrysler Coupe in his rearview mirror before Wheels hit the horn. He glanced into the mirror again and waved. Wheels signaled for him to pull over. Raleigh groaned under his breath.

"Who is it?" asked Mona.

Mona's flushed and moist face—a look he'd come to like on the dance floor—seemed less desirable to him now. "Wheels Henderson," he said. Mona started to turn, but Raleigh said, "Don't look. Just…"

Just what? Think of something. How the hell am I going to explain this?

"Just sit tight," he said at last, pulling across the intersection, angling the Model A toward the curb.

Wheels drove past them and parked. With his left hand out the window, he signaled to Raleigh to come forward.

"Just be a minute," Raleigh said to Mona, turning off the engine and setting the brake. He climbed out and walked toward Wheels. "Hello, old man."

Wheels waited until Raleigh was beside the window. He was chewing gum. "So it's true."

"What's that?" Raleigh looked down at the bobbing, crooked front teeth, rather than meet his friend's glare. He knew they were far enough away that Mona couldn't hear, but he kept his back to her anyway.

"All the bullshit I've been hearing about you and Mona Garrison."

Raleigh tried to marshal his pounding heart. "What have you heard?"

"That you're doing something with her… I don't know. I told Sammy White he was crazy and that I'd pop him one if I heard him say it again."

"What'd he say?"

Wheels checked his rearview mirror, took a long look at Mona. "That you've been hanging around with her, taking her into that vacant apartment above the Osprey Club."

"*What*?" Raleigh felt an ache in the pit of his stomach. How many people thought this? What was he doing to Mona's reputation? And his own?

"Hey, you asked," said Wheels. "Like I said, you won't be hearing that from Sammy White again."

Raleigh took a deep breath and gazed over the top of the Chrysler. "Look, Wheels," he began, "Mona is working for my aunt, okay? She cleans her house on Tuesdays. I give her a ride into town and take her home in the afternoon."

Wheels squinted up at his friend, clearly not satisfied.

"Here's the deal, okay?" said Raleigh, his voice pinched and partly stifled by nerves. "Mona is a great swing dancer. I didn't know this till... I found out recently. She's not just great—she's phenomenal. I can't describe it. I know she's...she's..." He was tired of calling Mona feebleminded. She was one of the nicest girls he knew, and lately she'd been acting and speaking more like girls her age. Still, there was no denying she was in grade school. "I know she's *different* and all that, but I've never seen anything like it. Anyway, I got it into my head that she and I could win the dance contest at the Puyallup Fair this fall. Win the one hundred dollars. And on top of that, we could beat Sally and Ted. They came in third last year, remember?"

Wheels's jaw dropped. "You're kidding me."

Raleigh could feel the heat rise under his skin. "No."

"So...you're..."

"After she's done at my aunt's house, I take her to the Osprey Club to practice."

"Practice? What do you mean practice?"

"Dancing. We play music on the jukebox."

"Wait a minute, wait a minute. You and Mona Garrison? You two are...?"

"That's right. She's teaching me. I'm not kidding, Wheels. She dances like an angel."

Wheels's brown eyes bored into him. "Are you nuts? What are you trying to do—get yourself arrested?"

Raleigh's head snapped back. "*Arrested*? For dancing? That's all we're doing." He grew more frustrated with each passing second. Was Wheels going to believe him, or not? Whose side was he on?

"Raleigh, she's in the fourth grade or some goddamn thing. You can't—"

"She's fifteen."

"I don't care if she's sixty. She's feebleminded. What do you think you're—?"

"She's *not*. I mean...she can't do schoolwork, but she's a lot smarter than people give her credit for. You don't know her like I do."

"Oh, shit. You *are* nuts. You're using her."

Raleigh raced around the front of the car, opened the passenger door and jumped in. "Listen to me," he bellowed. His tone was ferocious, unlike any he'd used before. "I'm not using her—okay? I'm using her dancing. There's nothing going on. I...I don't care what anybody's saying. She's fifteen. She's a girl. She likes to dance. She's agreed to dance with me at the fair, and we're going to win. That's it, period." Raleigh slung his elbow out the passenger side window and shook his head.

"Okay, okay." Wheels put both hands up. "Keep your shirt on."

Raleigh let a few seconds pass. "It's just the way it is," he said miserably.

Wheels rubbed his hands over the steering wheel. "Well, you sure have everybody talking."

"To hell with them," Raleigh muttered. The skin between his shoulder blades contracted. This meant his dad would find out. And the Garrisons, too. Did they already know something?

"What do the Garrisons say about this?" When Raleigh didn't answer, Wheels blew out a long breath. "Oh, shit. You're dead."

"I'm going to tell them," Raleigh said weakly. A faint whiff of courage produced, "They'll be okay with it."

Wheels shook his head. "This is the craziest thing I've ever heard. If it wasn't the middle of the afternoon, I'd say you were drunk."

"I shouldn't have told you," said Raleigh.

"And this is all to get back at Sally Springs? By the way, what'd she ever do to you?"

"Not to get back at her, to *get* her. To get her to notice me for once. Shit, you know I've had a thing about her since the minute I laid eyes on her. We're graduating next spring. So tell me, when do I get a chance?"

Wheels looked closely at his friend and raised his eyebrows. "You don't, old man. Don't you know that?"

Raleigh's heart sank. Part of him knew Wheels was right: Sally would always be with Ted. But wasn't there one chance left? Isn't there always room for that? He'd pinned all his hopes on Mona, because she was to Yelm what Ginger Rogers was to Hollywood. He'd discovered her. She could out-dance Sally and every other girl he'd ever known. So if he danced with her, surely some of Mona's excellence would rub off on him. Then he and Sally could share a love of dancing.

He'd imagined creating a moment for all of them: For Mona, who would be the star of the night, but also for Sally and him. Especially for Sally and him.

"You need to stop all this while you can," said Wheels.

"It's my only shot." Raleigh turned to Wheels. "Will you keep this a secret?"

Wheels let his mouth gape open.

"I mean it," said Raleigh.

"You're a real specimen, you know that? This has got to be one of the most harebrained ideas you've ever—"

Raleigh brought his arm inside the car and raised his voice. "Do you have any better ideas? If you do, let's hear them."

"All right. But listen, you better figure something out—quick. Your reputation's going to the dogs."

"Tell people Mona's cleaning my aunt's house. That's the truth. And I take her because we're neighbors. We live on the same road."

"And the Osprey Club?"

Raleigh searched the corners of his mind, trying to ignore the irritation in Wheels's voice. "Errands," he said at last. "I was running an errand when they saw me. It doesn't matter what." He turned rounded eyes on Wheels. "An errand for my dad or something."

"All right, boss. I'll keep your secret. I don't like it, though. It's putting me in a hell of a spot." Wheels shifted his weight. "Now, let me tell you why I stopped you. A bunch of us are going swimming Sunday afternoon at Lake Lawrence. It's supposed to be hotter than Hades this weekend. You might as well join us—you know, like you're normal or something. Might be the last party of the summer."

And a chance to see Sally in that orange bathing suit.

He remembered Sally's long legs and curvaceous figure as she strode ashore at the Pioneer Days picnic the previous August, sunlit droplets sliding down her skin, her wet hair streaked back like cast bronze.

"Well?" said Wheels. "What do you say?"

"What? Oh, sure. I'll be there."

"What's going on?" It was Mona's voice just above a whisper. The girl stood behind him on the sidewalk with her arms folded across her chest. Her brow was puckered with concern. "Are you all right?"

Raleigh jumped out of the car and ran to her side. He gently turned her toward the truck. "Oh, sure. Sure I am. Let's get you home." He opened the door, then trotted around and got in behind the wheel—not once looking in Wheels's direction.

CHAPTER EIGHT

AT THE LAKE PARTY, Raleigh greeted Sally, stole glances over his upraised Pepsi-Cola bottle, listened for the timbre of her voice. He couldn't sit facing her; not even behind sunglasses would he trust himself not to stare. He set his back to Sally, joined another group, and pretended she wasn't there. Pretended that Ted's voice was meant for someone else.

"What about you, Raleigh?" said a tan, bare-chested Joe Zandt. Zandt lay back on his elbows over an orange, blue, and white beach towel, legs outstretched, bare feet planted on the gentle slope. Small waves died among the pebbles at the shoreline a few feet away, producing an unending chorus of whispers.

"What?"

"The war. You going over to fight the Nazis, or what?"

Raleigh watched a thread of smoke rise from Zandt's cigarette. He thought he heard Sally's voice in the other group. "If we declare war, you mean?"

"Oh, we'll get in. You wait."

Raleigh shrugged. "I'll go. I'm not going to let that idiot brother of yours fight for me, if that's what you mean."

Zandt smiled. "That's Private Second Class Ronald R. Zandt to you."

Raleigh raised his Pepsi-Cola bottle in lieu of a salute. "Which goes to show the Army will take anybody. Ron couldn't hit the lake with a rifle from here."

Wheels rocked back with laughter. "Maybe with a tank he could."

Raleigh lifted his sunglasses and placed them in his hair. "Why'd he enlist, anyway? I thought he was going to become a commercial fisherman with your brother-in-law in Alaska."

"He was. But did you hear what they're doing over there? We get clippings from the *New York Times* from my uncle Aaron in Hoboken. The Nazis are burning all the Jewish businesses, and shit, arresting people—sometimes whole families. Ron says fishing can wait; dealing with Hitler and his thugs can't."

Raleigh nodded.

"As soon as we graduate, I'm going in," said Roy Fisher. "Maybe before, if I can talk my parents into it." The lanky senior-to-be tossed a pebble into the lake to lay emphasis on his words. "If Roosevelt'll get off the dime and declare war on Germany, I'll go in the next day."

"Or Japan," said Zandt.

"Or Japan," agreed Fisher.

Raleigh set his head back to take the sun against his face. He'd heard enough talk of war. But a few seconds later, he remembered his father leaning close to the radio the night before, listening to Edward R. Murrow's report from London. More than once over the past several months, following Murrow's "Good night, and good luck," his father had shaken his head and said one way or another: "If Britain falls, Hitler won't be stopped. It's now or never. What are we waiting for?"

Wheels said to Raleigh, "I just thought of something. If we declare war, you'll have to put your gigolo business on hold."

Laughter erupted all around. Raleigh smiled crookedly. "I might. If I do, there'll be a lot of disappointed women from here to Bellingham." More laughter. Raleigh decided to keep it going. "I wonder if that's a rank? Gigolo First Class? Hell, I could take that show right to Berlin."

Their small circle rocked back with raucous laughter. Raleigh felt a warmth unrelated to the temperature of the air or the blazing four o'clock sun.

"Now you're talking sense," said Wheels. "There's a place for everybody in the Army."

Raleigh smiled and spread his arms in the air. Fisher relayed to Sally's group what all the laughter was about: "Raleigh wants to be a gigolo in the Army." Sally laughed with the others.

Oh, is there any sweeter sound in all the world?

* * *

By late afternoon, half of Raleigh's classmates had departed. The group was down to eleven, including Sally and Ted. Fisher had left for an hour and returned with a case of Rainier beer, and someone else produced a pint of Hennessey. The towels were moved one by one to a shady patch in the pea gravel beside an aromatic stand of cedars, and it was no longer possible for Raleigh to keep the object of his desire out of view. At least five times since relocating, he'd formed the intention and rehearsed in his mind the features of a graceful exit. But something kept him there, albeit hidden behind dark sunglasses.

He allowed himself the relief of a short swim, then dropped down on his towel. He was donning a short-sleeved white shirt when Wheels tapped him on the arm. A suggestive nod pointed him fifty yards down the beach, where three people made their way over the stony shore to the water's edge. The youngest stumbled and reached down to catch herself. As they picked their way along, Raleigh looked at Wheels and felt a lump form in his throat. They'd brought her there to swim, to cool off.

Raleigh and the others were downwind and partly hidden by logs and boulders. It was clear the Garrisons hadn't seen them.

He imagined that his friends were staring at him. He folded his hands over his knees and looked down. The conversations of a few moments earlier had halted and died.

What now? Do they all suspect?

Wheels spoke up. "Hey, I heard she's working for your aunt this summer. Is that true?"

Raleigh nodded. "Yeah. Tuesdays."

"I saw you dropping her off there one time, but I couldn't stop. I was late for a dentist appointment. So what happened to the other lady? The one who cleaned Mrs. Moore's house before?"

"Ella Corning," said Ted.

Raleigh pulled out a tall, spindly weed, roots and all. Tossing it aside, he said, "Yeah. Her husband got a job in Seattle, so they had to move. She worked for my aunt for as long as I can remember."

Wheels wasn't done. "I heard somewhere your dad recommended Mona Garrison." He chuckled. "That's pretty keen of him. I mean, that's something she can do, right?"

"That *is* keen," said Sally. "I didn't know that. I like your dad."

Raleigh smiled as the others voiced agreement with Sally's sentiment. He turned and met Wheels's eyes over his upturned beer bottle. Wheels's eyebrows arched victoriously.

"And I provide the taxi service," said Raleigh, reaching for a Rainier himself. He popped the top and listened for what clues he might gather from the side talk of his friends, but there were none. He remembered the look on Wheels's face when he'd confronted him about the Osprey Club. What could he say if someone asked him what he and Mona were doing there? He had to come up with something. At last, an idea occurred to him. "I don't mind driving her there and back, but it can be all wet, too. Especially if I've got things to do. Dad says I'm responsible for her, period—no ifs, ands, or buts. Until I get her home, wherever I go, she goes."

"Well, summer's almost over, old man," said Wheels. "You can retire the halo and concentrate on football."

Raleigh and the others laughed. "You got that right," Raleigh said.

Fisher belched and said, "I'm going in. Anyone else?" He clambered to his feet. Others took hurried swallows of beer or snuffed cigarettes, and the whole group, save Raleigh, was in motion at once.

"I just got out," Raleigh said. He scooped up a beer bottle, three-quarters-full, in danger of tipping over onto Fisher's towel. "You guys go ahead. I'll hold down the fort."

Fisher didn't miss a beat. "Like hell you will." He leaned over, grabbed the Rainier bottle from Raleigh's hand, guzzled it, and threw the empty bottle, spinning circles of suds into the woods. He turned and headed toward the lake.

Over the laughter of his friends, Raleigh shouted, "Don't trust me, huh?" and "Let's see if I pass the ball to you this season!"

The others walked to the water's edge and beyond, jostling and laughing, and Raleigh, smiling, lay back, propping himself on his elbows. But soon enough the three figures standing alone down the beach stole his attention.

What are the chances? I bet the Garrisons haven't gone swimming here in years—maybe ever—and today of all days they show up. It's for Mona's sake. Probably hotter than a pistol upstairs in that house. I wonder if she can swim. Well, it doesn't matter. She can wade, anyway.

He relaxed and remembered Mona's smile as she rode beside him in the truck, listening to him talk; and the way her eyes turned serious when he would ask her a question, and she would answer as though nothing in the world were more serious; or when she cleaned Aunt Edith's house. These images could drift through his mind now that, thanks to Wheels, suspicions about him and Mona had been dealt with. He watched Mrs. Garrison instruct Mona, who stepped out of a long black skirt to reveal an enormous, outdated, ill-fitting black swimsuit.

Oh Lord, they're making her wear that?

A sharp pain began in his chest. He glanced at his friends to make sure they weren't watching. Mona looked like a child wearing an obese woman's swimsuit from the days before the Great War. Her slender legs didn't begin to fill the leg holes, and her arms hung forlornly out of great ovals cut in the draping cloth. A V-shaped fold of loose material covered her posterior.

How could they do that? They should have stayed home. They didn't have to subject her to this.

Out of the corner of his eye, he saw Ted jump on Fisher's back, forcing him under the water. Fisher let out a loud yelp. Mona spun around. She froze. Seconds later, she was covering her chest self-consciously, and struggling over the rocks as fast as she could go, splashing into waist-deep water. She slunk down and immediately turned her back to Ellington, Fisher, and the others. Mrs. Garrison was saying something to her that Raleigh couldn't hear. Mona shook her head, refusing to look, inching farther out into the water.

Raleigh was unaware of the smile forming on his face. When at last he felt it, he lay back, staring at the tops of the cedars, not trusting himself to avoid looking at her. He closed his eyes and remembered a conversation he'd had with his aunt two weeks earlier.

"I ran into Grace Garrison at the DAR dinner last night," Aunt Edith had said, reaching for Raleigh's arm. Her tone was secretive. "She's at her wit's end, worried sick about how to manage Mona."

"*Manage* her?" he'd replied in a hushed tone. The two moved by implicit agreement away from the stairwell for fear Mona, working upstairs, would hear them. "What does that mean?"

"Well, Simon doesn't know anything about girls, of course, and Grace feels now that Mona's a teenager, she's apt to..." Aunt Edith spoke with a nervous ardency that Raleigh knew from years past. "The feebleminded are—how do I say this? There's no shortage of men who will take advantage. You'll find these girls succumbing to temptation, adopting loose morals."

Raleigh tried to think of a response.

For some girls, maybe, girls who are severely—but not Mona. She's so much smarter than people think. And who would take advantage of her?

"I don't see it myself," Aunt Edith added, as though reading his thoughts. "She may be defective—oh, no doubt she is—but there's a strength there. I sense it. I hear it in her voice. I tried to tell Grace this, but she wouldn't listen." Raleigh stood staring at his unseeing aunt, a prisoner of her relentless odors. "She's a good worker," Aunt Edith continued. She seemed to shudder at an unspoken afterthought. "It's good that you're with her when she comes into town on Tuesdays, Raleigh. Don't let her out of your sight."

"No, of course not."

The sounds of laughter and splashing from the lake lifted him from his reverie. He turned onto his left side and rested his head on his hand.

I could go over there and ask the Garrisons about the fair. Nobody would hear me, but seeing me over there talking to them would prove that I'm a friend of the family, that I'm on the up and up where Mona's concerned.

He sat up and reached for his shoes. If Mrs. Garrison accepted his being alone with Mona, who could complain?

Simon and Grace Garrison stood several feet apart, leaning against the trunk of a fallen cedar that stretched far out into the lake. They were watching their niece. When Mona saw Raleigh approaching, she sank further in the water, letting her chin break the surface.

"Oh hello, Raleigh," said Mr. Garrison.

"Hi, Mr. Garrison, Mrs. Garrison. I thought it was you over here." Raleigh looked closely at Mrs. Garrison. If she'd heard rumors or held suspicions about Mona and him, he'd know in an instant. There was nothing out of the ordinary in her dour expression.

"It's a hot one, isn't it?" said Mr. Garrison.

"It sure is." Raleigh smiled. "I'm surprised you two aren't in the water."

"Oh, pshaw!" said Mrs. Garrison. "I haven't swum in twenty years. We came so Mona could take a dip before dinner."

"Ah. I see," said Raleigh. He turned to see Mona squatting in the water. She appeared to be inching away from them.

Raleigh set his back to the lake and whispered, "Speaking of Mona, I have a question for you. My Aunt Edith is delighted with Mona's work. I think I told you that. I'd like to do something special for Mona—a bonus. Edith can't leave the house, as you know. So what I came up with is the fair."

"The fair?" said Mr. Garrison. "I don't follow you."

"I'd like your permission to take Mona to Puyallup one day next month to take in the fair. I think she'd get a kick out of it, and it'll give her an idea how much Aunt Edith appreciates her hard work."

"Oh, heavens," said Mrs. Garrison, coloring. "I don't think that'll be necessary. No, not at all."

Raleigh looked into Mr. Garrison's gray eyes. Without thinking, he blurted, "You two would be invited, of course. We could make a day of it."

Oh, Lord. Say no, say no.

Mr. Garrison lifted his worn felt fedora to let some air inside. "No, that's all right. I'm up to here with fairs. But I think Mona would like that. She's—"

"What?" said Mrs. Garrison, turning to face her husband.

"Sure," said Mr. Garrison. "She'd have a swell time. Raleigh here will look after her."

"I'm sure he would," said Mrs. Garrison without conviction. "But I don't think it's a good idea. In fact, I won't—"

"Nonsense," said Mr. Garrison. "We were that age once. Let her take it in, for heaven's sake. The fair only comes around once a year."

Mrs. Garrison leaned toward her husband and cautioned between clenched teeth, "That's not the point. I've talked to you about this, Simon. I can barely keep things under control as it is."

"If you'd like to go along..." Raleigh repeated.

"Yes," Mr. Garrison encouraged his wife. "Go, if you want."

A deeper red stained her face. "No, thank you." Her rounded shoulders sagged, and an audible breath escaped through her nose. She looked at Raleigh and her husband as though confirming, in these two examples, something indecent and unpredictable about the gender. She addressed her husband: "I've told you why we can't be too careful. If we start here, it will—"

"Oh, for Pete's sake," Mr. Garrison interrupted. "It's the fair. What are you so worked up about?"

Mrs. Garrison frowned. "I can see I'm outnumbered," she said.

Mr. Garrison, who had repositioned himself against the log, with his arms crossed, said to Raleigh, "You'd have to keep a close eye on her. Don't let her out of your sight."

Raleigh nodded. "Absolutely."

Raleigh felt a wave of relief. "So, if it's all right, it'll have to be that last Saturday. I know Dad has plans for me on Sunday."

Mrs. Garrison thrust her lower jaw to the side angrily. "That's fine, Raleigh," said Mr. Garrison. "Mona'll like that."

Raleigh glanced around to see Mona in the same position as before. "If it's okay, I'd like to surprise her."

Mr. Garrison nodded. "Sure."

Raleigh cleared his throat, suppressing his guilt. He considered telling them about the dance contest, but it would only create more questions. Besides, he had told them he'd be with her at all times, keeping her safe.

CHAPTER NINE

IT WAS A QUARTER PAST TWO O' CLOCK on a rainy Sunday, September 7th. Raleigh stared out the windshield, bouncing and rocking behind the wheel. Mona sat with her left leg over her knee, tying her shoe. Sam Farmin, a neighbor, passed and waved. Raleigh waved back.

Mona's workday had been switched from Tuesdays to Sundays now that school had started. Raleigh was a senior; Mona had been enrolled on a trial basis in the fifth grade at Yelm Elementary School. Aunt Edith hadn't had a problem making the switch to Sundays. "Washington's blue laws don't mean a thing to me," she'd explained. "I'll employ who I want, when I want, and you can tell the governor for all I care."

Ed Becker had been no less accommodating. "We're closed Sundays, but I go in after twelve to clean, restock, and do paperwork. If you two want to practice, knock any time between noon and three." Both had made things so easy.

Chasing a random thought, Raleigh said, "I heard Brian Tanaka may be quitting the football team."

Mona sat up tall. "He is. His sister told me on the bus." Her voice rang with conviction. Raleigh opened his eyes wide. He'd never heard her talk like this before. "It's awful."

"Why? What did she say?"

Mona fixed Raleigh with a severe look. "Morton's won't buy vegetables from her father anymore because they're Japanese. Mr. Stoddard told them that some customers have complained."

"What?"

"Yeah. So now Brian has to go after school and help his father sell vegetables at the roadside stand near Dylan's Corner." Mona pushed her hair back over her left ear. "It's so unfair."

"It's probably because of the Japanese—their invasion of China and everything."

"What does that have to do with Mr. Tanaka?"

"Nothing. I mean, they're different, though—right? You can't—"

"They're people like anyone else."

Raleigh didn't know what surprised him more, the news about Mr. Tanaka or the depth of Mona's concern. How could he answer her? There was no answer. He stared out the windshield, but could see out of the corner of his eye that she was still looking to him. He took a deep breath. He thought of trying to describe the significance of the loss of Brian Tanaka to the football team, but that seemed out of place.

They drove in silence for several minutes. Raleigh glanced over at Mona, not once but three times in quick succession. Something had changed. He'd realized how much he liked her—admired her, even. Her gentleness, the way she carried herself, her compassion, her purposefulness. Even the sound of her voice.

Because of the humidity, her cheeks were still red and moist from dancing. Raleigh's breath caught at the sight of the top of one of her breasts where a button had come loose on her beige blouse. She turned and looked into his eyes. When he didn't say anything, she turned away again. The rising edge of her cheek—evidence of a smile—was visible as she stared out the passenger window at the passing fields.

Something else was different, too. Maybe it was that they'd gotten their dance routine down. She'd been a great teacher. No matter how many times he'd messed up, she had never complained. It was always, "Let's do it again."

"I was just thinking about the old man who wanted to dance with me," said Mona. "Do you remember him?"

Raleigh chuckled. "How could I forget? You could smell the whiskey on his breath ten feet away. I should have known something was up when I saw him stagger over to the jukebox."

Mona giggled.

Raleigh sang in his best crooner voice, letting the windshield wipers set the beat. "I'm confessing that I love you... Tell me, do you love me, too?" Mona covered her rising laughter with her hand. "Hiya there, doll," Raleigh droned, trying to mimic the drunken old man. "I couldn't help noticing you. If you don't mind, I'd like to... I'd like to have this next dance."

"He was nice," Mona protested.

"Ha! That's what you think." Mona's smile lingered as she slid down and rested her head against the back of the seat. They shared the smell of more than a dozen years of dust and grit in the closed-up truck, and the whine of its tired engine. "What you don't know about men could fill *The Encyclopedia Britannica,"* Raleigh said, repositioning his hands at ten and two on the steering wheel. The truck's translucent red steering wheel knob rested in the crotch of his right thumb.

Raleigh thought back three and a half weeks, picturing the way the old man's bleary eyes had ridden his wet, stuck smile down the length of Mona's body and up again.

"She's with me," Raleigh had said, stepping closer to Mona. He'd considered putting his hand out and would have done so if the man had taken one more step toward Mona. "Sorry, sir. We're not here to—she's with me."

"You don't say," the old man shot back. "Well, that's jim-dandy. But I believe that's my nickel's worth you're listening to there. That's Rudy Vallée. A man can dance to his own nickel, can't he?"

By this time Raleigh had motioned to Ed. Whipping his white towel over his shoulder, Becker walked from behind the bar. "Let's leave these two be, Ralph," he said, taking the old man by the arm. "They're here to practice. I told you that last time."

"I don't give a goddamn if they're here to pick peaches. I paid for that Rudy Vallée song." The old man's eyes jumped from Becker to Raleigh to Mona and settled somewhere near Mona's breasts. He pulled his arm free. "I should be able to dance to my own song."

"Ralph, you come on over here," Becker said, turning the old man. "These two are practicing for that big dance contest at the fair. You'll throw off her timing. I've seen you dance."

"I'm a hell of a dancer."

"Well, that's right. You're a hell of a dancer."

Becker looked back over his shoulder and winked at Raleigh and Mona. Pushing the old man along, he said, "Let me refund you that nickel, Ralph. It's only fair."

The wipers continued to clack across the windshield. "You didn't want him to dance with me," said Mona.

Raleigh looked over. Her eyes were closed. "No, I guess I didn't. Did you want to dance with him?" Her brow puckered, but she didn't answer.

"The fair is two weeks away," he said several minutes later, with the rattling truck a mile closer to the Garrison home.

"Yes," Mona replied, her voice far away. All of a sudden, she sat up straight and said, "Oh, Uncle Simon said you won the football game on Friday night. Is that true?"

"Ha! Where'd that come from? Yup. We beat Eatonville 14 to 6."

"Do you like football?"

Raleigh squinted at her skeptically, but her eyes shone with genuine curiosity. He chuckled. "Sure."

"Uncle Simon says you play until the end of November."

"That's right."

"I'd like to go to one of your games."

"What?" His insides churned as he imagined not just the high school but the whole league buzzing about Raleigh Starr and his feeb girlfriend… *"And look, she's in the stands!"*

"You want to see a game? A football game?" he said.

Mona smiled and nodded.

"Wait, why would you—" Then it struck him. It wasn't the game she wanted to see. It was him.

His eyes darted back and forth.

What's she thinking—that I'm keen on her? Or that I could be? I told her this was for the dance contest only.

He remembered how she had looked at him when he picked her up that morning and the Sunday before. He felt a sinking sensation. Had she averted her eyes out of coyness? Was her face pink from blushing and not sleepiness?

Mona sat up, awaiting an answer.

"Oh, I don't know, Mona. I don't think you'd like it. It's—"

"How do you know?"

"It's just that—"

"You like it."

"Well, yes, but—" He glanced at her questioningly.

"And Uncle Simon likes it. I think I would, too. Let me come. As a favor."

"A favor?" Raleigh said. "Listen, I'd rather focus on the dance contest, if that's okay. Football is—"

Mona's face clouded over. "You said you wanted a favor. When you asked me to dance…in the beginning."

A determined look crept into her eyes unlike anything he had seen before, although he'd seen something similar when she worked. He rubbed his hand over his mouth trying to hide his panic. "Okay, let me think. What about your uncle? Can't he take you? I go early. I can't—"

"I asked already. He said he doesn't have time."

Mona's tone told him she wasn't prepared to take no for an answer.

Raleigh glanced side to side as he tried to think of what to say next.

It's true, I asked her to dance as a favor, but I never thought…I never said anything about… And now she wants to…

"Why are you doing that with your eyes?" Mona asked. "What are you looking at?"

Raleigh cracked the window to let some air in. "Okay, listen. I'll think about it, okay? I need to think about it."

* * *

"You're an idiot!" Raleigh's sister Lauren stomped out of his bedroom with Raleigh in close pursuit.

"I need you to take her to one game. I owe her that."

"I can't believe you!" She spun on her heels rather than enter her bedroom. Pushing her hair away from her eyes, she shouted, "You know, I heard a rumor about this, but I didn't believe it. You can't do this to people, Raleigh. What were you thinking? That she wouldn't notice you? *Mister* Quarterback? You think you can take a fourteen-year-old gir—"

"She's fifteen."

"—a fifteen-year-old, feebleminded girl dancing, and she won't have feelings?" Lauren turned and walked into her bedroom. She threw her arms out at her sides and spun around. "You find her a job, and you don't think that will endear you to her?"

"I…"

Lauren sat heavily on her bed. "And this obsession over Sally Springs is too much. What do you see in her?"

Raleigh stepped into her room, glad that his father wasn't home to hear any of this. He closed the door anyway. "Just look at her," he said. "Sally's the most beautiful girl in this whole damn—"

"Sally Springs? You're kidding me, right? Open your eyes, Charlie."

"What do you mean?"

"She's average at best. You've got to get out of Yelm."

Raleigh searched his sister's face for a sign of jealousy or insincerity, but…

"Besides," Lauren continued, "she and Ted Ellington are inseparable. When are you going to get that through your thick skull? She's not available." Under her breath, she added, "thank God."

Raleigh stared at his sister in disbelief.

Lauren touched her forehead as though pushing against a headache. "You've certainly fouled things up this time." She picked up a pair of socks on her bed and threw them down. "For the first time in my life, I can honestly say I'm ashamed of my baby brother."

Stung, Raleigh made his way to the chair facing Lauren's desk. He spun it around and straddled it.

"What are you going to do?" she asked.

Raleigh looked up. "I don't know."

"You can't go through with the dance contest, you know. You've got to tell her."

"Tell her? You mean—oh, no, I can't do that. I've promised her. She's counting on it. Lauren, she… No, listen, we're going to win that one hundred dollars, and it's all going to be because of her. Besides, I've promised her we'd split the money."

"You're going to break her heart."

Raleigh thought for a moment. "We don't know each other that well. It's a schoolgirl crush is all. It can't—"

"Like your feelings for Sally? You don't know *Sally* that well either. You said so yourself."

He had to concede the point. He looked around the room for his next idea. When it came to him, he turned back to find Lauren waiting for a response. "We can still do the dance contest," he said. "But listen, this is where I need your help. I need you to talk to her. Take her to next week's game. If you're there with her, you can tell her I'm dating someone, or—"

"You want me to lie for you? Forget it." Lauren shook her head. "I can't believe you took her to that stinking Osprey Club—or that you took her anywhere dancing without a chaperone."

"We weren't dancing *that* way. It's practice. Besides, Ed was there most of the time."

"Most of the time. Ed Becker? Do you hear yourself? What do Mona's aunt and uncle say about this? Do they know?"

Raleigh drew in a ragged breath. "No, they don't." He didn't want to look at the evidence mounting against him. Staring down at his hands, he mumbled, "But they've given me permission to take her to the fair."

"What? They said yes to that?"

Raleigh nodded.

With a bitter smile, Lauren said, "You've got this all figured out, don't you?"

Fighting the urge to stomp out and slam the door behind him, he gripped the back of the chair. "I'm in love with her—with Sally—and time's running out. We're seniors. She doesn't notice me. If I can't... And besides, Mona loves to dance. I'm giving her a chance to do something she wouldn't get to do otherwise: to go to a dance, or to dance with a partner. If you could see her dance, you'd know how good she is. It's amazing."

"She's not a trick pony, Raleigh. She's a human being."

Over the next few seconds, Lauren seemed to shed some of her agitation. Raleigh told himself to keep quiet, to let Lauren have the next word. He looked down at his hands. He'd take Mona dancing someday—properly—after this was all over. Maybe in a couple of years. He'd ask the Garrisons for permission. He'd tell his father. She'd be old enough to go unchaperoned, or maybe he'd take a chaperone along anyway. It'd all be on the up and up.

Finally, Lauren spoke. "I'll take her to your next game, and I'll tell her the truth about you and your mooning over Sally. For the last three years, you've been dizzy over that girl—and you still are. And I'm going to tell Mona she doesn't have to go through with this silly dance contest if she doesn't want to. Those are my terms."

CHAPTER TEN

"COME ON, YOU STADIUM TIGERS! Cremate Yelm!"

The shout came as the teams ran onto the field. Lauren glanced back at a middle-aged man sitting two rows above them in the bleachers. His strange exhortation prompted a flurry of stunned laughter and halfhearted cheers from other adults sitting nearby. Mona leaned close to Lauren and made a face that was one part secret delight, one part "Should we be sitting here?"

"It's all right," said Lauren, patting her arm. She whispered in Mona's ear, "As long as we're quiet, they'll never know."

Mona nodded.

While unfolding a thick blanket and spreading it over the hard wooden bleachers, Lauren fumed over Raleigh's request that they sit as far from the Yelm crowd as possible. Still, she was glad Mona hadn't asked to move.

"So," she said when they had both settled on the blanket, "have you been to a football game before?"

Mona shook her head. Her smile lingered as she gazed at the brightly lit field. Dozens of players from both teams did calisthenics in unison, jumped up and down, threw footballs, ran routes, clapped and patted each other's rear ends. Dark-suited coaches carrying clipboards meandered among them, exhorting the players. Across the field, in two sets of bleachers set wide apart, students from the two schools, Yelm High School and the home team, Stadium High, were fronted by their respective cheerleaders and a few watchful teachers and school administrators. The Stadium High School band struck up the school fight song. "It's exciting, isn't it?" said Mona.

Lauren looked at her doubtfully. She'd never cared much for football or for any sport. "Sure."

"Do you see Raleigh?"

Lauren scanned the red-, black-, and white-clad Yelm squad. "There he is," she said, pointing toward a group of boys at the thirty-yard line. "Number 12."

Mona bent one way and another to look around the man sitting in front of her.

"There," Lauren added. "He just threw the ball. Do you see? He's talking to one of the coaches." She turned when Mona didn't answer. The younger girl's smile told her that, indeed, Mona had spotted her dance partner.

Raleigh took another practice snap and threw a tight spiral to Roy Fisher, who ran a slant pattern. Fisher caught the ball, tucked it under his arm, and ran a half-dozen steps against an imaginary opponent. By the time he'd turned around, Raleigh had taken another snap, dropped back five steps, and fired a pass to yet another receiver.

"Oh, he's wonderful, isn't he?" said Mona.

Lauren laughed. "They're just warming up. Wait till the game starts." Lauren sat back and sighed. She watched Mona lean one way and the other, her dark blue eyes bright with focused intensity and the wonder of newness as she seemed to study Raleigh's every move.

Don't you know he's only my idiot brother? Can't you see he's not available, anyway? That you two live in different worlds?

She inventoried Mona's features. Her angular face. Lauren had to admit it was pretty. Her thick lashes. Her body, even under a thick sweater, was shapely. And her engaging smile. That alone could bludgeon a boy's heart.

She's so vulnerable. Something's going to happen to her. I can feel it.

Raleigh completed another uncontested pass to one of his teammates, and Mona clapped. Lauren was not alone in scrutinizing Mona this time. Lauren smiled, mildly embarrassed, raising her eyebrows to the woman sitting on Mona's other side.

Doesn't she get that this is the warm-ups? I don't think she does—or, maybe she doesn't care. That's Raleigh Starr out there. That's all that matters to her.

Lauren sat back and covered her mouth with a hand.

Oh, dear. This is going to be harder than I imagined.

A fleeting thought, the unlikely image of Mona and Raleigh kissing, ran through Lauren's mind, startling her. She sought its destruction at once. "How do you like school this year?" she asked Mona.

Mona turned to her. Her smile evaporated. "I like it a little. It's hard, though. Especially reading and arithmetic."

"Those were always hard for me," Lauren lied. "Do you have the same teacher you had last year?"

Mona nodded.

Lauren was satisfied—her brother knew better than to kiss a girl in the fourth grade. She turned back as the play clock wound to zero. When the horn sounded, the two teams converged in tight packs around their respective coaches. Lauren looked up to take in the bleachers across the way. "Do you know Sally Springs?" she asked.

"Who?"

"Sally Springs. She's in Raleigh's class."

"No." Mona was fixated on number 12.

"That's her over there," Lauren said, pointing. "In the black coat with a green scarf around her neck, three rows up. Auburn hair." When Lauren was sure she had Mona's attention, she added, "Do you see her? The girl next to her is wearing a white coat."

"Yes. I see her."

Lauren checked herself.

Can I do this? Yes, I have to—for her sake.

She leaned close to Mona. "That's the girl Raleigh likes," she said confidentially. "He's been crazy about her for years."

Mona gazed at the distant figure for several seconds. Without saying a word, she turned her attention back to the field. Once again, she sat up tall and craned her neck to find Raleigh in the bunch. A slight smile marked her success.

What in the world? Didn't she hear what I said?

The captains for the two teams sauntered to the center of the field for the coin toss. The smells of mowed grass and popcorn hung in the crisp fall air. With all eyes awaiting the referee's signal, Lauren touched Mona's arm. "You understand me, don't you?"

Mona turned to her, seemingly unperturbed. "Yes."

"She's all he's ever wanted. It's pretty pathetic." Lauren was worried she wasn't getting through. "And another thing, Mona. You don't have to go through with this silly dance contest."

"Oh, but—"

"If I were you, I'd tell him to go jump in the lake. I mean, he's using you to impress Sally. Pretty obvious, isn't it?"

"I don't know. But I want to dance just the same."

"You do?" Lauren lowered her voice to a whisper. "Do your aunt and uncle know you're going to be dancing in the contest?"

Mona's face colored behind a mischievous smile. She put a finger to her lips and shook her head. "It's our secret," she said.

Lauren cursed her brother for implicating such an innocent girl in his silly ploy. And for being a sap where Sally Springs was concerned.

The Stadium High School crowd cheered the results of the coin toss. Behind them, the same baritone repeated his exhortation, "Come on, Tigers! Cremate Yelm!"

Against a crescendo of noise, Lauren leaned close again. "He doesn't—he can't love you, Mona. He loves Sally. Do you hear me?"

Mona's expression grew serious. "I know," she said. "I'm not good enough, anyway. I'm broken."

* * *

In the Starr kitchen the following night, there was "nothing left to negotiate." Mona Garrison was a sweet girl who deserved better. Raleigh was a jerk and a self-centered weasel. Lest there be confusion, Lauren would accompany Mona to their final dance practice at the Osprey Club and to the dance contest at the Puyallup Fair in two weeks' time. If Mona and Raleigh should win the contest, Mona would get seventy-five dollars to Raleigh's twenty-five.

The sound of the toilet flushing down the hall told them that their father would be entering the kitchen any minute. Lauren handed Raleigh a steaming bowl of mashed potatoes. "You got that? You're not going anywhere with her without me. I'll be driving her to Aunt Edith's from now on, too."

"Fine," said Raleigh.

"Fine is right."

"You don't have to snap your cap."

"Oh, I don't, huh?" Lauren shot back.

Raleigh dropped the potato dish onto the kitchen table with a bang.

"What's got into you two?" asked George as he rounded the corner from the hallway.

"Nothing," said Raleigh.

Lauren exhaled at the stove, wiping her hands with a dish towel. "Nothing," she said at last. "Nothing at all."

CHAPTER ELEVEN

THE LINE INCHED FORWARD. Lauren and Mona, arm in arm, heads bent, took two small steps and stopped. Raindrops suspended in their hair glistened green and gold beneath a buzzing neon sign: DANCE HALL. A flashing hand pointed toward the entrance around the corner on Grand Avenue.

"I should have brought an umbrella," Lauren said.

"We have an umbrella by the door," said Mona, without irony. Through the windowless wall of the dance hall came Fletcher Henderson's *Down South Camp Meeting*. The wail of Henderson's saxophone section competed with pipe organ music from the brightly lit carousel less than 200 feet away.

Raleigh gazed into the night sky, thankful for the rain cooling his cheeks and forehead. He could make out the blue outline of swollen clouds moving to the northeast. For him, they hinted at something ominous. He looked away and stared into the faces of fair-goers passing by in droves, the smell of cotton candy and popcorn hot in his nostrils.

It'll be fine. It's like anything else—like a game. We just need to get started, and all the butterflies will be gone.

He looked back at the line stretching another half block or more, disappearing into darkness. Relieved that he didn't recognize any of the faces visible in the glow of the sign, he flipped up the collar of his jacket. Sally and Ted were here somewhere, but he didn't want to be seen—not yet. He was about to plunge his hands into his pockets in search of his tickets when a man's voice called out behind him: "Any contestants? Any contestants back here? If you're dancing in the contest, move to the front. We'll start in ten minutes. We've started a second line on the right for contestants only." The man strode past and began to repeat his instructions.

Mona and Lauren turned. Raleigh smiled stiffly. "That's us," he said.

Lauren slid her arm free of Mona's. "All right, you two. I'll be there in a few minutes." As Mona and Raleigh stepped out of line and moved forward, Lauren called out, without much enthusiasm, "Good luck."

Raleigh pointed Mona around the corner, and they fell in behind a handful of skittering couples converging on the new line. A second door opened. A middle-aged man in a dark wool suit and a purple sash with JUDGE in white block letters raised his hand. "All dancers, listen up. Make sure you're checked in and have your numbers on before going out onto the dance floor. Come forward."

Raleigh's pulse quickened, and his mouth went dry. Staring at the back of Mona's neck, he wondered if she was as nervous as he was. She edged forward with the others; she seemed to be giving her whole attention to the judge's instructions.

Maybe not. Maybe with her condition... He inched forward almost touching Mona. *No. It's not her condition. She's brave! She's...amazing.* He remembered the strength of her voice during their early practices: "That's better. Try stepping closer to me on the third beat... That's it! That's it! Now you've got it!"

Suddenly he wanted to put his hands on her shoulders. *Isn't that what you do when you like someone? When you care for someone as much as—*

"Starr! Hey, Starr! Over here!"

Raleigh jumped at the sound of his name. He turned to see Dale Hood, the center fielder on the baseball team, and his girlfriend, June, waiting in line thirty feet from the door. When their eyes met, June waved, and Dale's hands went up in the shape of a question.

"Are you lost, man? That's the contestants' line."

Raleigh forced a grin. "I know."

Mona turned. Dale did a double take. He and June looked at each other, and Dale, wide eyed, mouthed to Raleigh, "What are you doing?"

Raleigh pretended not to understand. "Huh?" He glanced down at Mona. "That's Dale Hood," he explained. "I go to school with him."

Mona's eyes darted up to meet Raleigh's. "Oh. Okay." She turned back.

Raleigh winked at his classmate. "You'll see," he mouthed back. He pointed at the top of Mona's head. "Watch!"

It was Dale's turn to signal incomprehension, this time with his hands spread wide. "What the hell…?" he called out, biting off the end of each word self-consciously. Raleigh turned as the contestants' line advanced, but the distance was not enough to prevent him from hearing Dale's high-pitched protestations or the couple's random eruptions of sharp, embarrassed laughter.

Dammit, I knew this would happen. Raleigh bit down on his lower lip. *Oh, well. They'll see for themselves.*

They checked their coats then each donned their number, 31. Mona wore a long black skirt and white blouse, with a red barrette in her hair. Raleigh wore creased tan slacks and a blue and white striped shirt. They hadn't talked about what to wear, but Raleigh was pleased with her choices. Something neutral. Nothing "off." Let the other girls be flashy if they wanted to.

The first few bars of King Oliver's *Shake It and Break It*—banjo rhythm, trumpets in unison—blared from the loudspeakers as they crossed the lobby and were swallowed up in a mass of humanity converging opposite the southwest gate to the dance floor. They were soon separated by the pressing crowd. As they bumped and squeezed their way forward, he could feel the excitement of the other contestants and hear it in their voices. It looked as though Mona was trying to turn, and Raleigh thought he heard her call his name. But turning in that crowd was not an option, only going forward and spilling onto the vast dance floor was.

"I'm right here," Raleigh called out. He wanted to see her face, to make sure she was okay—wanted her to turn. She seemed to nod, as though acknowledging his voice.

What an odd feeling. I guess I'm being protective. Where's this coming from? Look at her. She looks damn good from the back, too. The way she carries her shoulders...

The needle was jerked off the record with a loud scratch, followed by a booming baritone. "Testing…testing." The same judge who'd greeted them at the entrance. "Contestants, keep the lines moving. We have over 150 contestants tonight, but as you can see there's plenty of room on the dance floor. As soon as you're in, start warming up."

The music restarted, only to be cut off less than a minute later in the same ham-handed way. "Listen up, everybody. Here are the rules: There will be five judges, including myself. We'll be walking around during each of the first five numbers. If we tap you on the shoulder, please grab your gal and exit through the nearest gate. The judges' decisions are final. Three couples will be left for the sixth and final number, from which we'll choose the winning pair, as well as second and third places. First prize is one hundred dollars; second prize, fifty dollars; and third prize, twenty-five dollars. Don't forget, all contestants receive a free bottle of Coca-Cola and a voucher for a Fisher's Scone courtesy of Eastside Buick. Good luck to all of you. Ladies and gentlemen, let's have a big hand for all the contestants."

To a loud and boisterous audience reaction—the onlookers numbered three hundred or more—Mona broke free of the current of humanity pushing her forward. The loudspeakers boomed with the brassy opening phrase of *Dippermouth Blues*.

"There you are," Mona said to Raleigh through a half-smile. She looked relieved.

The couples around them were already turning and beginning to dance. "You ready?" Raleigh shouted. Mona looked down self-consciously, nodded. She pushed her hair back over her left ear and nodded again. He took her hand and led her to a far corner of the rectangular dance floor. He was vaguely aware of the moving bodies all around them and the scores of people crowding the railing, cheering their favorites. As he leaned over and began to dance, turning sideways to Mona, taking her hand and spinning her past him, he realized how removed he felt, how far away everything seemed: the crowd, the other dancers, even Mona. Yet through it all, he felt the beat.

The spinning room seemed to contain his irregular breathing and a driving rhythm. He twirled Mona into his arms, embracing her; the floral scent of her hair was familiar and rejuvenating. He watched her as if in a blur, passing beneath his arm, felt her hand skim the width of his back and lock onto his left hand. But so far this was all happening *to* him, not because of him. He was in league with no one. He was alone.

It continued this way well into the second warm-up side. The sounds of feet scuffing and sliding over the floor entered his awareness, as did the swishing of skirts and dresses. These subtleties embellished the static that sounded, at times, like water filling a bathtub in an upstairs room.

Raleigh's breathing evened out. He focused on Mona's feet, her white ankle socks, her slender legs—on her twirling body and her fair, unsmiling face. She had so much energy. She did so much more than he. Oh well, he just had to hold his own, look like he knew what he was doing. That was the idea. Show her off.

He looked around the room for Sally, but he didn't see her. Then he followed the staring eyes of a woman nearby back to Mona. Mona had immersed herself in the music—had stepped away from him and, bending at the waist, had begun to rotate her shoulders and drive her arms down in that singular way. But it's too soon, he thought. He stepped forward and gently grabbed Mona's right arm, the way you might take the arm of a sleepwalker. She jumped.

"Let's save it for the contest," Raleigh shouted in her ear. He leaned closer. His lips touched her ear as he said, "I don't want people to see how beautifully you dance until the contest starts. This is still the warm-up. Okay?"

Mona blushed and nodded. A second later, Raleigh caught sight of Wheels standing at the railing waving at him. "Shoot," he said.

Mona stopped dancing. "What's wrong?" she asked.

Raleigh had to compete with the ascending notes of a clarinet solo. "That's Wheels over there," he shouted. "I'm sorry. I'll be right back."

Mona didn't answer. Her shoulders sagged as he raised his finger to signal "just a minute." He left her behind.

"What are you doing here?" Raleigh shouted, extending his hand to Wheels.

"You didn't think I was going to miss this, did you?"

Raleigh smiled. "We're going to win. I told you."

"So you say." Wheels gestured in Mona's general direction. "She looks pretty good."

Raleigh nodded. "She's very good. Have you seen Sally?"

Wheels leaned closer. "I saw her when I came in." He pointed. "Over there somewhere."

Raleigh turned and looked for an opening in the exuberant, packed crowd. He spotted Sally—and Ted. Their white bibs bore the number 26. Sally spun under Ted's raised arm, and in the split second before turning back, she smiled up at her boyfriend in a concentrated way. It was not her unfettered smile, but Raleigh loved it—imagined it transferred onto him, onto Raleigh Starr. Loved it more than he could say.

Wheels tapped Raleigh on the shoulder. "Listen, Dale Hood's outside. He's yapping to a bunch of the guys. They're having quite a laugh. All this shit about you and Mona."

Raleigh stared into Wheels's eyes, holding his breath.

"Bill said, 'Leave him alone. That girl's got a dynamite body, and he's probably going to get lucky.' He said he'd be happy to take Mona Garrison for the night, and no one should blame you for doing the same."

Raleigh looked away, a hot wave of shame washing over his face.

Wheels continued. "They're coming in, taking bets on whether it's true or not that you're with her."

Whether I'm with her? I am with her—but it's Sally I want to be with.

He looked at the strained neutrality in Wheels's eyes.

I'm with Mona. So this whole contest is... She has a great figure, and everybody thinks that's all I care about. They don't understand about the dancing, or that Mona is one of the nicest, sweetest girls around. I'm making a fool of myself, then, is that it? She's going to be a sideshow, and I'm part of it—I'm the reason for it. What was I thinking? They're laughing. What if Sally laughs, too?

Raleigh began to look around for the exit signs. There was one. He could grab Mona and be gone in under a minute. He could take her home. But he'd have to come back for their coats. He could do that—through the front door.

He remembered their first time entering the Osprey Club, how he'd fled with Mona on his heels. It would be the same thing all over again: hightailing it out of fear, driving away in silence. Having to explain again. And how would he explain it this time? That he was—or they were—about to be laughed at? Would Mona care about that? Her one chance to dance at a real dance, and would she run like an embarrassed child? No. If anyone were running away, it would be him.

"There you are," said Lauren, sidling through the standing-room-only crowd. "Where's Mona?" She gave Wheels a quick nod and looked left and right for her brother's dance partner.

"Out there," said Raleigh.

"You left her out on the dance floor?"

Lauren seemed to read something in his eyes, and for all he knew it was the truth: that he was contemplating a last-minute escape. He averted his eyes, unable to return her steady stare. She glanced at Wheels as though confirming the worst.

"Well, number 31," she cried. "Get your rear end out there and dance with her. You can't leave her there."

Raleigh looked back at his sister beseechingly. "I'm not sure I can. I think this may have been a mistake."

"*What*?" Lauren shouted. "What are you talking about?"

"You said yourself—"

Lauren's shaking head stopped him. "What about Mona? This isn't about you anymore. Hell—I mean heck—yes, this was a mistake. I told you that. But you've brought her here and you're going to dance with her."

Raleigh looked at Wheels and got no help. His sister was right.

Lauren turned to Wheels and demanded, "What did you tell him?"

Wheels stepped back and touched his chest with the tips of his fingers. "Nothing. I swear!" Raleigh knew Wheels was afraid of his sister. He didn't hold his friend to any greater standard of honesty than he would have imposed on himself had the tables been turned.

"Whatever you two were talking about can wait," Lauren shouted, competing with the music. She turned to Raleigh. "Get out there. She's waiting."

She's an amazing dancer. Who the hell am I to chicken out? Do I care if they laugh? They won't be laughing when that judge hands us a hundred-dollar bill.

Raleigh stepped away from the railing and pointed back at Wheels. "You watch. We're going to win."

Wheels hesitated, then played along. "You think she's that good, huh?"

Lauren nodded. "She is that good," she said gazing at the dance floor. "I've seen her." Raleigh turned and pushed through the crowd.

CHAPTER TWELVE

"I OWE YOU AN APOLOGY," Raleigh managed to say as he spun Mona close to him and let her go again.

Mona blushed but didn't look up. With the warm-ups done, she appeared to be concentrating on the music and her steps. At last, she shook her head.

Raleigh stopped dancing. "*Yes.* I was wrong to leave you like that. I'm sorry."

Mona kept her eyes downcast. She turned her back to him, her arms and legs moving to the rhythm, her head bobbing. She spun back and took both his outstretched hands. She gave no hint of wanting to accept, or consider, an apology. He felt the energy of the dance through her fingertips.

She stepped away. Moving toward him again, she batted her eyelids twice. It was the signal. She was ready.

He threw his hands up—his part of the "okay, okay, I won't touch you" maneuver. From there, the dance was hers, her moves unequalled, her legs and arms a study in uncanny syncopation. Dancers to their left and right turned to look. Some pointed. Raleigh knew it would be this way—she was stealing the show. He stepped forward and back to the beat, leaned left and right. By comparison, it was hardly dancing.

Raleigh reached for Mona's hand as she swept past him, twirling. He spun on his heel, moving her hand from one side to the other behind his back. When he faced her again, he glanced up to Dale Hood and June. They led a line of Yelm High School students along the balcony railing. He could tell they were looking for him—for both of them. Raleigh spun again and captured Mona's slender hands.

Stepping close to Mona, he considered reaching out to stop her, to tell her it was time to move to another part of the dance floor. He hesitated.

But we could be disqualified. No, we're not going anywhere.

He glanced at Mona as she wheeled beneath his right arm.

Look at her! She's the best dancer here.

Her performance seemed to unfold in slow motion. He knew every sequence.

What's to be embarrassed about? If anyone should be embarrassed, it's Mona, the girl with a dud partner. The word's out, anyway. So I took Mona Garrison to a dance contest. So what?

He told himself to concentrate on Mona and not make eye contact with any of them. He crossed over, changing places with Mona. Not looking at the others would be easier said than done.

Four couples nearby were eliminated in quick succession. The purple-sashed judges—three men in dark wool suits and two women wearing long, sparkling evening gowns—wandered among the dancing couples, but none seemed to be paying attention to him or Mona.

A female judge approached within several feet, stopped, smiled, and moved on. A few seconds later, the same judge tapped the shoulder of a young man dancing wildly with a partner who seemed to be compensating in the other direction. The young man straightened. After the initial shock, he and his partner accepted their fate.

They've seen her. They know she's a finalist—that she has to be.

Two more couples were tapped out, followed by another close to them. Mona was in the groove, her dancing as smooth and quiet as a flywheel. Raleigh swung his head around, unable to resist the temptation. Sally's head was just visible over the crowd. He watched her smile at Ted and turn under his outstretched arm. They disappeared from view.

He traded sides with Mona. Over her left shoulder, the Yelm contingent crowded as close as possible, hugging the railing, staring down at them, their faces either contorted with laughter or blank with disbelief. His eyes locked with Dale Hood's. Raleigh did the only thing he could think of: he saluted the center fielder with two fingers and turned away with the flow of the music.

A few moments later, Mona's eyes flashed in their direction, but she gave no hint of recognition. She looked left and right with her dancing, spinning, her brown hair flying out to the side; and it was all immediate, and contained, and it had nothing to do with any of them.

Mona pivoted past Raleigh and caught his hand when his arm was fully extended. Her body jerked. It was their first mistake. She recovered. As they turned on their heels, he looked up to see if any of the judges had noticed. Just then, out of the corner of his eye, he saw one of the male judges step close to Ted and Sally. The judge hesitated for a few moments, then tapped Ted's shoulder. Ted and Sally were out, just like that. Sally smiled up at Ted. They turned at once and made their way off the dance floor. Raleigh didn't have time to think about it. He swallowed a feeling of sympathy—banished it from his mind—and reached out both hands for Mona.

* * *

"This will be the sixth and final dance," announced the emcee, his voice echoing over the largely empty dance floor. "We're down to three couples—couple numbers 6, 31, and 48. Good luck to all of you. Let's give them a hand."

Mona, mere inches from Raleigh, stood with head bowed, unable or unwilling to look up. The other finalists smiled and waved to the audience, but Mona remained as still as a mannequin. At last, Raleigh took Mona's hand and tried to raise it. She would not allow her hand to go any higher than her chin. He gave up.

"It's all right," said Raleigh, smiling for the benefit of the audience. He leaned close to Mona's left ear. "They're happy for us. It's okay."

Mona didn't react.

Raleigh stood straight again, holding Mona's hand. He looked around at the sea of faces behind the railing and in the balcony, avoiding the spot where he knew Dale Hood and the others stood. He waved with his free hand. He caught sight of Sally standing a few feet from the northeast gate with Ted by her side. She wore her white bib, although the black stenciled numbers 2 and 6 were obscured by the way Ted held her so close. Raleigh's eyes met hers. He tried to find something positive in her expression, but he could see nothing beyond shock and disbelief—and distance. A seemingly unbridgeable distance. He felt a sudden chill. Had this all been a mistake? It wasn't *his* dancing that was keeping them out there. Why had he thought partnering with Mona would impress Sally, would make her like him?

"Here we go," exclaimed the emcee. "Let's swing, swing, swing!"

With the first beats of the Gene Krupa drum introduction to *Sing Sing Sing,* Mona stepped away from Raleigh, turned, and began dancing. The other couples followed suit. The final round was underway. Raleigh felt conspicuous dancing with just two other couples on the immense dance floor, the cheers of the crowd filling his ears. His legs felt awkward, as though he were unsure of the most basic moves.

It's because of her.

As he and Mona went through the opening steps of their routine, he pictured Sally's blank look. Forcing a smile, he twirled Mona one way and another.

She's judging me. She thinks I'm a fool for doing this.

Mona took his hand. He dared not look at Sally, at the way Ted held her.

Maybe if I talk to her again at school. If I explain that I did this for her.

He wound Mona into his embrace. He felt her soft posterior and her hard shoulder blades press against him, and for the first time ever she held his forearm, squeezing it. She stayed in that position for eight beats rather than four.

A shock of electricity raced through his body, bringing him alive to the here and now. When she spun out of his embrace, she gave no hint that anything was different. Had it been an accident? It had happened so fast. But there was no mistaking the fact that she had squeezed his arm.

Now it was Mona Garrison he thought about. Mona, the beautiful dancer. *Don't be an idiot.* She had only been thanking him, or telling him she was enjoying herself. Or maybe she had been telling him to pay attention, to get his mind back on the dance. They spun in opposite directions, crossed and caught each other's hands. Stepping past each other again, he glanced over at the other couples. They were older, maybe in their twenties. The women both wore bright smiles.

Raleigh took hold of both of Mona's hands and pulled her toward him, not once but twice. "Smile," he said, startling her. She looked up questioningly. "Smile," Raleigh repeated. They'd never talked about this.

Mona smiled tentatively at first. She pivoted and looked at the other women. Mimicking them, she let a warm, broad smile take shape and turned back. For the remainder of the dance, Mona smiled at Raleigh. He hadn't realized until then that her dancing could be even more mesmerizing. When they finished their signature "okay, okay, I won't touch you" bit and she stepped forward to join hands with Raleigh again, the audience cheered. They cheered more when the song ended. This time, when he raised Mona's hand in his, she did not resist. And something of her smile remained.

* * *

The Model A dipped as Raleigh pulled into the pothole at the end of the drive. He shifted down, grinding the gears. As the headlights swept over to the corner of the Garrison home, Lauren said, "You have to tell them. You can't keep it a secret."

"Oh, yes we can," answered Raleigh, bouncing behind the wheel. "Besides, we've already talked about it, haven't we, Mona?" His right hand brushed against Mona's leg. A rush of excitement ran through him. When she didn't answer, he looked over at Mona sitting on Lauren's lap in the cramped cab. Mona stared out the windshield disconsolately. Behind her Lauren's eyes glinted in the darkness.

"How is she going to explain having seventy-five dollars in her purse?"

"She doesn't have to. They won't know about it. Mona's going to hide the money—aren't you, Mona?" When he looked at her again, he couldn't tell if she was nodding or bouncing in place. "Is that right?"

Mona looked up at him, and there was no mistaking the nod.

"What are you talking about?" Lauren cried. "You're going to make a liar out of her, too? Oh, no you—"

"No. Not a liar. We're not going to talk about it. We went to the fair, period. That's all they need to know."

Lauren scoffed. "And you don't think they're going to find out? Are you serious? Half the town knows already. *Yes,* you're going to tell them."

Raleigh brought the pickup to a sudden stop in front of the Garrisons' door. He set the hand brake. "No, I'm not." He opened the driver's side door and stepped out. Mona slid behind the wheel and had one leg out when the porch light went on behind him.

"Yes, you are!" Lauren said.

Raleigh refused to look at his sister. The image of Dale, June, and the others was seared into his mind: withholding applause, their expressions rife with stunned disbelief and judgment. He'd had enough blame for one night. Besides, he was tired and didn't need to deal with this. The Garrisons might not care, but he wasn't going to take a chance.

This whole thing didn't go as planned, and I'm no closer to having Sally than I was before. She knows Mona won, not me. I was just the goofball partner.

Mona jumped to the ground. She straightened her skirt and turned. "Good-bye," she said to Lauren. "Thank you."

"Good night, Mona. Raleigh, I swear to God, if you don't—"

Her words were cut off by the slamming of the truck's door. The front door of the house opened, and Mrs. Garrison said into the night air, over the squeak of the screen door, "Hello, you two. Mona, come on up and get ready for bed."

"Hi, Mrs. Garrison," said Raleigh.

Mona ran up the two steps to the landing, stopped and turned back. "Thank you, Raleigh," she said.

As Mona stepped past her aunt and disappeared inside, Mrs. Garrison called over her shoulder, "Did you have fun at the fair?"

Mona didn't answer. They could hear her racing up the wooden stairway inside the house.

"Well," said Mrs. Garrison. Beneath the glow of the porch light, her plump face was distorted by points of magnified light on her cheeks and stark, grayish shadows cast by the rim of her glasses. "I hope she behaved herself."

"Oh, of course," said Raleigh. "Well, we better get going. I'll be by in the morning to take Mona to work."

He opened the door of the pickup, but as he did the passenger door opened and Lauren stepped out onto the running board. She twisted around to face Mrs. Garrison. "Raleigh has something he wants to tell you," she blurted.

"No, I don't," protested Raleigh.

"Tell her, Raleigh," said Lauren.

Mrs. Garrison took a half step out of the house. "What is it?"

"It's nothing," said Raleigh.

"Why don't you let Mrs. Garrison decide that?"

Raleigh wanted to turn to his sister. His conscience told him to face Mrs. Garrison. "It's no big deal," he said. More white showed above and below the irises of Mrs. Garrison's eyes.

"What is it, you two?" she asked. "What happened?"

Raleigh closed the pickup door. "Nothing happened. Well, that's not exactly true. Mona and I..."

Mrs. Garrison stepped beyond the screen door and crossed her arms against the cold. "What did she do?" she snapped insinuatingly.

"Tell her, Raleigh," said Lauren.

"Mona didn't do anything wrong. It's just... Well, Mona and I entered the swing dance contest at the fair, and we won. We—"

"You what?"

"Yes. We won a hundred dollars. I've given her seventy-five, and I have twenty—"

"Mona was dancing?" Mrs. Garrison stepped back and shouted for her husband through the screen door. She turned back. "You danced in public?"

He couldn't begin to understand Mrs. Garrison's reaction.

Well, yeah. It was the fair.

A vein bulged at the side of Mrs. Garrison's neck. She pushed her glasses up like a nearsighted pugilist preparing to fight.

"Answer me!" she thundered.

Raleigh felt the force of her words ten feet away. The muscles in his chest seized and left him, for a moment, unable to breathe. He reached back, letting his elbow come to rest on the hard, cold metal of the pickup. There was some comfort in that.

Mrs. Garrison moved to the edge of the porch. "What in heaven's name is wrong with you? Don't you know she's...damaged?" She glanced up at Lauren, by the look of things in search of understanding.

She seemed to know Raleigh was the proper target. "Yes, of course you do. And to think we trusted you."

"Wait a minute—" said Raleigh, straightening.

"What's going on out there?" bellowed Mr. Garrison from somewhere in the back of the house. His footsteps on the oak floor pushed Raleigh's heart up into his throat. Mr. Garrison opened the screen door at once and didn't hesitate to come onto the porch, closing both doors behind him.

Raleigh swallowed with difficulty. He wanted to say, "Nothing, sir. Your wife's upset, but she has no reason. You see, because all I did was enter the dance contest with Mona...and we won! We won a hundred dollars, and I gave seventy-five of it to... It was a swing contest, and Mona loves swing. She's very—she loves it. She had the time of her life. So did—and my sister here, she was with us. She can tell you everything, can't you, Lauren?"

He would have said this, would have met Mr. Garrison's understanding nods with a fearless and generous spirit, man to man, except Mrs. Garrison had, by the elevation of one eyebrow, stayed his tongue.

"Raleigh took Mona dancing. I've caught her dancing upstairs. I've told you about that. It's obscene the way she moves. She might as well be advertising herself for... And every man from Seattle to Vancouver will be after her."

Horizontal lines crossed Mr. Garrison's forehead and grew in intensity under the glare of the porch light. "What's this about, young man?"

Raleigh's explanation lacked the fearlessness and male bonding he'd imagined moments before.

"Why didn't you tell us you had this in mind?" said Mr. Garrison. "Or is this something you came up with on the spot?"

"Uh, no, sir. I don't know, sir."

"They've been practicing all sum—," offered Lauren, biting off the word as Raleigh's hand came down with a slap on the hood of the pickup.

He turned and gestured at Lauren as if to say, "What are you doing?"

"They're going to find out anyway," she said, embarrassed.

Mrs. Garrison had put a clenched fist over her chest and taken a step back. "No!"

Mr. Garrison took hold of his wife's arm and looked up at Lauren. "What exactly do you mean, Miss Starr?"

"Tell them, Raleigh," said Lauren.

"You've lied to us this whole time," said Mrs. Garrison. She stared off into the distance, setting a wan, fleshy hand against her cheek. Her eyes returned as she registered a new thought. "How did you know Mona could dance?"

Raleigh looked to Mr. Garrison for understanding. "One night, it was—I don't remember when it was. My truck broke down, and I was walking home. You guys weren't home. I saw Mona upstairs. She was dancing."

"So you watched her through the window," Mrs. Garrison said miserably.

"No. I mean, yes, but I just stood over there in the road. She had the window open. I heard the music."

Mrs. Garrison was at a loss for words.

"And what about this practicing?" said Mr. Garrison at last. "She said you were practicing all summer."

Raleigh looked down. "Yes, that's true. Mona taught me how to dance—her way."

"You mean... When?" asked Mrs. Garrison, finding her voice. "Was this when she was supposed to be cleaning Edith's house?"

"No. It was after she was done."

Mrs. Garrison lowered her brow. "I don't believe Edith permitted you two to dance in her home. Not for one minute!"

"It wasn't at her house," said Raleigh, averting his eyes. "I, uh, made other arrangements so we could practice for an hour or so before I brought her home. Look, I—"

"What other arrangements?" demanded Mrs. Garrison. "Although I'm not sure I want to know."

"We'll take this up with your father in the morning," said Mr. Garrison. "You tell him we want to talk to him, and we'll be by at eleven."

"You're never to come around here again," said Mrs. Garrison. "Do you understand me? Don't you ever speak to Mona again."

"Hold on, Grace," said Mr. Garrison. "Let's cool down a bit."

Mrs. Garrison skewered Raleigh with her look. "You have some nerve. *Shame on you!*"

"Grace, that's enough. Let's not get ahead of ourselves."

Mrs. Garrison's round eyes sparkled with tears. She looked up at her husband. "If you knew what her dancing was like, how inappropriate it is, start to finish, especially for a...you'd understand what I'm talking about. How are we going to protect her if... She's going to end up like her mother."

"Okay, okay," soothed Mr. Garrison.

Raleigh inched forward. "I'm sorry, Mrs. Garrison, Mr. Garrison, but...she's a wonderful dancer. There's nothing inappropriate about it." He turned to his sister for validation. Lauren nodded. "See? There's nothing—"

"You better get going, son," said Mr. Garrison. "You tell your father we want a word with him."

Raleigh's stomach churned. His breathing was shallow. He spread his hands, "If you'll let me explain..."

"There's nothing more to talk about tonight, son," said Mr. Garrison. "You go on."

Raleigh slid behind the wheel. When Lauren was in, he fired up the truck and began backing over the rough ground. He stopped and pulled forward again. He rolled down the window and spoke above the rumble of the engine. "What about tomorrow? I have to pick Mona up for work."

"Absolutely not," cried Mrs. Garrison. "I told you—"

"It's all right, Grace," said Mr. Garrison. He rubbed his cheek with the backs of his fingers. "I'll take her. I can be back by 9:30." He looked past Raleigh toward his sister. "Would you be able to pick her up, Miss Starr? When she's done, that is? Alone?"

"Yes, I'll do that," said Lauren.

Rather than turn the truck around, Raleigh backed the length of the drive. He and Lauren rocked over the potholes. As he angled onto Thompson Road, he glanced back at the house one more time. The porch was empty, the porch light off. Behind the dimly shining glass on the second floor, he could just make out Mona standing in the dark.

CHAPTER THIRTEEN

RALEIGH PICKED UP THE PHONE on the second double ring. "Hello?"

"I'm looking for a Pariah? A Mr. Raleigh Pariah?"

Raleigh recognized Wheels's voice. He carried the telephone from the hall table and leaned against the wall. "Funny."

Wheels laughed. "How the hell are you, old man? How's that knee?"

Raleigh winced at the memory of the sudden and unexpected blow he'd received at Monday's practice. "It's going to be fine. I'll be ready."

"You better be—last game and all. Our final chance to even the score with Aberdeen. I don't know what Ted was thinking. The whistle had blown, right? Everybody had stopped."

Raleigh watched his sister walk by in a hurry, eating a piece of toast. "Tell me about it. I was turning to go back to the huddle when he hit me. So, what's going on?"

"I've got some big news. Clarice Austen and her cousin Barbara are coming again Thanksgiving weekend. They're staying at Clarice's grandpa's place, and he's out of town. You know what that means."

"Keep it clean. This is a party line."

Wheels chuckled. "It's going to be anything *but* clean, old man. You can thank me now, or thank me later. I'm solving all your problems."

"How's that?"

"Actually, Barbara will be solving them, but...well, you get the idea."

Raleigh cleared his throat, turned around, and set his forehead against the wall. He could imagine his neighbor Mrs. Ottinger listening in, as was her habit. He thought of telling Wheels to drop the subject altogether, but he wanted to know more. He whispered into the worn, black mouthpiece, "Hey, seriously, tone it down, okay? I don't know who this Barbara is."

"Yes, you do. She was at the lake party. Both of them were. Don't you remember?"

"I don't remember much from that night." Raleigh closed his eyes. What did he remember? Mona dancing in her window, the way her arms had moved, how she'd spun, the shadows crossing her nightgown one direction and another.

"Short, blonde hair," said Wheels. "About five-five…blue eyes… curves."

Raleigh couldn't picture her.

Wheels continued, "Barbara Spade? From Seattle? Goes to Franklin? Volunteers at the Red Cross—remember? Visits old people and stuff. Drinks like a fish? Likes to laugh a lot."

"No, I don't remember her. So what's the deal?" Raleigh forgot about Mrs. Ottinger and felt an unexpected lightness—a surge of energy. He stood tall and stretched his back. He relished the fresh prospect: someone or some*thing* might help him forget his last and final humiliation where Sally Springs was concerned. But no, he realized a moment later, leaning against the wall again, he would never forget how Sally had spun on her heels not once but twice in the weeks following the fair—fleeing from the possibility of an encounter with him in the halls of the high school. And since then, not an acknowledgment, not a hello. It was as though she'd blotted him out of her mind.

All of a sudden, Raleigh awoke to the fact that his friend was talking. "…to meet us at the Green Lantern on the Friday after Thanksgiving, at two o'clock, and we'll go from there. Do you want me to pick you up?"

"Sure," said Raleigh absently. "That'll be fine."

"You okay?"

"Yeah. I was thinking of something, is all."

Wheels hesitated. "Look, I know what some of them are saying. Ignore them."

"Yeah."

"Whatever happened to Mona, by the way? Do you ever talk to her?"

"Nah."

"But you see her on the bus, right?"

"No, she doesn't ride the bus anymore. Her aunt and uncle take her to school."

"Ah. Okay. So, anyway, we're on for the twenty-first. And I'll see you tomorrow, old man, okay?"

Lauren's heavy steps on the stairway drummed above and behind him. "Sure. See you then."

"Who was that? Your idiot friend Leonard?" Lauren said as she stepped past him in the hall and disappeared into the kitchen. Two seconds later, she reappeared and headed for the front door. "I'm off to pick up Mona from work," she said.

Raleigh set the phone back on the hall table. "That's ridiculous—that I can't do that, I mean. It's been over a month. Why should you have to pick her up?"

"Oh, my brother," she said theatrically, "your days of picking up Mona Garrison are through." Lauren bounced on one foot as she struggled to put on her shoe.

"And why are you doing it?"

"Why? Because. Because I like Mona, and I don't want her to lose her job over the mess you made. Besides, Aunt Edith wants her to stay on. She and Grace Garrison talk, you know." Lauren bounced on the other foot. "They both made me promise you won't be in the truck or anywhere near it when I pick her up."

"Oh, wonderful."

Lauren lifted her coat off the hook near the door. "You asked," she said. "Not everybody hates you, though. I don't—and Mona doesn't. I don't think Dad does. He might… Oh, and did I tell you they moved her out of her old room? They put her in the unfinished attic room at the back of the house."

"Who? Mona?"

"Yeah. That way, you can't ogle her from the road. She didn't tell me this. Aunt Edith did. She didn't say why, but I know that's it." Lauren opened the door and stepped out. "Toodle-oo."

Raleigh followed her onto the porch. He felt heat rising against the inside of his face. "Tell me you're kidding—"

"Nope." Lauren opened the door of the pickup and slid behind the wheel. She called past the open door. "Mona likes you, though. She doesn't care. She's been begging me to sneak her off to your football game this Friday."

"She has?"

Lauren slammed the door and answered through the partially opened window. "Yup. I keep telling her no, but she's persistent. Last Sunday, she offered me seventy-five dollars if I'd take her. The seventy-five dollars she won at the fair."

"What'd you tell her?"

"I told her no, of course. What do you think?"

She backed and swung the Model A around. "Tell Daddy I'll back in about an hour." She pulled away.

* * *

"Hey, what do you have against Starr anyway?" the sandy-haired junior linebacker said, chewing a peanut butter and jelly sandwich. His question was buried in the chatter of juniors and seniors packed in the school cafeteria. On three sides, high pale green walls sent echoes cascading over the tables; through the windows on the fourth wall came steeply slanting spears of bright midday sunshine. Students in the second row of tables shielded their eyes as they ate.

Before Ted Ellington could answer, another varsity player, the center, said, "What do you mean?"

The linebacker answered, waving a glass of milk in front of him. "You didn't see him hit Raleigh at practice the other day? The whistle had blown, and Ted here blindsided him."

The center looked across the table at Ted. "That was you? I saw Raleigh lying there, but I didn't know who did it."

"It was an accident, okay?" said Ted, coloring but defiant. "I'm tired of people asking me. I didn't hear the whistle."

"If we lost our quarterback before Friday's game against Aberdeen, you'd hear about it a hell of a lot more than you're hearing about it now," said the linebacker.

The muscles above Ted's jaw pulsed. "I don't give a shit about Starr. Wouldn't have mattered to me if he *did* get hurt."

The two others looked at each other. The center said, "What'd he do to you?"

Ted answered over the top of his sandwich. "To me? Nothing. But maybe... I don't know. Sally hasn't been the same since the dance contest. She won't talk about it, but she's acting different. It's like she's jealous of him winning or something."

* * *

"Do you take sugar?" asked Mrs. Garrison.

"No, thank you." The prim, square-faced woman raised the cup to her lips. As she sipped, wisps of steam slid, ghostlike, past her temple. Not five minutes earlier, Martha Robinson had climbed the porch steps of the Garrison home and introduced herself as deputy director of Family Services, Washington State Department of Health. "And this is Jewel Ballard," she'd added, nodding toward the woman standing at her side.

"And what about you?" asked Mrs. Garrison as she relinquished the second cup of tea. "Do you take sugar, Miss Ballard?"

"It's Mrs. Ballard," answered the guest, who, sitting at the opposite end of the couch, forced a thin-lipped smile with evident difficulty. Her gray-green eyes seemed to entertain the idea of Mrs. Garrison without assuming any obligation to look at her, at least for the time being. She put her cup on the coffee table between a copy of *The National Geographic Magazine* and a pile of Mona's schoolwork. "Yes, if it's not too much trouble," she said.

"Oh, I'm sorry," said the deputy director, glancing from Mrs. Garrison to her husband and back again. Simon Garrison sat in his favorite chair at an oblique angle to the couch. The gray light from the window behind him cast his midday shadow on the side of the radio cabinet. "I thought I told you about Jewel. Did I not mention I might be bringing her along? She's a guardian for several of our clients in this area, and I thought she could answer any questions you might have about guardianship."

"Guardianship?" said Mr. Garrison. "What's this about?"

"Mrs. Robinson mentioned it when I called," said Mrs. Garrison as she crossed the room with a double-handled sugar bowl and silver spoon. "She said it's something we might consider. Letting someone else be responsible for Mona—her education, medical care, and such." Mrs. Garrison delivered the sweetener and retreated to the overstuffed green armchair. Avoiding eye contact with her husband, she turned, knees and all, to face Mrs. Robinson.

"Yes," said the deputy director, "I mentioned guardianship when you told me how much trouble you're having with Miss Garrison."

"Trouble?" said Mr. Garrison, sitting up. "It's her schoolwork we're concerned about."

Mrs. Garrison bowed her head, evidently in an effort to collect herself. When she looked up at her husband, her expression bore evidence she had failed the attempt. "Simon," she said. "You know it's so much more than that. There's—"

"You told me you called Family Services to talk about her schoolwork," said Mr. Garrison.

"I did. That's part of it, isn't it? But sneaking out, carrying on with boys and such? We're not controlling her. That's the plain fact. I called Mrs. Robinson to find out what our options are."

"It's an understandable problem," said the deputy director. Mrs. Ballard nodded in agreement while sipping her tea.

Rather than return her husband's stare, Mrs. Garrison produced a handkerchief from under her sleeve. She used it to blow her nose.

"If I may," said Mrs. Ballard at last, "is Mona's feeblemindedness hereditary? Do we know that?"

The Garrisons gave concurrent and contradictory answers.

"What are you talking about, Simon?" said Mrs. Garrison. "You know your sister is simpleminded, and so was your Uncle Ted."

"Wrong on both counts," muttered Mr. Garrison. His sunken eyes seemed to look back over the decades. He fidgeted and gave no sign of wanting to defend his position further.

"I most certainly am not," snapped Mrs. Garrison. She turned back to the guardian. "The answer is yes. Her mother's been institutionalized in Oregon—a former burlesque dancer until she got hooked on narcotics."

"The reason I ask is—"

"I didn't tell you," interrupted Mrs. Garrison, fixing round eyes on the deputy director, "we caught Mona last Friday night coming home from a high school football game she had snuck out to see. Can you imagine? We have no idea how she got there, and she won't tell us."

"Good heavens," said the deputy director.

"Has she developed? Physically, I mean?" asked Mrs. Ballard uncomfortably. She cradled her teacup in her left hand, lifting it now and then to relieve the heat.

"Yes, but she's in the fourth grade!" cried Mrs. Garrison.

"She's also fifteen years old, for crying out loud," said Mr. Garrison. He struggled to his feet. "I thought this was about schoolwork," he repeated. He pulled a watch out of his pocket, read the time, and looked up again. "She's been told again and again she can't read, she can't do things. Is it any wonder she gives up?" Under his skeptical gaze, the three women established a blinking, ocular sisterhood confined to their side of the room. "I'll be in the barn if you need me."

With the banging of the back door, Mrs. Ballard spoke. "You don't know what else may have happened. She says she went to the game, but you don't know who she might have been with...who might have taken advantage of her."

"Exactly right," said Mrs. Garrison.

"For years," continued the younger woman, setting her cup down, "it's been the policy of Washington State to curb hereditary feeblemindedness...and the problem is the one you mentioned. When these people are out in society, we don't know what might happen. I have three feebleminded youngsters and one adult under my care, and I've had others in the past. Fortunately, I have no pubescent girls at present. It's a vexing problem."

"We've lost control," said Mrs. Garrison, breaking above a whisper. "I didn't think—"

"I've told Jewel about the dancing and the Osprey Club," interrupted the deputy director. "To me, that's much worse, much more of a concern. To think—taking this girl to a bar on the Lord's day."

"We couldn't believe it when we heard it," said Mrs. Garrison. "The boy—well, this is no excuse, but he's a motherless child. We never thought he was capable of something like this."

"You've spoken to his father?" asked the deputy director.

Mrs. Garrison nodded. "It's a good family. That's what we can't understand."

"We must protect these children," said Mrs. Ballard formally, with deep feeling, putting her tea on the coffee table. "Both from others, and from themselves. It's not their fault. Don't misunderstand me."

"You're right, of course," said Mrs. Garrison, her face beginning to color unevenly. A few moments later, she spoke through tears. "I don't know what to do. And Simon is no help."

"I'm so sorry you're going through this," said Mrs. Ballard.

Mrs. Garrison sniffed. "Do you have children of your own, Mrs. Ballard?"

The question had an unexpected effect on the guest. She began to brush imaginary lint from her lap. "I lost my daughter and my husband in an automobile accident three years ago," she said with a coolness in her voice that neither listener would have taken as authentic. "So, the answer is no."

"Oh, I'm sorry," said Mrs. Garrison.

The deputy director sat up as though straightening her spine. "Perhaps we should talk about the custodial school. They've expanded their capacity and—"

"The custodial school?" said Mrs. Garrison.

The deputy director smiled perfunctorily. "Yes. Western State Custodial School. It used to be The School for the Feeble Minded. It was in Medical Lake for years, but they've added a new facility in Buckley, a few miles from here."

"Yes, I knew that," said Mrs. Garrison vaguely. "It never occurred to me... Well, not until this year, anyway."

"With a girl like Mona, we have to ask ourselves if she wouldn't be better off taking life skills courses with other feebleminded children and teenagers," said the deputy director. "She'd be safe there. It's a locked facility. There's a great deal to do, and you wouldn't have to worry about things like this happening again."

"No, I suppose not," said Mrs. Garrison, deep in thought.

"And they've added a new dormitory," said the deputy director.

Mrs. Ballard picked up her tea again. Her voice betrayed a degree of indifference. "This isn't something you have to decide today. It's one option."

"I'd want to talk to Simon about it. And Mona, too," said Mrs. Garrison.

"Of course," said the deputy director.

"Another option—and the two aren't exclusive—is guardianship," offered Mrs. Ballard, "You would have to—"

"My reason for bringing up the custodial school," interrupted the deputy director, "is not just that Mona is at risk, but she seems to have gone as far as she can in regular school." She picked up the pile of Mona's schoolwork and thumbed through it. Each page, in the upper right corner, bore Mona's name untidily rendered in green crayon in her own hand.

"I meant to ask about that," said Mrs. Ballard. "What can you tell us about Mona's progress?"

Mrs. Garrison was drying the corners of her eyes with her tissue. "Her mother had her in and out of school when they lived…when they were homeless in Portland. We started Mona in the second grade, but by the third she was floundering. We held her out for some time, then tried again last year. They recommended we try fifth grade this year, so we did; but she's back in fourth again. We'd hire a tutor if we could afford it."

"She's repeating fourth grade, and her work is unsatisfactory," said the deputy director matter-of-factly. She looked at Mrs. Garrison for confirmation and received it. "She can't keep taking fourth grade indefinitely."

"Would you like me to tell you about guardianship?" said Mrs. Ballard, subdued but sitting forward.

"Yes," said Mrs. Garrison. "I'll try to remember what you tell me so I can tell Simon."

"First, there's no cost to you. I'd file the petition on behalf of Mona, a minor. If appointed, I would be paid by the county."

Mrs. Garrison snickered self-deprecatingly. "Well, that's a relief, seeing as we barely have two pennies to rub together."

CHAPTER FOURTEEN

"IS YOUR DAD OVER the whole Mona Garrison fiasco?" asked Wheels around a wad of chewing gum. He removed his coat and slid into the booth opposite Raleigh.

Before Raleigh could answer, a waitress approached with two glasses of ice water, menus wedged under her arm. "Hello, fellas," she said. "Two today?"

"Four actually," said Wheels. "They'll be here in a few."

"Can I get you something to drink?"

"Two Pepsi-Colas," Wheels ventured. Raleigh nodded. "Oh, and some potato chips."

"I think the storm's blown over at home," Raleigh said, opening his menu. "Thanks in part to Mrs. Garrison."

"Mrs. Garrison? I thought she was the one hammering you?"

"She was. But she overplayed her hand. Told Dad that none of this would have happened if Mom were still alive."

Wheels cackled. "No shit?"

"That didn't go over real well," Raleigh said in a mock strained whisper. "That's all Dad talks about. He doesn't say anything about the contest or the Osprey Club. I couldn't leave the house for a couple of days, but it would have been a whole lot worse if Mrs. Garrison hadn't crossed that line."

Wheels smiled crookedly. "Crazy old biddy."

"The guys, now that's a different story. The football team—in fact, the whole school, from seniors on down... They don't..."

"Give it another month. It'll blow over. Besides, I didn't see anyone complaining when you hit Fisher in the end zone the other night."

Raleigh put down the menu. "Even the teachers act different. People are afraid to talk to me—maybe they don't want to be *seen* talking to me. Either way, I'm ready to get out of this hellhole. Graduation can't come soon enough."

Wheels watched the waitress set two more places at the table. When she was gone, he leaned over and asked in a hushed tone, "What about you and Sally?"

Raleigh scoffed. He picked up his fork and began to turn it over and over. "Me and Sally? What are you talking about? There is no me and Sally—never will be." Raleigh didn't blame Wheels for asking, but he swallowed back some anger just the same. "She won't talk to me anymore."

"That's crazy."

"What's that look for?" asked Raleigh. "Do you know something?"

Wheels had trouble holding Raleigh's gaze. "No. All right, Clarice called me last night. She said Barbara wants to know if you're still hot on Sally Springs. That's all. I told her you weren't."

"What does she know about Sally Springs?"

"That's just it. I'm afraid I told them about you. I was drunk. It was at the lake party, when Rollins brought the White Horse. They wanted to know who you were, and why you were so glum, and I'm afraid I spilled the beans."

Raleigh's eyes flashed across the table. "What'd you say? That I was sick over Sally? And she didn't give a hoot about me?"

"Not exactly," replied Wheels. "But yes, that's pretty much it. But they were drunk, too, and I didn't think they were listening. When Clarice mentioned it last night, hell, that's the first time I remembered it myself—telling them, I mean."

Raleigh stared out the window past the Green Lantern Café sign. A woman and young boy waited for cars then crossed the street, no doubt heading for Wolf's grocery store.

Is there anybody who isn't talking behind my back? I've been dizzy over her all right, but something's changed. I think I'm done.

He nodded to himself.

In fact, I'm sure of it. She doesn't even have the guts to face me.

Raleigh looked back to find his friend braced for a verbal attack. "Hey," Raleigh said, picking up his water glass, "don't worry about it. It's no big deal."

"I should have kept my goddamn mouth shut."

"No. It's all right." Raleigh took a long drink. "So this girl wanted to know about me, huh? What do you make of that?"

Wheels warmed to the new topic. "You're going to like her, old man. Curves out to here."

Raleigh laughed. "Better than teeth out to there, I guess. My fate is in your hands, I'm sorry to say."

Wheels swung a knee onto the seat cushion. "You won't be disappointed. These Seattle girls are..."

"Pips?" Raleigh volunteered.

Wheels hesitated. "I was going to say reliable."

Raleigh's laughter filled the café.

"Here you go, fellas," said the waitress. Raleigh watched his friend's eyes follow the woman's hand from her tray to the table and back. As he reached for his Pepsi-Cola, someone turned up the radio behind the counter. "Chef Tony never misses the war report," the waitress confided in a low voice. "He'll turn it down as soon as it's over."

Raleigh and Wheels exchanged glances.

> *The United States today suspended economic assistance to France's North African colonies and broadly hinted that diplomatic relations with the Vichy government might be severed because of increasing Nazi domination of French affairs...*

"He's like my dad," Wheels said. "Listens every day at two and six-thirty." Wheels gave his menu a desultory looking-over, front and back.

Raleigh turned around. The two men and one woman at the counter listened with unfocused eyes, staring beyond their plates. Behind them, out of sight, a conversation reshaped itself into a friendly argument over the survival of the British Isles.

> *After devoting the morning to the European situation, Secretary of State Hull met with Admiral Kichisaburo Nomura...in another talk designed to find a peaceful solution*

of Japanese-American tension in the Pacific. The Japanese had received new instructions from their foreign office during the night.

"If it's not one thing, it's another," Wheels said, slapping the menu with comic indignation. He grabbed a handful of potato chips with his left hand, and with his right he plucked the gum from his mouth and stuck it under the table.

"Hell of a world, isn't it?" Raleigh said, smiling and reaching for the bowl of chips. He more than matched Wheels's handful. "Thank God we've got Private Second Class Ronald R. Zandt standing at the ready."

Wheels, unable to control his laughter, keeled over and spit a mouthful of potato chip crumbs over the tabletop. "Ha!" he cried. "That's hilarious. General Ronald R. Zandt." He picked up a napkin and began to scrape the crumbs toward his side of the table. He stopped chuckling long enough to produce a slow, nasal voice. "Uh, it's damn near lunchtime. Let's...uh...kill us some of them goddamn krauts."

"Hello, Leonard." Wheels looked up. Two bright-faced, fresh-smelling girls stood at the end of the table, to Raleigh's left. The one on the right, Clarice Austen, wore a large brown wool coat with a missing button. She had a full face with dimpled cheeks and eyes that narrowed to slits in the service of her smile. She wore her brown hair in loose curls parted down the center of her scalp. Her companion, dressed in an open, dark gray coat with a silver starfish broach, was a trim, shorter figure, with blonde hair set in finger waves, bright blue eyes, a strong, well-shaped nose, and alabaster skin stained with patches of pink, as though she'd been running.

"Hello there," said Wheels, hurrying to clear the last of the crumbs from the table. "Clarice, Barbara, you remember Raleigh," he said as he slid over to make room.

Raleigh did the same. Blushing, Barbara Spade sat next to Raleigh. "Hi," she said.

"Hi."

"This is great," said Wheels. "You guys know each other, but Mr. Amnesia over here doesn't have a clue." Clarice and Wheels laughed together, knocking shoulders.

Making like a couple already.

"You were pretty far gone," said Clarice. "Do you remember us at all?"

"Yeah," interjected Barbara, slapping Raleigh on the arm. "Do you remember me? Or were you just thinking about that other girl?"

Raleigh turned to find the pink blotches gone, replaced by a fetching smile and a full, open, expectant expression. Her long lashes seemed to keep the question alive.

"Uh, well…not exactly," said Raleigh, covering his mouth with the tips of his fingers. "I wish I could say I did." This last he said over rainbows of laughter.

"I told you," said Barbara to Clarice.

Barbara leaned forward and began to take off her coat. Raleigh reached to assist. He felt a sudden, unexpected surge of pleasure: the sight of her soft, argyle sweater pulled tight, the smell of perfume released from a hiding place warm and protected.

"Thank you," said Barbara. "Well, I remember you." She colored again. "And I'm glad you're feeling better." She placed her coat on her lap and half onto Raleigh's lap, as well. Raleigh couldn't tell if this was intentional or not. He decided not to move it. What was the harm?

"How was your trip down?" Wheels asked.

Clarice and Barbara giggled at some secret between them. Barbara said, "Long. Too damn long."

Their laughter brought stares from the two men at the counter. With the war report droning on in the background, Barbara leaned into Raleigh's shoulder and Clarice slid her hand toward Wheels's leg under the table.

Raleigh wondered if this explained Barbara's coat over his leg. "So, how are things in Seattle?" Raleigh asked Clarice in a quiet tone. "Quite a change from Olympia I bet." He'd remembered that much, that Clarice was the daughter of a friend one of Wheels's mother, and they had moved to Seattle from Olympia a couple of years ago. Barbara Spade was a second cousin and friend of Clarice's from Franklin High School.

"It's aces," said Clarice. "There's so much more to do."

Raleigh faced Barbara, focused on her up close. "How long have you lived there?"

"Born and raised," said Barbara, smiling. "So, let's see...that makes twenty-four years."

Clarice and Wheels guffawed and immediately covered their mouths, aware that others in the café were listening to the war report. Raleigh grinned. "Twenty-four, huh? You don't look a day over twenty-three."

Barbara leaned on him again, giggling. This time she was slow to straighten. Was she going to put her hand on his leg? Was that next?

"What can I get you two?" said the waitress who appeared at the end of the table. She looked over her order pad from Barbara to Clarice and back again.

Clarice whispered something into Wheels's ear. He nodded. As if on cue, Raleigh felt Barbara's fingers drumming against the outside of his leg under her coat. He didn't dare turn to look at her.

"I guess we're running late," Wheels said.

Barbara bent close to Raleigh's ear, pressing her ample chest against his arm. "Clarice's grandfather will be back between five and six," she whispered. "We've got his place all to ourselves for a couple of hours."

Wheels looked at him expectantly. Barbara's fingers stretched over Raleigh's knee. Raleigh was glad her coat was exactly where it was.

* * *

Lauren lifted the heavy skillet from the burner with two hands and set it off to the side with a loud clank. The bacon grease sizzled against the side of the pan. "Breakfast is ready!" she shouted at the top of her lungs.

"I'm right here," said Raleigh.

Lauren turned with her hand over her heart. "Don't do that!"

"Do what? I've been here for five minutes. Serves you right for listening to the radio while you cook. Remember what Grandma used to say: if you can do two things at once, you're only half as good as you think you are." Raleigh turned the page of Friday's *Daily Olympian*. "Where's Dad?"

"Burning the garbage out back. He's eaten already. Did you get your homework done?"

"Yes, Mother."

She dropped a plate of eggs, potatoes and bacon on top of the newspaper. "Oh, that's right. I keep forgetting you're a horse's behind."

"Thanks," said Raleigh, admiring the breakfast and unfolding one of the white linen napkins that came out of the cupboard on Sundays.

A minute later, Lauren slid into her chair. Her plate held a single egg. "Who was the letter from?" she asked.

"What letter?"

"The one you got yesterday."

"I got a letter? You're kidding. I never get mail."

Lauren got up, went to the hall, and came back tossing him a hand-addressed envelope. "Looks like a girl's handwriting to me."

Raleigh put down his fork. He looked at the return address. There was no name, just: *3222 S. Plum St., Seattle, Wash*. He knew it was from Barbara.

He'd promised to call her if he could figure out a way to pay for it. If he couldn't—well, that was the idea. He couldn't.

"Want to read it out loud?"

"No." Raleigh smiled out of one side of his mouth as he tore the envelope open. The handwritten letter was written on Red Cross stationery.

> *Dearest Raleigh,*
>
> *I've been thinking a lot about you. I think you're nice. I want you to know I've never done anything like that before. I don't know what got into me. I hope you liked it though, and you're not mad at me.*
>
> *Clarice and me are planning to come to Yelm again during the Christmas break. I would love to see you—if you want to, that is.*
>
> *Yours affectionately,*
>
> *Barbara*

"Well?" said Lauren.

Raleigh reprised the half-smile, folded the letter and reached around to put it in his back pocket.

"Gosh, I wish some Clark Gable-type would write me a letter," said Lauren, just warming up. "Dear Lauren, kissy, kissy, kissy. Kissy, kissy, kissy."

On the heels of her words came a news report over the radio in the parlor. Raleigh and Lauren fell silent.

> *This is John Daly speaking from the CBS newsroom in New York... The Japanese have attacked the American naval base at Pearl Harbor, Hawaii, and our defense facilities at Manila, capital of the Philippines...*

Lauren put her fork down and got up from the table. She stood over Raleigh and touched his shoulder with a trembling hand, then walked slowly out the back door.

* * *

Something in the way his father stood, leaning on his rake, staring into the quiet, smoke-heavy garbage fire, made an odd impression on Raleigh. He felt as though he were gazing at a photograph of an unreclaimable moment, something he might remember—that he hoped he would remember. And his father was not a part of him, but of the fire, and the tall, striated grasses of the field behind him, and of the worn shed that kept the wind from the flames. Raleigh advanced on the man—crossing paths with his sister, who was returning to the house in slow deliberative steps. George Starr grew larger in his son's eyes with each step, but it was not until Raleigh came within the fire's circle of heat, and could smell the garbage burning, that the spell broke.

Still clutching Barbara's letter, he spoke to the man who had raised him. George looked up, his face gone as pale as the oversized tan trousers that crimped and puckered up and down his legs. His eyes turned away a moment later and settled back on the fire; and Raleigh knew that look, and could name it. He had seen it a handful of times—when his father lost his job at the mill, for example, and when his mother's doctor left the house that last time—but then, being younger, he could not have named it.

The two men—for Raleigh felt grown—stood without speaking. George rubbed the stubble on his chin and grimaced once, but remained quiet. The gentle soughing and exhaling of the fire seemed to soothe Raleigh, who thought of the multitude of times he had stood watch over the burning garbage, and wished now to do it a thousand more times.

God help me.

He leaned forward and dropped Barbara's letter onto an active flame.

CHAPTER FIFTEEN

1942

ON HIS WAY to the quartermaster's tent, Raleigh squinted across the airfield through weltering heat waves toward the wide expanse of the South Pacific. He listened for the drone of approaching P-40s. It had been forty-five minutes since word had come down: The morning's target had been reached. The squadron was heading back, all planes accounted for.

That doesn't mean some weren't shot up. Chances are we'll be rebuilding at least one engine tonight.

He checked his watch.

It's early. Give them an hour.

Raleigh wiped his sweaty, grease-stained hands with a rag before entering the quartermaster's tent. When his eyes adjusted, he saw it was packed with more than a dozen men taking advantage of the shade to read letters from home.

"Hey, Starr, yours is over there," someone said, pointing to the corner of a desk occupied by the mail clerk, Sandy White. White, from Cheyenne, the only man in uniform, held out an envelope as he approached.

Raleigh nodded a thanks while studying the handwriting on the envelope. It was Lauren's. He swung the rag over his shoulder and sauntered back out into the blazing sunshine. Slapping the unopened letter against his thigh, he made for the relative cool of the palm forest. Beneath broad, windswept fronds, he sat on a patch of coarse island grass, tore open the envelope, and pulled out the letter. A second, smaller piece of folded paper fell out and began to blow away. Raleigh scooped it up deftly. He opened it. All but the signature was written in Lauren's hand:

Dear Raleigh,

You are a dear. Please be careful. I know my dream. Do you remember you asked me? I want to go to Glacier Park, to see it for myself. I saw pictures in the magazine.

Mona

He read it three times and touched the thick scrawl of the signature with the tips of his fingers. "Mona," he said out loud.

He looked up, fighting back a sudden upwelling of emotion. Where was it coming from?

He imagined Mona standing before him, smiling up as she had at the dance contest. Her face shone in the afterglow of the dance, her eyes bright with affection. For the first time, he imagined leaning down to kiss her, and her rising to meet his kiss. He closed his eyes.

I'm out of my mind!

He slapped the trunk of the closest palm tree.

What the hell is wrong with me?

He jumped to his feet, turned one way and another, and laughed out loud. "Okay, I admit it," he shouted toward the landing strip, "I'm nuts! Okay? All right? Can we agree?" He kicked the sand, reached out and leaned against the same palm, shaking his head as though he'd seen a monkey do a cartwheel.

* * *

May 20, 1942

Dear Sis,

I got three letters last week, two from you and one from Aunt Edith that Mrs. Fuller wrote for her. You have no idea—or maybe you do—how much it means to me to hear from home. A fellow can only take so much boredom and blistering heat, and there's been plenty of both here. Sleeping is next to impossible except around 3 to 6 in the morning, when it begins to cool off. If we're not up repairing planes at that hour, you can bet I'm sawing logs.

The scuttlebutt is we'll be moving ████████ *████. The Seabees are already at work on a* ████ *on* ████████.

I'm happy to hear you're getting out a bit. I've always liked Doug, and it's nice to see his patience paying off. He knows he's a lucky guy, and I couldn't agree more.

Aunt Edith tells me you're still driving Mona to work and picking her up on Sundays. That's swell. Please tell Mona hello for me, and thank her for the note.

Oh, and tell Dad he'd want none of this. I know him well enough. He'd be like the flyboys around here, grouching about too little flight time.

On a lark, some of the fellas and I are building a motorcycle (you heard right). If it runs—and why wouldn't it?—we'll be using it to chase macaques off the runway before the flyboys drop in. How's that for excitement? Well, that's all for now. Be good and write again soon.

Always and forever, your bro-bro,

Raleigh

* * *

Mona looked at Lauren. "Read it once more."

"Here," said Lauren, "let's read it together." She set the letter down between them and straightened its creases. "You can read this. Follow my finger: 'Dear Sis… I got…three letters last week…two from…'"

Their voices melded in the closed-up cab of the pickup at the side of Thompson Road. Neither woman looked up from the letter, not when

Jake Stedden passed on his way to town, and not when Sam Farmin passed in the other direction with a friendly honk—not once.

* * *

"What do you think, Starr? Can we save the patient?"

Both men stood on ladders reaching into the bowels of the P-40's Allison engine. Raleigh grimaced with the effort to loosen a bolt without stripping it. "Not if we can't straighten the housing on this scavenge pump," he said at last. He pulled his hands free. "You want to take a pull at that, Steve? You were raised on corn, right?"

"That's right," said the burly Buckeye, a cigarette hanging from his lip. "Bring that flashlight over here, will you?"

The two machinists continued to attack the stubborn bolt, oblivious to the slow, winding buildup of the air raid siren. They were used to several such drills a day. But when the radioman's strident "This is not a drill! This is not a drill!" began blaring from the speakers, a shock ran through Raleigh unlike anything he had felt before. He straightened involuntarily, nearly toppling from the ladder. His eyes met the Ohioan's in a moment of mutual disbelief, but seconds later both men were running for the gun locker.

The first reports of the antiaircraft guns thundered from the far end of the island and echoed off a nearby hill. Hunching over an M1 and a box of clips, Raleigh took three running steps toward the sandbag-reinforced foxhole but was stopped in his tracks by the *thud-thud-thud-thud* of bullets pushing up the earth only feet in front of him. With his heart in his throat, he spun and scrambled to the far corner of the avionics repair and maintenance shelter, diving out of sight as the first low-flying Zero screamed overhead. The roar of its engine was deafening.

Oh God, this is really it. This is really happening.

Raleigh looked up to see Lockhart picking himself off the ground and racing to the foxhole. It was fifty yards away—fifty yards of exposed, open terrain. It seemed like a hundred and fifty.

I won't be going over there.

As he searched frantically for the next best alternative, the first bombs began to fall. A fireball rose above one of the parked P-40s, and its severed wing flew up and landed on top of another plane. Bits of dirt and sand began to rain down around him. The air filled with the smell of burning fuel.

Two more Zeros angled in, letting loose a volley of machine-gun fire. Visible paths of destruction ripped through the commander's Quonset hut and shredded one corner of the infirmary tent to Raleigh's left. When the dust cleared, two men lay in pools of blood, and Raleigh recognized one of the pilots who had been trying to get to one of the remaining P-40s.

Exhaust billowed from the manifolds of three Warhawks as their propellers spun. The planes veered together onto the runway in a desperate attempt to get airborne. The sudden acceleration of their Allison engines added to the cacophony.

Prone in the grass at the corner of the maintenance yard, Raleigh rolled onto his side to adjust the rifle's shoulder strap. *Jesus, this is incredible. This is really happening.* Trying to command his heart to slow down and his tight chest to relax and let him breathe, he settled over his weapon and squinted down the barrel in the direction of the airstrip. "C'mon," he whispered as the tiny circle of a Zero's cowling came into view, a gray dot in the silver-blue September sky. It was more than two miles off but would be within range in a matter of seconds. Raleigh cleared dirt and sand from the rear sight and settled over his left elbow, concentrating on the target. He ignored the flashes of yellow from the Zero's machine guns. He'd expected them. The pilot was after the scrambling P-40s—no mistaking that.

Raleigh fired off a round. Then another. Then another. He banished from his mind the sudden realization that he was firing a weapon at another human being. *Calm down,* he told himself, bringing the sight down on the target again. But he couldn't calm down. He tried to concentrate on the smooth, hard surface of the stock against his cheek. *Breathe.*

The Zero was over the end of the runway. It climbed to clear two airborne P-40s. Where was the third? It dipped again and made a run at the parked warplanes. Raleigh continued firing. The siren above his head began to wind down. He heard the *bang-bang-bang-bang-bang* of nearby antiaircraft guns and saw crisscrossing tracer bullets following the Zero across the horizon. No effect—at least none he could see. The Zero screamed out of view over the tops of the palm trees to his right.

Shit, if the antiaircraft guns can't hit them, we're in trouble.

Raleigh couldn't see the fifth Zero sweeping in from the southwest, but there was no mistaking its direction from the bullet paths intersecting the earlier angles of attack. He jumped up and fired at the flashing metal coursing over the field a split second behind the roar of its radial engine. This time, as the Zero banked hard to starboard to realign itself with the other marauders, he spied the head of the Japanese pilot. He fired off another round—with no time to aim.

I've got to get a better angle. His heart still pounding, he slumped back against one of the supports holding the camouflage netting. As he changed clips, he looked down the length of the runway to see a crumpled P-40 propped on its nose, burning furiously. *He didn't make it.* A thick column of black smoke rose into the cloudless sky. Suddenly, all his energy left him. He wondered if his heart, so furiously throbbing, was pumping blood at all.

He dropped his head back against the post. Closing his eyes, he heard his father say, "You ever seen a fire like that, son?" He recalled the smoke rising over the line of trees ringing the Garrison farm. "That's not a slash fire," he'd said to his father. "That's the tool shed next to the barn." A thin, tired whirr came up from the Model A's engine as it jostled over the potholes of Thompson Road. He'd looked back for a moment to watch the spinning dust cloud trailing them, then spun around as an idea occurred to him. "There're no kittens in there. Those days are gone."

"I'll help with the fire, son," his father seemed to say. "You better get to those wounded men."

Raleigh's eyes shot open. Mechanically, but with a low, guttural growling, he climbed to his feet and sprinted for the closer victim. As though he had broken through the line and was running for the goal line, his legs stretched and bent over the hard, sandy soil. He nearly stumbled and caught himself with his left hand, keeping his head low and holding his rifle high with the other. Small arms fire popped from the foxhole and, not far beyond, he felt the all-enveloping *bang-bang-bang-bang* of the AA guns. A sudden memory: Wheels, on the day they enlisted, squinting one eye shut in the sunshine, squatted down over his parents' fresh-cut lawn. "This may not be such a clambake. You keep your head down, Raleigh—you hear?"

Raleigh skidded to a stop. Two lines of exploding soil raced toward him. A hail of sand and dirt blinded him, but he managed to stay upright. Squinting out of one eye, he could still make out the shape of the wounded man lying in the open. He staggered toward him. The gunfire intensified, and he knew another Zero was closing fast. Without pausing, he threw his rifle over his shoulder and leaned over to pick up the man, sliding his hands under each arm. It was Jack Forester, the company cook. He felt Forester push with his leg, trying to help.

"I've got you, Jack," Raleigh shouted. He pulled the man toward the cover of the tents and lean-tos near the edge of the palm forest. Forester continued to push with one leg while dragging the other.

Two men relieved Raleigh of his burden, and others scrambled toward the second wounded man—or was he dead? It was the pilot. Raleigh had acted out of something like instinct. Without deliberation, maybe without thought. He spotted the thick trunk of a palm tree.

Over there. I've got to get over there.

He dove headfirst behind the swollen base of the palm tree, his vision all of a sudden limited to the flecks of sand: black, gray, tan, and white. *Could this be the world? These tiny pieces? Could I find a way to make this the world—here, where nothing moves?*

The pinging of bullets tearing through the P-40s on the ground roused him. He leaned out to see a Zero flying straight over the runway, its guns blazing. As he rolled over to clear his rifle from his shoulder, the Zero exploded in a fireball, raining debris onto the airfield. He rolled back. A second later, he heard the roar of an Allison engine and saw a P-40 banking to the right and climbing back into the azure sky for more. Raleigh glimpsed the tail number: 15. It was Al Lamson—Al, the playboy from San Diego. He felt a connection to Lamson he had never felt before, and he knew in that instant it would last a lifetime.

A moment later, Raleigh was up on one knee again, steadying the barrel of his M1 against the side of the tree. He eyed the approaching Zero with a new sense of confidence and possibility. The plane passed behind the smoke cloud at the end of the runway, turned north, and lowered its nose. The pilot unleashed the Zero's 20 mm cannons, slowing the plane. The destruction to Raleigh's right was instantaneous and horrific—P-40s torn apart, one exploding in a fireball, great swaths of earth hurled a hundred feet in the air or more.

Raleigh leveled the front and rear sights of his M1 on the Mitsubishi fighter's windshield and raised the barrel to adjust for distance. He felt the recoil of first one bullet and then another. Over the front sight, he saw the flash of tracer bullets streaming past the plane. As the Zero continued its assault, Raleigh fired again and again. He squeezed off the eighth and last round in the clip.

Dammit.

Suddenly, he saw it: a smoke trail, thin at first, but getting thicker by the second.

Had he done it? Had he hit the engine? One of them had.

The Zero's engine was already coughing and sputtering by the time the plane passed overhead and disappeared over the foliage beyond.

A cheer went up from the foxhole. Raleigh turned to see Steve Lockhart looking at him with his fist raised in the air. But in the next instant, Lockhart's body writhed through a thin veil of dust, and the other men in the foxhole collapsed backwards in a grotesque dance of death. The trees behind the foxhole quivered under the barrage of bullets. In the time it took Raleigh to comprehend what was happening, the next Zero had completed its carnage. It climbed steeply, made a barrel roll, and angled south, tailed by a P-40 a few seconds behind. The Warhawk banked hard to port, its supercharged engine roaring in close pursuit.

The dogfight was visible from the airstrip. Over the next ten minutes, a close observer would have seen two Zeros shot down over the sea, while the remaining four disengaged and fled west. Before the fight was over, one Warhawk was forced to land on its belly, with the tip of its starboard wing blown off, and two failed to return. Al Lamson returned in one piece in the 15, as did Chuck Brown in the 22 and Fred "Steady" Trout in the 6.

But Raleigh was not an observer. He had set off at a sprint for the foxhole. In the minutes that followed, while the war raged above their heads, he and three others took orders from the medic—and it was all he could do to keep from vomiting.

CHAPTER SIXTEEN

"I HOPE I'M DOING THE RIGHT THING," said Mrs. Garrison as she leaned over the kitchen table and placed her signature on a line indicated by Jewel Ballard's finger.

Mrs. Ballard turned the page and pointed to another line. "And right here."

"What's this?" asked Mrs. Garrison.

"It's a Waiver of Notice and Consent to Guardianship. This will be filed with the court to show that you've approved me as Mona's guardian and waived notice of the hearing. It's a standard form."

While signing, Mrs. Garrison said, "You didn't mention all this paperwork when you were here with Mrs. Robinson. It's for the best, though. You'll take good care of her, won't you?"

"Of course I will, but remember, she'll be at the Western State Custodial School. They'll have day-to-day responsibility. My job is to advocate for her and see that decisions are made in her best interest."

"I don't feel like I can keep her safe anymore," said Mrs. Garrison, sinking into one of the kitchen chairs. She sought the guardian's eyes. "I'm lying awake at night."

"I understand, Grace. May I call you that?"

"Of course, dear," said Mrs. Garrison, reaching for Mrs. Ballard's hand.

Mrs. Ballard took it as a sign to sit. She was pulling a chair out when Mona appeared in the passageway.

"Oh, there you are," said Mrs. Garrison.

Mrs. Ballard pushed the chair back in. "Hello, there," she said with an assumed familiarity.

Mona stood beneath the arched passageway connecting the living room to the kitchen in her heavy winter coat, carrying a beige pasteboard-and-leather suitcase. Her cheeks were flushed, her eyes puffy. She took a step back when Mrs. Ballard approached with her hand extended.

"This is the guardian I told you about," said Mrs. Garrison.

"I'm Mrs. Ballard. It's nice to meet you. My, you're a pretty thing. Your aunt has told me all about you."

Mona set down the suitcase. She glanced at Mrs. Ballard's hand and averted her eyes, refusing to shake it.

Mrs. Garrison left the kitchen table and stood close to Mona with a hand on her left arm. "Mrs. Ballard is trained to help people like you, Mona. Do you remember me talking to you about this?"

Mona stared to the side.

"She's been moody lately," said Mrs. Garrison to Mrs. Ballard. "Haven't you, dear?"

Mona didn't answer.

Dispelling a long silence, Mrs. Ballard said, "Your aunt and I have been going over some paperwork. May I show it to you?" She returned to the kitchen table and waited for the other two, then picked up the bundle and showed them to Mona. "These are legal documents. They're going to make me your guardian. Your aunt has signed on this page, and on this page. See?"

Mona nodded sullenly.

"And there's another line here for your signature," said Mrs. Ballard, fumbling to find the page. "Here it is."

Mrs. Garrison's blue eyes bulged behind her rimless spectacles. "Can *she* sign it?"

"Yes," replied Mrs. Ballard. "It's not mandatory, of course. Some people can't sign their name at all—but we know Mona can, can't you, dear? This says you agree with your aunt and don't object to the court appointing me as your guardian." She reached for the pen and offered it to Mona.

Mona looked at her aunt questioningly.

"Go ahead, dear," said Mrs. Garrison.

Mona signed her first name on the line and, after urging from both Mrs. Ballard and Mrs. Garrison, added "Garrison" in a much rougher hand.

"All right," said the guardian, straightening the papers and placing them in her briefcase. "Are we ready to go?"

Mona looked across at her aunt. "Will you and Uncle Simon visit me?" she said, her eyes glistening with unspilled tears.

"Of course we will, dear," said Mrs. Garrison, opening her arms to Mona. "I told you that last night."

Mona stepped away to avoid her aunt's embrace. "And will you tell Mother where I am?"

Mrs. Garrison exchanged oblique glances with the guardian. "Yes. Get your suitcase, dear. We'll see you sometime next week."

"I want to say good-bye to Uncle Simon."

Mrs. Garrison frowned. "No. The doctor says he needs as much sleep as possible, and I don't want you catching his flu bug. You two go on, before I change my mind."

* * *

October 5, 1942

Dear Raleigh,

We were so happy to get a letter from you today…

Mona came out to the truck yesterday to tell me she's quitting Aunt Edith's. She wanted me to come in with her so she could explain it to Aunt Edith and not mess it up. I went, but she did fine. She told us she's moving to the Custodial School at Buckley where, as she puts it, "other students are slow like me." She thanked Aunt Edith and told her she hoped she could work for her again. Something tells me this wasn't Mona's idea, not at all. Anyway, it will free up my Sundays, won't it, brother-of-mine?

Lauren

* * *

Mona sat up. The Buick's windshield was a riot of raindrops and sinuous water trails. It was easier to see out the side window. "Is this the school?" she said, looking up at the wet stone facade.

"No," said Mrs. Ballard, depositing her car keys in her purse. "We're in Olympia. There's something we have to do first."

Mona leaned back. *Olympia? Why didn't you tell me we were going to Olympia?*

"Don't get too comfortable," said Mrs. Ballard. "By 'we,' I mean you. We have to get you tested." She extracted a manila envelope from her briefcase.

A shudder ran up Mona's spine. "Tested? What do you mean?"

"Oh, it's nothing. It'll take about an hour." Mrs. Ballard looked at her watch. "I'll be back for you at ten thirty. Let's go. He's expecting us." Mrs. Ballard exited the car and walked around the front, sidling between parked cars with the manila envelope over her head to keep the rain off her blonde hair. She opened the passenger door. "Come on. Don't make a scene."

Mona straightened her back and took hold of the side of her seat. "But...what test? I can't take tests."

She should know that. Isn't she the one who said—?

Mrs. Ballard leaned down and jerked the hand away. "Don't be silly."

Mona's feet were planted on the floorboard. Increasingly frightened, she said, "I want to go home."

"No. You can't go home. You're under my care. Please, get out of the car. I'm getting soaked here."

Mona's face tightened. "What test do I have to take?"

"The school requires a current IQ test, okay? And I need a medical report for the guardianship hearing. It's the same for every child in my care. Once we get this done, we can be on our way. Come on. I'll buy you a Pepsi-Cola when we're finished."

Mona stared blindly out the windshield, felt herself quaking deep inside. "I feel fine. I don't need to see anybody."

Mrs. Ballard squatted next to the open door, smiling. She lowered her voice. "Look, dear, it's going to be fine. We'll have you out of here in no time."

"No. I don't want to."

"You don't—" Mrs. Ballard stood again, adjusting her dress. She glared down at Mona. "Things are going to be much easier for you when you learn your place. I will not be talked back to, do you understand?"

She looks like she might hit me.

Slowly, Mona put one foot out of the car. And then another. Mrs. Ballard backed up, and Mona stepped up onto the sidewalk. When Mrs. Ballard murmured "That's better," Mona turned away and folded her arms.

Mrs. Ballard stepped around Mona and straightened the girl's collar. "We'll just get this done and be on our way," she said. "Be brave."

Five minutes later, they stood shoulder to shoulder on the third floor of the Century Building. FELIX ABERCROMBIE, M.D. was written in a thick serif across a translucent, undulating glass panel that rattled precariously each time Mrs. Ballard knocked on the door. She tried the door a third time. "Hmmm. He said he'd be here." She checked her watch. "This isn't his regular office," she said as she lifted her purse and began to dig through it. "I wonder if he expected us at the clinic?"

The lock clicked and the door opened. A short, square man with gray eyes, bushy brows, and a saucer-sized bald spot at the top of his head appeared in the doorway. He wore an unbuttoned lab coat over a gray suit with a high-collared white shirt and a purple-and-gold floral tie. Behind him, the lights in the waiting room were off.

"Good morning, Mrs. Ballard," he said through yellowing teeth. His eyes shifted to Mona and back again.

"Hello, Dr. Abercrombie. This is Mona Garrison, your nine-thirty appointment."

The scent of Abercrombie's hand soap drifted into Mona's nostrils, along with his sour, coffee-laden breath. His eyes seemed to open wider than normal for Mona. "I see. Good morning, Miss Garrison." He stepped back and opened the door wider. "Come in, come in."

"She's nervous," said Mrs. Ballard. She looked at Mona. "But it's going to be fine."

"Of course it is," said the doctor.

Mrs. Ballard escorted Mona into the waiting room, then said, "Dr. Abercrombie, if I can have a word with you in the hall?"

"Of course." He left Mona hugging herself in her thick coat in the center of the room. As he stepped into the hallway, he pulled the door partially shut behind him.

Mona could hear them plainly. "I need both an IQ test and a physical exam on this one," Mrs. Ballard whispered. "She has a history of making herself available to boys."

Mona's hand flew to her mouth. *What! I do not! Why would she say that...to a doctor?"*

Abercrombie's whisper was softer and more effeminate than the guardian's. "I see. And do you suspect...?"

"Not necessarily, but I want to find out. And, of course, Western State needs the usual report confirming that she's psychologically incapacitated—IQ below seventy-eight. Anything above that and I'm not going to be able to place her there."

What does that mean, below seventy-eight?

"Of course." The doctor paused, then said something else.

Mona tried to hear what he was saying, but it was no use. She looked nervously around the room. An old, threadbare couch in a red-and-white plaid fabric occupied one side, two wooden, straight-back chairs, the other. The chairs were separated by a small end table with a single magazine on top, its cover torn off. There was nothing on the dusty white plaster walls save an outdated calendar from 1939. Through an open door, Mona saw what looked like an uncomfortably high bench in the center of a small, windowless room. She leaned over to get a better look. The bench was covered in black leather, with two perforated leather straps like the ends of belts hanging to the floor. But it was not the straps that kindled her alarm. It was two oddly shaped polished steel appendages extending like mechanical arms from the end, angling up two feet or more above the surface of the bench to end in something like a cup or pocket.

* * *

> *Wheels dropped by last Friday. He was home on leave and wanted news of you. Dad and I filled him in as best we could. His battalion is shipping out for England soon. He says to tell you he's learned to shoot like Ron Zandt, whatever that means. Despite the nice-looking uniform, he seems like the same old Leonard Henderson to me.*

I'm delighted you're having fun with the motorcycle. Dad says he's got enough spare parts around here to build you one, but I did him one better. I told you Doug's selling used cars, didn't I? Well, guess what? He took a motorcycle in trade the other day, and I've talked him into saving it for you. It's an "Indian" or something like that. Doug says it needs work (it doesn't run), but if anyone can fix it up, I told him you could. Anyway, happy early birthday, Raleigh!

If you haven't guessed already, we miss you terribly. Stay safe and come back home as soon as it's over. You're in our prayers.

Your loving sister,

Lauren

* * *

On the hour-and-ten-minute drive from Olympia to Buckley, Mona sat with her tear-wetted face turned away from Mrs. Ballard. Only once did she change position, when Mrs. Ballard skidded to a sudden stop at an intersection.

Mrs. Ballard was a nervous, self-critical driver who made a dramatic production of the routines of driving—downshifting, for example, or pulling away from a stop sign. These seemed to tax her memory of things automotive, and she mumbled to herself and looked about—in the mirrors, through the side windows—like a startled hen.

She was a woman who arrived at destinations road-weary and bitter, with tight-set lips and gray shadows under her eyes. She would examine herself in the rearview mirror after a trip of any length, making corrections by working her mouth back and forth and patting the sides of her face.

"This is it," she said, staring in the mirror, the car still running. It wasn't until she began drumming on her cheeks that Mona sat up, setting her eyes for the first time on the imposing Spanish-style building.

"I don't want to be here."

Mrs. Ballard began to apply lipstick and roll her lips, still gazing in the mirror. "It's going to be fine. Listen, we're going to check in at the office first, and they'll assign you to a dormitory. I don't know... With an IQ of seventy-five, you'll probably be in W4. We'll get someone to bring in your suitcase." The guardian patted her wavy hair above each temple, turning her head one way and another. She looked at Mona, smiled consolingly, turned off the car, and reached into the back seat for her briefcase. "You're going to have to learn to do what I say, Mona. Things will go so much better for you if you do."

"I don't want to go to school here."

"It's always hard the first day, no matter what, but give it a day or two and you'll be fine."

"Please. I don't want to be here."

"You'll make lots of new friends here—you'll see."

I won't make any friends here. You're lying.

"No, I don't—"

"Mona, listen to me." Mrs. Ballard's face fell and she looked tired. "Your aunt has given me a power of attorney, and in a few days I'll be your guardian. My job is to protect you from harm, and that's what I'm going to do. You'll be safe here. I promise."

Mona opened her mouth wide. "But I don't want you to be my guardian," she shrieked.

"I know—but please, just give me a chance. I want you to think of me as a friend."

"No. Please take me home."

Mrs. Ballard looked into the rearview mirror again, this time to check her teeth for lipstick stains. After rubbing her tongue over her front teeth and checking them again, she said, "This is your home now."

Mona's face hardened. "It's not."

"It's both your home and your school until you turn twenty-one. Then we'll find someplace else to put you."

Twenty-one! No one said anything about—

"No! I don't want to live here. Don't you see? Please take me home."

Mrs. Ballard lifted her purse from the seat cushion between them and reached for the door handle. "That's enough, Mona. We're going in. It's been a long day. Let's get you settled."

"I want to talk to Aunt Grace."

"Come on."

"Please. I don't want to live here. I'm afraid. I will pay you! I will give you seventy-five dollars. *Please*!"

With one foot out the door, Mrs. Ballard twisted around. The teeth behind her smile were half in shadow. "Seventy-five dollars? Where'd you come up with a figure like that?" She exited the car and was straightening her dress when a man in his mid-twenties wearing bright white pants and a matching short-sleeved shirt appeared at the top of the landing.

He said something Mona couldn't hear, but Mrs. Ballard answered him, "Yes, please." He turned and went through the large, dark double doors and emerged again with another man, a dark-skinned man in his early thirties, with short-cropped hair and strong, muscular forearms. He too wore the all-white uniform. The two trotted down the steps and strode side by side around the Buick to the passenger door.

Mona jumped when one of the men, the white-skinned one, opened the door next to her. "Let's go," he said.

Mona tried to scramble to the driver's side of the car, but she was stopped by a vicelike grip on her arm. She tried to pull her arm free, but it was no use. As the darker man yanked her back and tried to pull her out of the car, she screamed, "Let go of me!" She was able to brace herself against the window frame with her left hand. "Leave me alone!" she shrieked.

Why are you doing this? You're hurting me! Who are you? Take me home, Mrs. Ballard!

The first orderly separated her hand from the window frame. There was nothing to hold onto now. The two men dragged her from the vehicle as she continued to struggle, locking her left foot around the doorframe. They carried her from the car in a prone position, then brought her upright and locked both of her arms behind her back. Mona turned to see Mrs. Ballard climbing the stairs toward the main office as though nothing were happening. Mona opened her mouth to call for help, but the orderlies jostled her roughly just then, hurting her right shoulder. Her face slowly, inevitably, melted into tears.

CHAPTER SEVENTEEN

1943

SATURDAY, JULY 17. They were spread out, three girls to a row. Loose-fitting blue chambray shirt dresses with open collars and matching cloth belts. Identical black leather shoes with white anklets, scarcely visible among the feathery leaves of the carrot plants. Bent over, swinging hoes, eradicating weeds. You could not tell most of the girls apart except by the color of their short-cropped hair. They worked late into the morning. Once, briefly, the sun appeared at full strength to tax their energies.

"What we don't use feeds the soldiers at Fort Lewis," they'd told Mona and the other girls, inspiring them, bringing proud smiles and nervous giggles to the breakfast table.

An overseer's chair sat empty at the shoulder of the road, with an open book lying face down on the seat. Ten minutes earlier, the school gardener, Mrs. Templeton, had stood up from the chair, stretched, and called out to the closest girls, "I'll be in the greenhouse for a while." She'd ambled away, taking a shortcut across a wide alfalfa field, bending between strands of barbed wire and disappearing behind four white sheds a quarter mile away. Except for one or two girls, the overseer's absence hadn't made a difference in their work. Even a chatty flock of geese circling, drifting toward the fallow field next door, did not divert them.

* * *

He thought he'd put the questions to rest the night before.

What would people say if they found out? Of course, they won't find out. How could they? This isn't like the dance contest. I'm not putting a number on my chest and marching out on a dance floor. Besides, I'm not going to see her. I'm just going to check out this school. I owe her that much.

He raced eastward between tall stands of fir and cedar, across a checkerboard of light and shadow. The motorcycle vibrated beneath him, its roaring engine a source of satisfaction. (He'd fixed it in less than two days. Lauren was right; he had a way with engines.) The back of his khaki dress uniform billowed in the wind.

It would be better not to see her. I won't even get close. I'll turn around at the gate.

He hadn't expected to see the teenage girls in their blue chambray dresses scattered throughout the carrot rows. "What the devil?" he muttered. He engaged the clutch and rolled to a stop within a few feet of an abandoned chair.

She can't be out there—can she?

He stood up, straddling the seat, gazing at the field and its occupants. At first, no one seemed to notice him, until one girl looked up. Then a second. And a third. Like dominoes, they all turned in relation to their distance from one another up and down the rows. Mona stood, held her hoe in her right hand, and shielded her eyes with her left.

Oh my God, is that her?

He thought his heart would burst the instant he saw Mona drop her hoe and begin to walk toward him, stepping over the plant rows. The other girls watched in silence as she passed, touching her bangs, brushing bits of vegetation and dirt from her dress.

He switched off the bike, set the kickstand, dismounted. He managed two steps toward the open gate in the barbed wire fence before he stopped. As she continued toward him, his thoughts flew in all directions. Should he be doing this? This was crazy. Why hadn't he turned around twenty minutes earlier?

He scanned the field for a teacher or other adult, then looked toward the gated drive. No one. The white sheds and the greenhouse in the distance seemed, for all the world, abandoned. He turned back, ran a hand through his windblown hair. Mona looked up between steps. He waved. She touched her bangs again, smiling.

Are you nuts? Did you just ride fifty miles to see this girl? God, but she has beautiful eyes. And her gentleness—she is the same as always. When she walks, it's like her feet hardly touch the ground.

With Mona a few yards from the gate, he moved toward her again.

What else can I do? I'm here. But she's feebleminded—remember that. Get her talking, and then you'll remember how impossible this is. Make some excuse for coming, then get the hell out of here.

He imagined the freedom and relief of the road, the wind on his face washing away the last of Mona Garrison—of this silly infatuation. The smile he wore when she stopped a few feet in front of him on the edge of the road was one part hello, two parts good-bye.

She didn't speak for several seconds. When she did at last, it was in a hopeful, parched croaking tone that touched him: "Is the war over?"

Raleigh shook his head. Stepping closer, he gazed into the two deep pools of blue he remembered so vividly. So fierce was his staring, she looked away at her friends in the field.

Show me, Mona. Show me your handicap. That's what I need. Show me how we're so different that I have no business being here at all, caring for you this way.

"Mona, talk to me. Say something."

Mona looked at him, confused.

"Please."

She glanced to the side and fastened on his eyes again. "I did. I asked you if the war was over...although I know it isn't."

"Something else. I need you to say something else."

Mona looked around. "I like your motorcycle?"

Raleigh laughed in spite of himself. He pivoted away and covered his mouth with his hand.

That's precious. How can you argue with a good-looking girl who likes your motorcycle? It's no use. If I thought I was confused before... Wait. She's wondering... She deserves to know what I'm doing here.

"I'm on leave. I've been reassigned. They're making me a maintenance instructor on the B-29. I'm going to Maxwell Field in Alabama for training on the seventh. So I thought I'd come say hello."

It appeared to be a lot of information for Mona. She stopped smiling and nodded self-consciously.

"How have you been?" Raleigh asked.

Mona's face brightened. "Good."

"Do they treat you all right here?" After she nodded, he looked around again, searching for any sign of a supervisor. Some of the girls had walked in from the field and stood more or less in a line on the other side of the fence. He waved and most waved back. Approximately half he recognized as mongoloids. Their flat smiles were full of joy.

Probably not a lot of visitors around here.

"You look good, Mona," he heard himself say.

She smiled and looked down at her feet.

As he tried to think of what to say next, she whispered, "So do you."

A bemused smile lifted her cheeks. He pushed her shoulder good-naturedly. "Aww, you're just saying that." He told himself to keep it light—to remember that she was just a friend.

Mona giggled.

"So," he said, "do you want a ride on my motorcycle, or not?"

Mona's eyes and mouth opened wide. Her grin was ecstatic. "*Yes*. Would you?"

Raleigh looked over each shoulder for any sign of an adult. He hadn't known what to expect, but it hadn't been a group of teenage girls left unsupervised in a field. "Of course. Let's go." Could it hurt if he took her to the bottom of that hill? It was about a three-minute ride.

Mona climbed on the rear fender rack, pushed her dress down tight and wrapped her arms around Raleigh as though she'd done this a thousand times. He kick-started the bike, made a sharp U-turn in the road, and with Mona laughing and waving to the other girls, they sped off.

He rode in an amorphous fog of uncertainty and pleasure. Despite their brief conversation at the turn-around—

"To say I've missed you is a complete understatement," he shouted.

"What?"

"I've missed you."

"You have?"

"Yes. Sorry about the noise. Are you all right back there?

"Yes."

It seemed to end as soon as it began. Mona letting go of his waist and the bike rising up with her dismount were as unwelcome as any sensations he could imagine.

"That was so much fun," she said.

He drank in her smile.

Oh, Mona. If only… You have no idea how beautiful you are to me.

"Thank you," she added.

"You're welcome." To relieve the pressure building in his mind—the temptation to say something stupid—he glanced past her at the faces beyond the barbed wire. An idea struck him. He said, "What do you suppose they're so interested in?"

Mona turned to see and spun back. "Would you, Raleigh?" she said excitedly.

"I don't see why not."

She jumped up and down and waved them out of the field. "Do you want a ride?" she called out. "Come on! Hurry!"

The rides began with squeals and ended in applause and hugs. Six girls took a turn. One made a show of sitting backwards on the bike, earned the laughter of her friends, before getting off and declining to go further. Three others came over to touch the motorcycle before they, too, shook their heads.

"Is that it, then?" said Raleigh. "No one else?"

Those who had declined colored and shook their heads. About half said, "Thank you."

Surrounded by a dozen or so girls standing in the road, Raleigh regarded Mona. Her smile deepened. "I guess I better get going," he said over the low rumble of the engine.

In the distance, unseen, Mrs. Templeton came running toward the barbed wire fence at the far end of the alfalfa field. She ran at first with an arm raised, then lowered it and sprinted as fast as her fifty-year-old old frame would go. Her screams were lost to the distance, to the girls' chatter, and to the revving of Raleigh's bike.

Raleigh looked down to engage the clutch and put the bike in first gear. He was surprised to feel Mona's body suddenly against his side, her arms encircling his neck, her lips pressed to his cheek. Without thinking, he enveloped her in his arms and drew her closer. He felt her breasts against his chest, the narrowness of her waist, her lithe body. He could smell her skin, and he wanted more. She didn't let go. For a time, he didn't either, but then… *No. You don't have the right. And besides, where would it go from here? I'm taking off in a few days.*

He edged her away gently.

"Thank you, Raleigh," she said. "Thank you for coming."

"Of course. It's been great to see you." Raleigh felt the stabbing pain of absence before he had traveled an inch. His eyes explored the contours of her face, the fading freckles, the arching brows, the delicate turn of her lips—but with his next uneven breath, he began to rebuild his protective wall. *She's a friend. What do you do with friends? You say good-bye and leave them alone.*

He began to form the words, but what came out of his mouth was, "Would it be all right if I wrote to you from Alabama?" One of the girls nearby giggled behind her hands.

"Yes. I would like that," said Mona.

Raleigh nodded. The girls made way as he released the clutch and rolled forward. Ten seconds later he was racing across the valley, kicking up a funnel of dust, beating himself up mercilessly.

* * *

Aren't we a pair? Isn't that what she'd said?

Three days had come and gone since he'd ridden his motorcycle out here. Raleigh started the truck, let the wiper sweep away the silver raindrops, turned it off again. The red-roofed buildings of Western State Custodial School crouched in the valley below, beneath lowering clouds. The surrounding fields seemed to gather in the dark remnants of the morning. Raleigh rubbed his unshaven chin and watched a lone car turn into the crowded parking lot of the school's administration building, its brake lights ablaze. She was in there somewhere. What was she doing? What was she thinking?

He tipped back his beer, drained it, opened the window, and tossed the empty onto the gravel and grass margin of the turnout. Cool, fresh-smelling air washed over his face. He held out his hand. The rain had all but stopped. He opened the door and got out. Standing on the running board, leaning into the crook of the door, he stared virtually unseeing at the state-run school.

Aren't we a pair?

* * *

I'm going to write to you every day, if that's okay—at least as long as I'm able. I said I'd write from Alabama, and I will. But today I'm on a crowded troop train stopped for no good reason a few miles south of Portland…

Seeing you was the best part of my short trip home…

CHAPTER EIGHTEEN

MEN WALKED NAKED, or wrapped in towels, from the showers. Throughout the barracks, some snapped trousers into readiness, others buttoned shirts or set collars aright. The mirrors at each end of the long quarters reflected men three and four deep adjusting ties or combing oiled hair.

The faint movement of air through the barrack's open windows set tolerable limits on the odor of aftershave, Old Spice, and Barbasol. If you wanted, you could tell yourself some of "that smell" was from the summer azaleas hemming the parade grounds.

"So, tell me about this place," said Raleigh, as he stuffed his razor, toothbrush, and shampoo into a zippered brown leather case on his bunk. "Is there dancing?"

Corporal Ray Tanner, an overnourished Texan with broad, pink shoulders, a wall-like torso, short black hair, and an ineradicable five o'clock shadow, answered: "Oh, there's dancing all right, and these Alabama girls are—how do you folks say it up there in Oregon? Eager beavers?"

The comment sparked laughter on either side of the room.

"I don't know. I'm from Washington," Raleigh said.

"You like to jitterbug, Starr?" said another enlisted man who was buttoning his creased khaki summer trousers and cinching his belt.

"Sure," said Raleigh. "What's not to like?"

Four men, dressed and ready to go, strode down the aisle bound for the door. "Abyssinia," the man in front said. He wore his garrison cap at a rakish angle and walked with a bounce. "Don't blame us if the prettiest dames is taken by the time you fellas get your lazy asses in gear."

"Taken ill, you mean," said one of the men under his breath.

"Keep dreaming, big shot," someone else yelled in a thick drawl.

Laughter drowned out the first half of the PA system announcement. The men stopped all together.

"Private Raleigh Starr to the post commander's office, on the double."

Raleigh shot upright, dropping his accessory bag on the floor. "What the hell?"

"*Post* commander?" Tanner said. He rolled his eyes and whistled. "What'd ya do? Make out with his daughter?"

Raleigh turned in disbelief toward the speaker above the door. He was met by the stares of men of every shape and size, frozen in place.

"Jesus, Starr, what are you doing? Fixing the old man's car? Me, I'll stick with the B-29."

Raleigh couldn't imagine what this was about, that is, until it occurred to him: something had happened to his dad or to Lauren.

He scooped up his summer dress shirt from the foot of the bunk and ran as fast as he could for the door. Within seconds, he was running at full speed down the gravel path toward the PC's office, buttoning his shirt.

He raced across the busy parking lot, almost getting hit by a DeSoto pulling out of a parking space. He stopped to get his bearings. Which building was the—there! Rather than retrace his steps, he ran across a triangular patch of newly seeded grass and leapt over a low hedge, landing a few feet in front of the administration building's concrete steps. He bounded up the steps and tore through the heavy double doors, skidding to a stop in front of the building directory.

Third floor. Room 318.

He jumped up the stairs three at a time, losing no speed on the landings. At last he stood in front of an ornate oak door marked Col. Jerald P. Black, Post Commander. A sheet of paper taped to the door said: KNOCK BEFORE ENTERING.

Raleigh tried to catch his breath. He knocked.

"Come in."

Raleigh stepped inside and saluted. "Private Raleigh Starr, sir."

The lieutenant rose from his desk and knocked on another oak door at the back of the waiting room. He entered the colonel's office without being summoned, closed the door briefly, and not completely, announced the visitor, and reappeared a second later. "He'll see you now."

"Thank you." Raleigh's heart went from racing to flailing. He entered the office, stood at attention, saluted. "Private Raleigh Starr, sir."

"At ease." The commanding officer, a thin man with graying brown hair, pockmarked, oily red cheeks, and a tapered mustache, looked up from his writing. He didn't make eye contact with Raleigh or return the salute. He rocked back in his chair and squeezed the bridge of his nose as if to buy time against some unpleasantness. Finally, he shook his head and swiveled in his chair to reach for a cigarette burning in an ashtray at the corner of his desk. The cigarette, once puffed, seemed to provide the impetus to go forward. "Have a seat," he said. Raleigh complied. The officer picked up a piece of paper. "You're Private First Class Raleigh Arnold Starr, is that right?"

"Yes, sir."

"Hometown: Yelm, Washington."

"Yes, sir." Now Raleigh was sure it had something to do with his father. He imagined his father pinned and dying beneath his overturned tractor partway down the ravine at the north side of their property, near where Raleigh had played as a child. His heart slowed at the image. He had difficulty breathing. "Sir, is it my—"

He was interrupted by the sight and sound of papers slapping down on the desk in front of him. What was it?

A form of some kind. Raleigh looked up.

"Read it," said the colonel, biting on a speck of tobacco.

With the first words—IN THE SUPERIOR COURT OF THE STATE OF WASHINGTON IN AND FOR THE COUNTY OF THURSTON: STATE OF WASHINGTON, DEPARTMENT OF HEALTH V. RALEIGH ARNOLD STARR—any thought that this concerned his father or sister vanished. But what was it? And what did it mean, the State of Washington versus Raleigh Arnold Starr?

Raleigh picked up the papers and read on:

TEMPORARY RESTRAINING ORDER and
ORDER TO SHOW CAUSE

Based on the Findings of Fact and Conclusion of Law entered on even date herewith, it is hereby:

ORDERED, ADJUDGED and DECREED:

1. That respondent RALEIGH ARNOLD STARR (DOB: 2/3/24) be, and hereby is, restrained and enjoined from entering upon the confines, legal boundaries, structures, leaseholds, roads, or premises of petitioner Western State Custodial School, 2120 Ryan Road, Buckley, Washington (legal description attached as Exhibit A);

2. That said respondent be, and hereby is, restrained and enjoined from contacting in person, or by telephone, telegraph, letter, proxy, or by any other means, and shall not be in, nor remain, in the presence of, nor come within 1,000 feet of, one MONA VICTORIA GARRISON (DOB: 4/10/26), a mental defective and resident of Western State Custodial School, for any reason whatsoever, from the date of this order until the same be discharged by order of this court;

3. That this order shall become a permanent restraining order within thirty (30) days hereof unless, on order to show cause, the same has been discharged by order of this court; and,

4. Respondent RALEIGH ARNOLD STARR be, and hereby is, ordered to show cause, if any he has, why this temporary restraining order should not become a permanent restraining order for the safety and protection of MONA VICTORIA GARRISON.

VIOLATION OF A RESTRAINING ORDER WITH ACTUAL NOTICE OF ITS TERMS IS A CRIMINAL OFFENSE AND WILL SUBJECT THE VIOLATOR TO ARREST.

DONE IN OPEN COURT *this 30th day of August, 1943.*

/s/ William A. Wilcox
Judge, Thurston County Superior Court

Raleigh looked up again.

"Well?" said the colonel.

Raleigh rubbed his mouth with his right hand. Words, the ability to speak, seemed to have escaped him. He felt the prickle of a searing shame around his eyes and at the sides of his face. "I… There must be some mistake. I didn't do anything."

The colonel folded his hands and set his elbows on his desk. "Do you know this Mona Garrison?"

Raleigh looked at him, stunned at the sudden collision of his private and military worlds. "Yes, sir. She's a neighbor—*was* a neighbor, I mean."

"And she's feebleminded, is that right?"

"Slow. Yes, sir. She has trouble in school, sir." This meant he couldn't see her again? Or talk to her?

I'll die if I can't. She's everything to me now. She's all I've—I love Mona.

He thought of the letter he'd mailed out the day before, of how he'd finally gotten up the nerve to tell her how he felt.

My Dearest Mona,

I can't tell you how much I miss you. I've finally let myself believe what my heart has been telling me for a long time. You are the most wonderful girl in the world, and I love you…

His breath caught. He'd sent it care of the custodial school.

She won't get it. They'll throw it away.

The colonel pointed to the papers in Raleigh's hand. "Go to the back there."

Raleigh thumbed through the pages until he came to a newspaper clipping taped to the last sheet. The headline read: YELM SOLDIER ACCUSED OF INAPPROPRIATE CONTACTS. He recognized the font and style of the *Daily Olympian*. His heart sank, when he'd thought it could sink no further.

A voice in his head told him not to read the article, but catching the colonel's eye, he saw what was expected of him. As he read, it began to dawn on him what these allegations and the news coverage must be doing to his father, to his reputation.

Oh, shit. Why couldn't I have left her alone?

"This is all a mistake," Raleigh said. "It's been misinterpreted. It says here a supervisor saw us kissing. That isn't true. I didn't kiss her. I hugged her—well, actually, she hugged me. You see, I had—"

"It also says you've been writing her letters. Lots of them. Is that true?"

Raleigh's eyes searched the colonel's desktop for an answer. He drew in and expelled a deep breath, slowly, leading to an awkward silence. "Sir, if I can explain—"

The colonel raised his hand. "Save it, Private. I don't know what happened, but it appears the court was satisfied, and that's what we're going to go on." He sucked on his cigarette. Smoke streamed from his nostrils as he continued. "Under no circumstances are you to contact this Mona Garrison again. Is that clear?"

"Yes, s—"

"Starting today. That's an order."

"Yes, sir."

The colonel regarded Raleigh closely. "I'll be honest with you, son. When I read this, I expected you to be a degenerate. I figured I'd be writing you up for a Section 8, but I see that's not the case. At least I don't think it is." He managed one more puff on his cigarette and tamped it out in the ashtray. "Normally I'd leave this to the first sergeant, but we had something similar come up last year. The local press got ahold of it. I'm not going to go through that again. I'm ordering you to be seen by the staff psychologist. I'll tell Smith to arrange it. He'll be in touch." The colonel followed his words with an expectant glance. "That's all—oh, and tell Lieutenant Smith to come in here on your way out."

Raleigh exited the building in a daze. His feet carried him back toward the barracks while his thoughts remained on Mona, on the newspaper article. "Friends of the accused disclosed to the *Daily Olympian* that Mr. Starr has had contacts with the feebleminded girl over the last several years."

If I stop writing her, she'll think I don't care. Will she know about the restraining order? Not likely. Maybe it's better this way. I've been a fool long enough.

* * *

The phone at the other end rang twice, and his sister's distant-sounding voice said: "Hello?"

The operator said, "Go ahead."

"Lauren? It's Raleigh."

"Raleigh? Is that you? Where are you?

"Alabama. Listen—"

"Oh, my. This must be costing you a fortune."

"Listen, I only have a couple minutes. I need you to do me a favor—a big favor."

Lauren hesitated. "It better not be what I think it is. Raleigh, you have no idea how people are talking around here. Last night—"

"I know. I saw the article. I know about the restraining order."

"Mona's guardian called. Why'd you do it, Raleigh? Why'd you go out there?"

"Never mind that."

"What do you mean, never mind that? It's about the only—"

"I need you to do this for me, Lauren. You need to talk to Mona—"

"*Mona?*"

"You've got to contact her. I can't. Tell her I can't, and that I would if I could."

"*What*? *Are you crazy*? What in the world has happened to you?"

"I'm serious. I need you to do this. I'll explain later."

"The answer is no. If you knew what was going on around here, how people are talking, you'd—"

"It doesn't matter." Raleigh turned in the phone booth, stared unseeing at the cars filling at the Texaco station across the street. "Okay, yes, it matters, and I'm sorry about it. I'm sorry if you and Dad are embarrassed. But Mona, she's not going to understand. I was writing to her, and now I can't."

"Oh, Raleigh."

"She won't hear from me. I need you to tell her that I'd write if I could, but I can't. Can you tell her that?"

"No. You don't understand. I could... I'll call Mrs. Ballard. I'll give her the message, but that's all I'm willing to do."

The operator's voice came on. "Twenty seconds."

Raleigh leaned back against the glass. "All right. If you'll do that? Tell her it's important that Mona knows why I've stopped writing."

"Raleigh," said Lauren, her voice resigned and plaintive. "Why are you doing this? You could have anybody."

If you only knew how untrue that is.

"Good-bye, Raleigh. Take care of yourself."

With the operator confirming that the call had ended and asking if there was anything else he needed, Raleigh thought of things in a new way: Our experiences are, for the most part, unique to us; we carry them alone, understood by no one but ourselves. Certainly, it was true of our loves and deepest desires.

Mine, and mine alone.

CHAPTER NINETEEN

PUFFS OF STEAM rose from electric irons up and down the rows, and Mona's back ached. Over each girl's left shoulder a black electrical cord swung from a hanger. Most of the girls—Mona included—wore a blue bandana to keep strands of hair from sticking to their foreheads, and out of their eyes. A few of the ironing boards squeaked and complained. It was the only noise in the large rectangular room besides an occasional cough, or the respirations of steam, and the clunk-clunk of the implements set down to free the hands to shift the white sheets a foot or two at a time. There was no music. There wasn't even a sound from outside, for the barred windows were shut. The air smelled of scorched cotton.

A door opened. "How's it going in here?" Mona and the others turned to see the familiar thirty-year-old attendant from the Midwest who had been assigned laundry duty supervision from day one. His name was Horowitz. He had a relaxed air with the girls in the ironing hall. They were the advanced girls, the stable ones.

Mona wiped her forehead with the back of her wrist and gave Horowitz a quick smile before returning to work. The hour wasn't up, and it was the attendant's habit to chitchat with one or two of the girls during the last ten minutes of the shift. She looked behind her to see the number of sheets left in her basket. At least four.

He greeted a fifteen-year-old, redheaded girl from Wenatchee, and began to tell her a joke that Mona couldn't quite hear. Something about a monkey. Mona shifted her sheet forward remembering the first time he'd picked her out for his friendly banter. Within minutes, the conversation had taken a serious turn. He'd revealed things that she hadn't asked about, and at first she didn't understand. But she came to know what a conscientious objector was, and how the government, unsure what to do with conscientious objectors during wartime, assigned them work in mental hospitals and custodial schools like this one.

Mona looked sideways at Dorothy Lambert, a fellow seventeen-year-old who, since transferring from Eastern State Custodial School in March 1943, about six months earlier, had become Mona's closest friend and confidante. The shorter Dorothy had a severe nose and large, soft, brown eyes that could harden into something fierce, like broken glass. Her straight blonde hair was all but hidden under her bandana. Dorothy looked up as though drawn by Mona's glance. She nodded once, and then tipped her head toward the wall clock above the door. What Mona saw in her expression was hope, a feeling Mona shared. The two were waiting for the same thing: mail. Dorothy, for a letter from her beau—as she called him—Cory. It had been a week since she'd found a letter from him at the foot of her bunk; on the next bunk over, it had been twelve days since Mona had received a letter from Raleigh. Twelve days—after receiving a letter almost every day, sometimes two letters a day, throughout August and the first ten days of September. Then the letters stopped coming. Why?

Since arriving in Alabama, Raleigh had shared things about his feelings that made her realize that what she had felt before was merely a prelude to something deeper. He was not a boy. He did not live in her memories of their dancing, or his exuberant, youthful voice riding over the rumble of the school bus. He had dreams today—fears, hopes. She began to discover these, could see them even in his most mundane descriptions of life in the barracks, of the things people said to him, of the boredom he felt on duty and off. And because he shared these, she dared to dream not only of the day she would finally get out of here, but of the future she might have with Raleigh.

Mona listened to the tone of Horowitz's voice and felt a pulse of hopefulness. It was no mystery why. He had agreed to read their letters aloud. It had been Dorothy's idea. She'd asked him, and he said, "Sure, I don't know why not." Dorothy couldn't read any better than Mona, although between them—before Horowitz came to their aid—they had helped each other decipher words that might have been lost. They might have gotten the gist, but in the fractured and stumbling efforts heard too much their own struggling voices, not the voices they longed to hear. Now they only had to approach Horowitz in the cafeteria between one and one-thirty, and if he wasn't called away, he would sit with each of them, one at a time, and read.

Horowitz laughed.

Please, God, Mona thought, *let there be a letter today.*

"Listen up, everybody!" Horowitz had both arms in the air. His smile revealed two neat rows of white teeth with a single gold imposter. "Mrs. Gentry's crew clearly miscounted. They've overfilled the baskets. That's not your fault. Let's break for lunch and pick up the rest tomorrow."

It was all Mona and Dorothy could do not to trample the girls in front of them squeezing through the double doors. Once they made the long, dark hallway, they set off at a run toward the dormitory wing. Mona stripped the bandana off her head as she flew through the door marked W4. But then she realized that there was only one envelope, and it was on Dorothy's bunk, not hers. She stopped and let Dorothy run ahead, her aching heart rising in her throat, tears coming into her eyes.

Dorothy stood at the foot of her bunk with her unopened letter in her hands. She looked back at Mona. "I'm sorry, Monski," she said.

Mona knew she would break down if she tried to answer. Should she look under her bunk? Could it have fallen on the floor? But how many times in the last week had she done that—looked frantically under her bunk, and under Dorothy's and the one on the other side, lifting the spare blanket at the foot of her bunk to make sure it hadn't slipped under there? No, not again. She had to accept the fact there were no letters.

This is wrong. Has something happened to him? He works on engines. He told me it's not dangerous—that he feels guilty about the other soldiers like Wheels and Fisher doing the real fighting.

"I know he's written," she said miserably. "I know he has." She formed then dismissed the idea that Horowitz had somehow taken her letters, was playing a trick on her. He wasn't like that.

Dorothy walked back to her and put a hand on her arm. "Maybe the mail's been delayed in Alabama. Are you sure he hasn't shipped out somewhere? That would explain—"

Mona shook her head. "It's a seven-week course. They're waiting for a squadron to arrive from Nebraska."

Dorothy caressed Mona's arm.

Mona remembered the last letter from Raleigh. There had been no hint of a problem. "Some of the boys and I are driving down to Mobile in the morning to see Spanish Fort and Fort Blakely, a couple of old Civil War sites. I recall reading about the siege of Fort Blakely in Mr. Adams's class. Tomorrow I'll write and tell you all about it. Gosh, wouldn't it be great if you were here and we could see these things together?"

She felt her insides turn, and a hot rage began to consume the tears that threatened to spill. She imagined the white envelopes with Raleigh's large blue scrawl piled on a table in the school office. "They've stolen my letters! He *has* written!" A protective instinct kept her from dwelling on the other possibility, that the school had thrown the letters out, or burned them.

I've got to get them.

Mona stepped away from her friend.

"What is it?" cried Dorothy. "What's wrong?"

It was a blur, the running, the slipping around corners, the half-falling, half-jumping down stairs, even her arrival at the outer reception window, panting furiously. She gripped the edge of the counter and leaned toward the talk-through. "I want my mail—*please!*"

A thirty-something female receptionist at a desk at the far end of the small room jumped in her chair, and dropped her pencil on the floor. She sat stunned for a moment, then raised her head and scanned Mona's uniform beyond the counter. Her eyes narrowed. "What are you doing down here? Get back—"

Mona, for the first time in her life, didn't care what anyone thought. There was only one thing that mattered, only one needful thing. "I want my letters! I know you've got them!"

The receptionist rose from her chair, coloring. "I don't know what you're talking about." Without turning her back to Mona she crossed the room and knocked loudly on a door at the back wall leading to an interior office. "You have no business being down here. What's your name anyway?"

Mona slapped the glass divider with a single blow. "You know my name! Give me my mail!"

The receptionist reached toward phone perched on the corner of a table. "Now settle down. We'll get someone to help you.

"Just give me my mail!"

"I don't have your mail," the receptionist said weakly, picking up the receiver. The door at the back of the room opened and a square-shouldered man in a brown, double-breasted suit entered. He wore his light brown hair in a flattop, and walked with a heavy step.

"What's going on out here?"

Mona's heart sank. She had seen this man once before, on the day she'd arrived at the custodial school. He'd reviewed the paperwork handed under the glass divider by Jewel Ballard, while Mona, surrounded by two orderlies, her shoulder throbbing, stood trembling where she stood now—in the foyer. The memory sapped her strength, but not her determination. Still breathing heavily, she waited for the receptionist to answer his question.

He released Mona from his glare long enough to check the school's main entrance doors a few feet to Mona's left. She knew why. He wanted to make sure the doors were shut and locked.

"This young woman," began the receptionist, "is a Level 4. She's insisting we have her mail."

The two behind the glass looked at each other for answers.

Mona could tell they knew who she was, and she believed they knew where her mail was. She hated to be lied to. The man had barely begun to speak when Mona shouted, "I can prove it! I can prove he's been writing to me! Let me call his sister. She'll tell you." She felt a tear drop onto her cheek and wiped it away as quickly as she could.

The man widened his stance and placed his hands on his hips, pushing back the hem of his suit jacket. "Residents are not allowed to use the phone. You know that. And you're not supposed to be down here. Get back to your room—now!"

"I can call my guardian," Mona protested. "She said I could. Either you—"

A shocked look came over the receptionist's face, enough to draw Mona's attention momentarily.

But Mona ignored her. "Either give me my letters or let me call her."

The man's face reddened. He stepped forward, shouted through the talk-through. "Go to your room!"

Mona swayed back, but squeezed the edge of the counter holding herself in place. She smelled peanut butter and coffee on his breath. "No! You...you give me my letters. They're not yours!"

He stared through the hole nonplussed. A slow smile signaled the return of his composure. "Miss Fletcher, please call the orderlies and have Dr. Scofield come at once—with phenobarbital."

Mona's heart quaked. She knew exactly what phenobarbital was and had seen its effects dozens of times. But her anger, now fully unleashed, could not be undone. Would she ever hear Raleigh's voice again, would she ever be reassured that he still cared about her, and thought about her? If she lost Raleigh, this place would be unbearable.

"I don't care what you do to me, but I want those letters. I know you have them!"

The man turned to the receptionist. "Get this girl's file, Miss Fletcher. I want it on my desk in five minutes. And call her guardian. Who is that, by the way?"

"Jewel Ballard."

The man nodded. "Tell her we've administered phenobarbital to her client this afternoon on orders from Dr. Scofield. The staff will monitor her condition for the next forty-eight hours and will notify her if there are any complications."

Mona felt an irresistible sob rising in her chest, followed by the contents of her stomach. She forced both back, but not without doubling over and letting out a silent scream. A fresh tear dropped to the floor. She could hear footsteps approaching beyond a door next to the reception desk marked STAFF ONLY. She gasped and stepped back.

"Why are you doing this?"

A second later, one of the large main doors to Mona's left opened, letting in a broad swath of sunlight and the sound of a car door shutting in the parking lot. Beyond the door stood a smiling, middle-aged man in a light gray suit. He was holding the door for someone else. His hand was extended, but the other person was not in view.

To the right of the counter, the staff door opened. Dr. Scofield, a balding man in his mid-forties wearing a physician's tunic, entered the foyer. He carried in his right hand a porcelain basin containing a large steel hypodermic needle. Two male orderlies rushed in behind him. The first was untangling a straightjacket. The second fixed his eyes on Mona.

She jumped back. Twice she'd seen girls restrained and taken to the ground, even punched by orderlies. The last girl she'd seen taken out of the cafeteria in a straightjacket was never seen or heard from again.

Mona had no time to think. She raced toward the exit and brushed by the man in the gray suit. She could see the parking lot. An instant later she collided with the woman who had been behind the man in the gray suit—and who was carrying a pink birthday cake. Both Mona and the woman screamed, but Mona kept running. As her feet drummed on the steps of the landing, she heard the clang of the metal cake pan hitting the ground.

CHAPTER TWENTY

"ALL RISE! The Superior Court of the State of Washington for the County of Thurston is in session, the honorable William A. Wilcox presiding."

Judge Wilcox, a balding man of average height in his mid-sixties, with broad, strong hands and athletic shoulders, turned at the door to his chambers and climbed the steps to the bench. He stood for a moment gazing at the empty seats in the gallery of the courtroom. "Have a seat," he said with a habituated smile. Still standing, he looked over his glasses in the direction of the defense table. Some color came to otherwise pale cheeks. "It's good to see you again, Mrs. Ballard."

"Thank you, Your Honor. How are you this morning?" Her tone was partly deferential, partly familiar. She touched the side of her head in her characteristic way and let a self-conscious smile transform heavily painted lips.

"I'm well, thank you." Judge Wilcox sat down. Holding his glasses to the light and looking through them, he exchanged a similar greeting with the deputy prosecuting attorney of Thurston County, Bede Stoddard.

"Okay, let's get started," he said. "For the record, we're here on the matter of the State of Washington versus Mona Victoria Garrison, case number 4-173-16. Representing the Institutional Board of Health we have Bede Stoddard, deputy prosecuting attorney, and representing the ward we have her guardian appearing *pro se*—is that right?"

"Yes," said Stoddard.

"It is, Your Honor," said Mrs. Ballard.

The judge scratched the side of his head and seemed to shift into a more serious mood. He opened the court file. "Okay, Mr. Stoddard, if you'd care to begin..."

Stoddard rose at the plaintiff's table. "Yes, Your Honor. This is a motion for declaratory judgment seeking authority to sterilize the respondent, Mona Victoria Garrison, age seventeen. This matter—"

"And Miss Garrison's presence has been waived by the guardian, is that right?" interrupted Judge Wilcox.

Mrs. Ballard made a halfhearted attempt to stand. "It is, Your Honor. The respondent signed a consent to eugenic sterilization when I became her guardian, and a waiver of notice. In my judgment, Miss Garrison would not understand these proceedings, nor would she be able to participate in any meaningful way."

"Very well. Sorry to interrupt, Bede. Go ahead."

"This matter was referred to the Institutional Board of Health by the superintendent of Western State Custodial School. Miss Garrison is an inmate at the facility and has been since last October. She is feebleminded, with an IQ of seventy-five. The record shows she has poor self-control where men are concerned and therefore is at high risk of becoming pregnant. Mrs. Ballard, in her affidavit, describes her as an attractive girl of seventeen who has—and I quote—demonstrated a propensity, without regard to the rules, to engage in inappropriate or salacious behaviors with at least one nineteen-year-old male."

"You're referring to Private Starr, I believe," said Judge Wilcox.

"Yes, Your Honor."

"Mrs. Ballard can speak to that in a minute. The Institutional Board of Health, at the behest of the guardian, seeks a declaratory judgment authorizing the guardian to proceed with a sterilization, which we feel is in the best interests of the inmate.

"As the court knows, last year our state supreme court struck down Washington's compulsory eugenics law in the *Hendrickson* case. However, it did so strictly on procedural grounds. The court ruled that compulsory sterilization is substantively within the police power of the state. If I may quote from the opinion, Justice Driver writes:

> *The purpose of the statute is to protect society from the burden imposed upon it by permitting mentally defective, morally degenerate, and criminally insane persons to reproduce their kinds.*

...The legislature, in the interest of public safety, morals, health, and welfare, has the power to authorize the sterilization of defectives.

"In the present case, Your Honor, we have an inmate who, prior to *Hendrickson,* signed a consent to sterilization and waived notice of the hearing before the Institutional Board of Health. We believe this takes us outside the scope of *Hendrickson.* Compulsory sterilization—if we can call it compulsory—should proceed. We are asking, therefore, for a declaratory judgment authorizing the guardian to arrange for the immediate sterilization of Miss Garrison."

Judge Wilcox removed his glasses. "So you're saying I have authority to order the sterilization regardless of our supreme court's holding in *Hendrickson*?"

"That's right, Judge," Stoddard said.

"Very well. I'll hear from the guardian. Mrs. Ballard?"

Mrs. Ballard stood, coloring. She pulled closed the jacket of her navy blue ensemble. "May it please the court, I was asked to be guardian for this young lady when her former guardians, her aunt and uncle, found they could no longer control her. Mona Garrison is indeed an attractive, fully developed young woman who has shown herself to be incapable of controlling her sexual urges. When I first met the family, I learned she had been traipsing off with this same young man to a local bar to dance, of all things. The boy, it turns out, had been watching her dress and undress through her bedroom window—I suspect with Miss Garrison's knowledge. She would also sneak out of the house and run off to watch him play football."

"Has Private Starr stopped contacting Miss Garrison?"

"It appears so, Your Honor—for the time being, anyway. It's early, of course."

"Yes. Go on, Mrs. Ballard."

"And I'll note for the record that three weeks ago Miss Garrison tried to run away from the facility, once again in connection with the same young man... As Mr. Stoddard points out, Miss Garrison signed her consent for CES at the time I became her guardian. You'll find that in the court file."

"This is the basis for today's motion, is that right?" asked the judge.

Mrs. Ballard looked at the deputy prosecutor before answering. "Yes, Your Honor."

Judge Wilcox thumbed through the court file. "Point me to that language, if you will," he said.

Mrs. Ballard sat and began to sift through her file. "Here it is," she said. "It's on page three of the Consent to Guardianship signed by Mona Garrison on September 27, 1942. I filed this on October 9, 1942."

"I see," said Judge Wilcox. "Let me... Give me a minute to read this." When the judge finished reading, he looked up. "This appears in a long list of rights the ward is giving up: the right to contract, the right to vote, the right to marry, the right to consent to or refuse medical treatment...?"

"Yes, that's right, Your Honor."

"And it's your position that this language..." The judge read from the document: "By signing this Consent to Guardianship, you are granting to the guardian the sole right and authority to decide whether a procedure authorized by chapter 53, Laws of 1921, p. 162, Rem. Rev. Stat. section 6957 et seq., is warranted, and you further waive notice of any and all hearings before the board of health in conjunction therewith—that this language gives you the basis for today's motion?"

"Yes, Your Honor."

"And it looks like her aunt, Grace Garrison, signed a similar document on the same day."

"Yes, that's right."

Judge Wilcox sat back, looked from Mrs. Ballard to Mr. Stoddard. "All right. Do either of you have anything further before I rule on the motion?"

Mr. Stoddard stood up. "No, Your Honor."

Mrs. Ballard also stood. "The problem of hereditary feeblemindedness is ongoing, Your Honor. People like Miss Garrison are prone to accidental and unwanted pregnancies, to say nothing of planned ones. The rest of us end up bearing the costs of raising these children or institutionalizing them—which also is at our cost. Many, as the court knows, become wards of the state. It's in Miss Garrison's best interest, as well as the state's, that she be sterilized at this time."

Mrs. Ballard picked up a sheet of paper from the table in front of her. "Perhaps through no fault of her own, Miss Garrison has violated the visitation rules of Western State Custodial School to make herself available to a persistent and irresponsible young man. We may have succeeded in stopping this individual, but there will be other men attracted to her and to whom she is attracted. Also, I'm going to have to make other arrangements for Miss Garrison when she turns twenty-one, as she'll no longer be eligible for confinement at the custodial school. I fear she is likely to get pregnant."

The judge looked at Mr. Stoddard. "Do you have anything to add?"

"No, Your Honor."

"Very well. Have a seat, Mrs. Ballard."

* * *

Jewel Ballard emerged from the bathroom of the third floor of the courthouse. With quick steps, the soles of her shoes beat quarter notes across the marble floor. She was reading something in an open file and nearly stumbled into a larger woman in a mauve two-piece suit waiting by the elevator. "Oh! Excuse me… Beatrice?"

"Hello, Jewel," said Beatrice Treadwell, another guardian employed by Thurston County. "What's wrong? You look upset."

"I am. You don't want to know."

"Sure I do," Treadwell said.

Only then did Mrs. Ballard come to a complete stop. Her shoulders drooped. "It's my Garrison case—remember, the gal who—"

"With the soldier. Yes, I remember."

"Right. Anyway, I moved for authority to get her sterilized, but Judge Wilcox denied the motion. He said she couldn't have understood what she was signing when she gave consent."

Treadwell registered surprise. "You got her consent?"

Mrs. Ballard glanced to the side self-consciously. "I included language in the Consent to Guardianship form. But it was a waste of time."

"That's too bad. I hadn't thought of trying to get consent up front. I figure it's hard enough to get people to agree to the guardianship."

"Yes, well…"

"So you're going to have to talk to the people at the custodial school, right? They're the ones who left those girls unattended."

"Oh, my *gosh*!"

"What? What are you thinking?"

"I can order the sterilization myself. Why didn't I think of that? I don't have to go through the Institutional Board of Health." Mrs. Ballard's eyes grew wide, taking in new possibilities. "Under my normal guardianship powers."

"What are you talking about? I thought the Supreme Court said—"

"No, they outlawed compulsory sterilizations by the state. The judge talked about that. But *I* can arrange the sterilization. That's the difference."

Treadwell seemed to shrink back. "Oh, I don't think…" she said weakly. "That doesn't sound right."

"Of course it is. I have the same authority to consent to medical treatment that Mona would have."

"Yes, but…why did you file the motion if you thought—"

"I was just following the old procedure." Mrs. Ballard smiled mysteriously. "As long as it's in her best interest." Mrs. Ballard placed a hand on her friend's arm as if to thank her. "I've got to get going."

"Wait, Jewel. What are you doing? Why are you so adamant about this?

Mrs. Ballard's face registered surprise. "Adamant? Well, if I am, it's because I've been through this before—and believe me, once is enough. I inherited the case from Sylvia Drake—a fourteen-year-old mongoloid girl who'd gotten pregnant from a hospital attendant. Thank goodness she lost the baby, but she was devastated and confused. She wouldn't have been able to keep it—couldn't have cared for it in her wildest dreams—and I ran myself ragged trying to make arrangements for the child. No, I don't plan on going through anything like that again."

"But where will you find a doctor?" asked Treadwell. "I don't think there's a doctor in the state who'll touch it."

Mrs. Ballard pursed her lips then nodded. "Don't worry. I know someone."

* * *

Two days later, on a blustery Thursday morning at 2:45 a.m., Mona was awakened by the night nurse, Theresa Douglas. Mona blinked her eyes open. "What? What are you doing?"

Nurse Douglas put a finger to her lips and whispered in a husky voice. "It's nothing. I've got orders from Dr. Abercrombie to give you a shot this morning."

Mona's body shuddered as though touched by an icy finger.

"What? What are you talking about?"

The nurse brought a metal object out of her pocket. "These are orders from Dr. Abercrombie. He said to give you a shot at 2:45 this morning. It'll calm you."

Oh my God! What is that?

Mona slid up in bed and started to shout, but Nurse Douglas put a rough hand over her mouth. Mona looked past the square-faced nurse. Two male orderlies stood at either side of the foot of her bed.

"Do *not* make a scene—do you understand?" Nurse Douglas said.

What are they doing? I've got to speak. There's been a mistake. I've got to explain to them.

Mona nodded. The nurse removed her hand. Mona whispered for the sake of the other girls sleeping nearby. "What do you mean? I don't need a shot. I'm not sick."

Nurse Douglas began to push up the left sleeve of Mona's nightgown. "Just do what you're told, Mona."

Mona jerked her arm away. "Leave me alone!"

The nurse signaled the orderlies, who stepped in and held Mona down. The wild turning of her head and thrashing of her legs were to no avail. The orderly who held her left arm squeezed it so tightly Mona cried out in pain.

No! Please don't! Please! Let me go!

Nurse Douglas raised the silver hypodermic needle and squeezed a little of its liquid into the air.

CHAPTER TWENTY-ONE

1946

"IS RALEIGH STARR HERE?"

The man's voice was nearly drowned out by the constant patter of rain on the corrugated roof, and a talkative runoff that splashed in the puddles at the bay doors. An October wind brought hissing complaints from the giant fir trees that fronted the City of Yelm maintenance building across the street from Rainier Auto Repair. "You found him," said Raleigh, working beneath a dark blue Buick Super Coupe. He'd removed a Chesterfield from his mouth. "What can I do for you?" Dipping his chin in close quarters, Raleigh was able to make out two shiny black leather shoes, blue and green argyle socks, and the cuff of gray slacks.

"You can give me that twenty bucks you owe me."

Raleigh recognized Wheels's voice at once. He slid out on the creeper. "I'll be damned." He rose to his feet and took a rag from his back pocket to wipe his hands. "What? Did you get expelled from the U or something?"

"Not yet." Wheels laughed. "Give me time."

When Raleigh had cleaned and re-wiped his hands, he shook Wheels's hand enthusiastically. "So how you been?"

Smiling, Wheels said, "Depends who you ask. I got no complaints." He looked around the shop. "So this is the job Lauren's husband found for you, huh?"

"Doug or Lauren. I'm not sure who pulled the strings." Raleigh offered his friend a cigarette. Wheels shook his head, leaned over, and looked under the Buick's hood. He jiggled a loose hose clamp as Raleigh asked, "You down for the weekend?"

"Actually, it's the other way around. I came to drag your sorry carcass up to the university. I knew you'd say no if I called, so here I am."

Raleigh rubbed his hand over his head.

"I know, I know," said Wheels. "You've heard it all before. Free money. GI Bill. Anyway, I didn't come here to pester you. Come tomorrow night. We're having a party with a couple of the other dorms—a mixer. At least you'll see what a college party is all about."

Raleigh was looking for a reason to say no when Wheels started backing out of the bay, pointing a finger at him. "I'm off to my parents' place for the night. I'll pick you up at ten tomorrow morning. Oh, and I'm taking Clarice Austen. She says Barbara Spade's been asking about you. Who knows, maybe she'll show up. Ooh la la, huh?"

Raleigh cocked his head and squinted good-naturedly. "Yeah. Lucky me."

Barbara Spade. It wasn't like he hadn't thought about her since coming back from the war—thought about calling her, about driving up there. But what would he be getting himself into? And how would he explain about the letters she'd written to him overseas, to which he'd given no reply? Combat stress? Would that be his excuse?

It was always about the bedroom with Barbara. He'd told himself more than once: *She doesn't know what she has going for her. Good looking, kind-hearted, generous, funny. Somehow that's not enough.* That look in her eye; the way she used to nibble his ear lobe and giggle breathily to let him know what she was thinking about. *Why's she that way? Isn't that the man's job? She's a year younger than me for crying out loud.* He thought of Mona then, of her gentle acceptance of him, without presumption. At the end of a long sigh, he tried to push her out of his mind again.

Raleigh went back to work under the Buick. With his nose less than four inches from the dark, dirt-encrusted oil pan, he pictured Barbara's radiant smile, her eyes closing for a kiss, the way she would sit up effortlessly, without hurting him, and put herself in motion. He knew she sought her own pleasure at these times, could tell from the frown that would slowly, inevitably form. It didn't matter. Left alone, he could trace his feelings back to Mona, could imagine her in Barbara's place—her warmth, her weight. It would have been so different, he told himself. Making love with someone he adored beyond anything else in the world. So perfect.

While reaching past the oil pan for the oil filter housing, he imagined himself gently pulling Mona down to kiss her. He would feel her hair brushing his temples. He would whisper, "You understand me, don't you?" Her nodding would tickle his face.

* * *

Raleigh waited in the car until Wheels waved him out of the vehicle. Wheels and Clarice stood on the trellised porch of her North Seattle duplex.

Raleigh got out of the car, put on his suit jacket, and started up the walk. "What is it?" he said, over the scraping of his hard soled shoes and the scattering of gold birch leaves at his feet. The sun had slipped behind the Olympic Mountains and a cool breeze wafted from the west.

"Barbara's not ready," Wheels said in a low voice.

"She just now showed up," Clarice said, rolling her eyes. "This morning she calls to say she's not coming. Twenty minutes ago she calls and says to wait for her, she's coming after all. Now she's in the bathroom putting on her face."

Wheels smiled crookedly at Raleigh. "Can you tell they had a falling out?"

Clarice banged him with her hip. "It's not that. We just live different lives. I haven't seen her for four or five months." Clarice began to bite her fingernails and examine the results.

"No problem," said Raleigh.

"No, but if we don't get a table because of her," said Clarice, "I'll wring her neck."

"Hi, there. Wring whose neck?"

The three turned at once to see Barbara in the doorway, one hand high on her hip. She wore a tight-fitting blue-and-white dress with a light white cardigan thrown over her shoulders. Bangs of wavy blonde hair angled over her forehead. Her teeth shone white in the dim light.

"What a nuisance I am," she said, stepping across the porch and down two steps, spreading her arms wide to embrace Raleigh. "Wonderful to see you."

"It's great to see you, too," he managed, stealing a glance at Wheels over her shoulder, and letting his hands come to rest on her hips. Her perfume took him back to the soft bed in the spare bedroom of Clarice's grandfather's house, the two of them lying on the dimpled white bedspread, his hand cupped over one bare, ample breast. It was the last time he had been with a woman. He breathed in her scent hungrily. Barbara seemed to notice and leaned her head against his.

"We better get going or we'll be late," said Clarice. "Barbara, do you have a coat or a purse or anything?"

Barbara brought her face nose to nose with Raleigh and spoke to him as if they were alone. "I have everything I need right here."

Clarice raised her eyebrows, cleared her throat, and sidestepped around them.

"Okay, let's go," said Wheels. He looked at Clarice, who continued to stare in disbelief at Barbara.

Following them down the walk, Raleigh heard Wheels whisper to Clarice, "Who needs a party, huh?"

Raleigh watched Barbara duck into the back seat, then followed her in. She scooted close so that the whole of his upper arm came to rest against her breast. "You probably don't know I wrote to you during the war," she said. "So many letters got lost… It doesn't matter that you didn't write back. I wanted you to be safe, to come back in one piece."

Raleigh didn't answer. If he'd built up a resistance to wanting Barbara, or to going too fast with her again, it was quickly melting.

Barbara pulled the hem of her dress down and said, "I hope they have dancing. I want you to hold me, Mr. Starr." She slid the tips of her fingers between his knees.

Raleigh smiled and slid his hand over her kneecap. He pulled her leg over hard against his. *She wants to pick up where we left off five years ago. Hard to say no to that.* But a second later he was struck by the memory of Mona's half-sweet, close breath as she embraced him on his motorcycle and thanked him for visiting the custodial school. He seemed to smell it again as though it were happening now. What had triggered this? Was it something in Wheels's car? It wasn't Barbara's breath, which he never liked very much, or her perfume. Perhaps her shampoo? He'd experienced this three or four times before. Each time it had come for no apparent reason, but he welcomed the memory and found her breath, so vivid in his nostrils or in his brain, more desirable with each occurrence.

"Of course, I want to dance with you, too," Barbara said. "I can't do it as well as that girl you won the contest with. Clarice told me all about it. What was her name? But people say I dance pretty well."

Raleigh's heart lumbered to a near stop. On the drive up from Yelm, he'd promised himself he wouldn't think about Mona. Not again. Maybe that's why he'd said yes to this whole thing—to turn the page once and for all. To quit obsessing about Mona, about what might have been. The restraining order was permanent. The Garrisons hated him, and so did Mona's guardian.

"What's wrong?" asked Barbara.

"Nothing."

Clarice turned in the front seat. "Mona. Wasn't that her name? Mona something?"

Raleigh nodded somberly. "Yeah."

"Mona Garrison," said Wheels as he checked for traffic and pulled out into the street. Wheels's eyes sought Raleigh's in the rearview mirror. "Whatever happened to Mona, Raleigh? Did you ever hear?"

"No," Raleigh answered. He looked at his friend squarely. *What are you doing?* He asked silently. *You know about the restraining order.*

But Wheels had looked away. "She's probably in a home somewhere," he said.

"You can bet she's dancing, wherever she is," said Barbara admiringly. "I would have loved to have seen her dance."

Anxious to change the subject, Raleigh said to Barbara, "How about you? What have you been up to?" He felt her body sink back in the seat.

"Not much. Nothing interesting."

"Try me."

"I'm working three days a week at Bartell Drugs. I want to be the store manager there someday. Other than that I take care of my mom, walk the dog, that sort of thing. Like I said, it's pretty—"

"Do you still volunteer at the Red Cross?"

Barbara smiled widely. "You remember? That's sweet. No, I stopped shortly after VE Day. I volunteer at the VFW on Sunday mornings, for the pancake breakfast." She poked Raleigh's arm and giggled. "You should come by sometime. We'll fatten you up."

Raleigh snickered. "I do like pancakes."

"Pancakes is my middle name," said Wheels absently, swinging his head left and right to look for traffic at an intersection.

Clarice was busy checking her makeup in the mirror of her compact. Wheels fell silent. Barbara leaned over and whispered to Raleigh behind her cupped hand. "You can… If you want to, I mean. You know, like before."

Raleigh set his head back on the seat and closed his eyes. Against his better judgment he squeezed her knee, then opened his eyes and faced her. Barbara smiled, then motioned him close with her finger. He could feel her breath against his ear. "My roommate is out of town this weekend."

* * *

Six weeks later, Raleigh was called in on a Saturday to work on a Ford Super Deluxe. He was on a smoke break, listening to the UW-Oregon State football game on the radio. The Huskies were on the Beavers' four-yard line, down 13-10 with twenty-eight seconds left in the first half. It was second and goal.

"Raleigh," one of the other mechanics called out from the office. "Phone for you."

Raleigh took a last drag on his Chesterfield and flicked the butt into the gravel parking lot. *I guess my break's over.*

He wiped his hands on a dirty towel on the way to the office.

"Starr here," he said into the black handset.

"Raleigh, it's me."

"Barbara?" From the sound of her voice something was wrong. "What's the matter?"

"I need to see you," she said.

"What do you mean? What's up?"

"I need to talk to you in person."

"Are you all right? I'm at work. Where are you?"

She hesitated. "I'm in Seattle. I—oh, Raleigh." She began to sob.

Raleigh looked around the office to make sure no one was listening. He turned his back on the open door leading to the service manager's office. "Are you sick? Did something happen to your mom? What's going on?"

"Raleigh… I'm pregnant."

He froze inside, staring blindly at the pinup girl calendar on the wall.

Pregnant? No, this can't be. One time, and I… This has to be some kind of a mistake.

He cupped his hand over the mouthpiece. Struggling to keep the words in the right order, he said, "What are you talking about?"

"I know," she cried. "I know. I can't believe it. I told the doctor it was impossible. Oh, Raleigh. I'm so sorry. What are we going to do?"

Barbara Spade? Is pregnant?

With his fingers half-buried in his stiff, heavily oiled hair, he stared out the window into the somber, gray December light. *How could I have been so stupid?*

CHAPTER TWENTY-TWO

WHEELS THREW HIS HEAD BACK and blew a long stream of blue cigarette smoke above the heads of Roy Fisher and Joe Zandt. Two tables over, a group of people sang *Joy to the World*. Raleigh looked over his shoulder to see how quickly the tables in the bar at the Yelm Lions Club were filling up. In the corner by the fireplace, a large, heavily tinseled Christmas tree sparkled brilliantly when people passed by, setting the tinsel in motion.

"So we were stopped twenty miles outside New York harbor, right?" said Wheels.

Raleigh tipped his bourbon back, letting the ice slide against his upper lip. He had been watching the camaraderie slowly melt Wheels's expression: the relaxing of his knitted brow, the easing of the vertical stress lines that bisected his right temple—features he'd brought back from Europe.

"We're waiting for the other troop ships to unload. The word goes around we're going to be stuck for the night, while those other SOBs have a time of it in Manhattan." Wheels turned his half-full glass on the tabletop, as though unspooling the rest of the story. "The captain comes on the loudspeaker around dusk and says, 'Listen up. You men have earned a show, courtesy of Uncle Sam's Navy. Clear the fore and aft gun decks. We're going to light up the sixteens.'"

"You're kidding me," said Fisher.

Wheels chuckled and put his hand over his heart. "Swear to God. The captain says, 'I've bet Captain Stevens on the CL-54, which you boys can see lying a mile south of us—I've bet him a bottle of

J&B we can turn this bucket thirty degrees with the guns alone."

Raleigh struggled to keep his bourbon in his mouth as the others erupted with laughter. Suddenly, they were the loudest table in the bar.

"I'm not joking," Wheels cried, the stress lines gone. "He called for battle stations, and fifteen minutes later the fore and aft sixteens are blasting away in opposite directions. I've never heard or seen anything like it. The night sky lit up like ten in the morning."

Wheels squinted and drew a long, slow puff on his cigarette. He coughed out a laugh with Raleigh and the others. "Sure enough, we started to swing, although the guy next to me swore it was the current. With each blast, we looked like a goddam ghost ship. You could see a couple thousand of us—grunts and crewmen—lining every inch of the upper decks, cheering and waving like schoolboys."

"Some war, huh?" said Fisher, a cigarette poised an inch from his mouth.

Wheels appeared suddenly and inexplicably pensive, and against the way the others also sat back and seemed to look within themselves, Raleigh slapped the table. "I'd love to have seen that! I'll bet the captain caught hell, though."

It was enough to rekindle the light in the men's eyes.

"Maybe not," said Zandt. "Shit, with the war over, it's a good way to off-load ordnance—as long as they don't hit anybody."

Nodding, tapping ashes into ashtrays, and examining their drinks, none of his former classmates seemed to notice the six young women in elegant, floor-length evening gowns—dark blues and reds, one olive green—winding their way through the tables toward them. The jukebox beyond the empty dance floor began playing *White Christmas.*

"You fellas are a sight for sore eyes," said the one in green.

Raleigh looked up into the smiling, heavily made-up faces of three of his old high school friends. With the first hint of their perfume in his nostrils, he jumped to his feet, as did the other men, offering their places at the table and reaching for more chairs.

When he'd settled one woman into his chair, he turned. That's when he saw her. She was waiting in the back of the group, her green eyes fastened on him. He felt his heart grow full making the drawing of his next breath difficult. "Sally?" he said without thinking.

She came forward holding a gin and tonic—silver liquid against the red sparkles of her gown.

Raleigh tried to think of something to say, wanted desperately to utter just the right words. Was it to lay claim to her for the night the way Ted had done for a lifetime so many years ago? But nothing came. He stood with his mouth open.

"Hello, Raleigh," she said, her voice almost drowned out by Bing Crosby and the surrounding noise.

The other men turned. "Hi, Sally," said Wheels. As a group they greeted her, each saying her name, each making eye contact. They took turns shaking her hand. She had lost the most in the war of any of them.

"Hello, all," she said. She stepped forward, half-stumbling in her tight dress. "Oh, my. Merry Christmas." She raised her glass, brought it to her lips and drank deeply.

Some of the men answered the toast, Raleigh among them. He finished the last of his drink. When she was done, Sally licked her lips, smiled, and folded herself into a chair held for her by Wheels.

"I'm ready for another one," said Raleigh. Sally had no sooner arrived than he needed a break—time to think. "Can I get anyone anything?"

"We've ordered," said Peggy.

Sally chuckled. "Not yet." She took another drink as though in a hurry to get drunk.

As he crossed the crowded room, Raleigh saw his sister and her husband enter the bar with another couple. The four stood hunched in the bright entry with sparkling wet hats and coats, smiling at each other and the festive setting. He'd expected her. Lauren wouldn't have missed the Lions Club Christmas party for anything.

Raleigh scanned the mirror behind the bar until he spotted Sally's auburn hair in the crowd. She was nodding at something one of her friends was saying and laughing—and beside her Wheels laughed, too. Raleigh thought at first he could hear her laughter, but then he realized no, that was someone else. The room seemed to billow with chatter on the verge of coming apart. The clinking of glasses, the scraping of chairs, low guffaws and high, and merry ripples competed with the jukebox—*White Christmas* ending, Duke Ellington's *It Don't Mean a Thing* beginning.

Raleigh shook his head.

All the thousands of times I've dreamt of sitting at the same table with her, of hearing her say my name.

"You all right?" asked the bartender.

He looked up. "What? Oh…yeah. Never mind. Can I get another Jim Beam on the rocks?"

When had Ted been killed? 1943? Shot down over Sicily.

Raleigh pictured two uniformed officers, a driver and a chaplain, on the porch of Sally's parents' home on Fir Street, where Sally lived during the war; Sally coming to the door in a loose, workaday dress, her long hair down and disheveled, her expression—well, whatever it might have been, it would have crumbled at once.

Why am I trying to guess at this? I can no more imagine what she went through than… Sally had her own war. Like everyone else.

By the time he made it back to the table, Wheels and Sally were on the dance floor, as were most of the others. The music was louder. The room vibrated with energy. Raleigh sat back, took a drink. To get his eyes off Sally, he watched his sister and Doug, each carrying two drinks, making their way to their friends at a table in the back. He saw Lauren look twice at Sally on her way past the dance floor. She turned and seemed to seek out her brother's face in the crowd, and when she found him, she locked eyes with him and tilted her head suggestively in Sally's direction. Raleigh nodded.

I see her. Believe me, I see her. He studied his best friend and the erstwhile girl-of-his-dreams dancing. Did it mean anything? Not as far as Wheels was concerned. He'd met someone—was head over heels for a gal from Wenatchee that he'd met at the U, Cindy Wallace or Walton. In fact, he was driving over there in the morning. But what about Sally? With Ted gone, was the door that was always shut to Raleigh potentially opened?

"This is the guy you should be dancing with," said Wheels a few minutes later, shouting to be heard over the noise and music as he and Sally approached the table again. "I'm a terrible dancer."

"No, you're not," said Sally. "You're a perfectly good dancer." She pronounced "perfectly" as though it had three f's.

She felt for the edges of her chair before sitting, looking as if she were blind. Raleigh retracted his legs to make room. She picked up her drink and drank deeply through her straw. Relief shone in her eyes. "Besides," she said, glancing at Raleigh, "I'm not sure I could keep up with Raleigh." She seemed to have to work to keep her eyes focused on him.

Raleigh looked away. Was this the look she'd given him years ago when he'd told her he couldn't stop thinking about her? It was close enough. For Raleigh, the room went dead for a few seconds.

"Are you kidding?" said Wheels. "You could keep up with anybody."

Sally laughed sarcastically. "What do you think, Raleigh?"

Their tablemates began to return from the dance floor. Over the scraping of chairs, Raleigh leaned forward and said to Sally, "I've got two words for you: Puyallup Fair." He didn't know why he'd said it—a vain attempt to make her jealous? She and Ted had lost the dance contest to them, after all. He felt the blood rush to his face and wondered if he shouldn't have said, "Here are my two words: Barbara Spade—oh, and by the way, she's informed me she's pregnant," and had it over with.

Wheels threw his head back and laughed.

Sally giggled over her straw. "Puyallup. Isn't that three words all by itself?"

"I thought you were going to say 'Mona Garrison,'" cried Wheels. A second later, he was looking from Sally to Raleigh and back again, evidently wondering where the gaiety had gone.

"There's a name from the past," Sally murmured into her drink.

Raleigh didn't know what to say. Wheels was drunk. Raleigh looked across the table and found Sally staring back at him. An uncomfortable smile crossed her face.

"So, shall we give it a try?" she said.

Exactly everything. That's what he would have given for this moment five years earlier—or six, or seven. Everything. All of him. Without a moment's hesitation. He looked intently into her eyes.

She seemed to understand. She nodded and drank the rest of her gin and tonic, sucking the last drops through her straw. Maybe she was screwing up her courage to dance with him.

"C'mon. Let's do it," she said, reaching her hand across the table.

A slow tune was playing, Glenn Miller's *Moonlight Serenade*. Raleigh took Sally's hand, and they made their way through the maze of tables to the crowded dance floor. She shouldered her way into the dancers, turned, and stopped with her face inches from his. She embraced him tightly. Her forehead was pressed to his cheek, and at once she began to lift her face up as though preparing to kiss him.

Raleigh pushed her gently away. "Are you all right?"

"Oh, sure I am, Raleigh," she said behind heavily lidded eyes.

They began to sway to the music. She looked down as if to collect herself or to push something back. Raleigh took her right hand in his left, wrapped his right arm around her waist. The movement of her hips—the feel of them—was delicious. It was unbelievable. After all these years, it was happening.

She moved closer to him, much closer. She began to watch the other couples. "How have you been, Raleigh?"

"I've been all right."

They danced in silence for a while. He felt her eyes, wide open, looking up at him again. He knew what he had to say. "Listen, I'm sorry about—"

She let go of his left hand, and her soft fingers pressed hard against his mouth.

"Shhhh!" she said. "Don't. Just hold me close. Okay?" A few seconds later, she laid her head against his shoulder. "This is what I want."

"Okay."

Is this what I want? What does it matter? All that time—all those years when it was Sally this and Sally that. And here we are...dancing...and Ted is dead... And Barbara is pregnant.

"What about you?" she said a minute later, absently. "Was it bad? You were in Pacific, weren't you?"

"Guam, in the end." He remembered Steve Lockhart, remembered the dozens of crewmen who came back wounded—or worse, blood-splattered gun turrets, planes torn to pieces. He didn't want to talk about it. Any of it.

She tipped her head back to look at him. Without a word, she lightly touched his chin with her fingertips. She smiled consolingly.

Her shoulders sagged, and she seemed to shrink an inch or two as she leaned into him again.

Moonlight Serenade was followed by a fast number. Sally pulled away and shook her head. She wanted none of it. Raleigh started to lead her off the dance floor when he felt a pull on his fingers.

"Buy a girl a drink?"

Raleigh chuckled. "You sure? You're a lap or two ahead already."

She slapped his arm good-naturedly. "Yes, I'm sure. Nobody holds their liquor like Sally Ellington."

By ten thirty, Sally was proving her point. She had danced with each man at the table at least twice, and more times than not she was the first on her feet.

"It's a great party, isn't it?" she said to Raleigh during a break in the dancing.

Before he could answer, her foot caressed the side of his leg. He waited a beat or two to make sure it was intentional. She had taken off her shoe and was brushing his calf up and down, leaving no doubt.

Raleigh swallowed. "Yes." He looked around the room, wondering if anyone was watching. He pulled his leg away, then, unable to resist, extended it again where she could reach it.

A furtive smile played at the corners of her mouth as she raised her glass and drank. Her hair, which had come loose during the dancing, fell over the left side of her face.

The emcee announced it was time for the Christmas tree raffle. In a booming voice, he invited everyone to come forward and to "get ready to pick a gift out from under the tree if your number is called." The room erupted with excited chatter and the yelps of wooden chairs being pushed back.

"Give it to me."

Raleigh looked up to see Wheels's open hand extended across the table.

"What?"

"Give me your ticket." He turned to Sally. "You, too. Give me your ticket."

Sally seemed to know what Wheels was up to. She dug in her purse and handed him her ticket.

Raleigh stared quizzically across the table. The others were all getting up and moving toward the lighted Christmas tree. He got it; Wheels was giving them a chance to be alone. "Oh, sure," Raleigh said at last, leaning over and digging into his pocket for the ticket. "Thanks, old man."

Wheels took the ticket, tapped the table twice like a gambler, got up, and walked away.

Raleigh felt a pang of remorse. He should have told Wheels about Barbara and the baby. He would; he just needed to find the right time.

Sally averted her eyes and seemed to color. "Well, well," she said. "You two were always best friends, weren't you?"

"None better." He watched reflected octagons of light from the glass ball above the dance floor sweep across Sally's face.

She tapped the end of her straw against the lonely ice at the bottom of her glass. "I could either have another one," she said, "or we could…you know."

Raleigh blinked.

I know? I know what?

"I'll get you another one," he heard himself say. He started to get up.

"No, wait," said Sally. "I guess what I'm saying is… Well, I don't know if you're seeing someone. Do you have a girlfriend? I'm sorry. I'm drunk. That's so forward of me."

"No, it's all right," said Raleigh, sitting back down. Should he tell her about Barbara?

"I know you had it bad for the Garrison girl once. You know, I never blamed you for that. Not like the others."

You never blamed me?

"It was silly and all, but—well, nothing makes sense, does it? Not in this world. At least, I can't… She was pretty enough… Probably still pretty. Is she pretty, Raleigh?"

You're soused. Why are you talking about Mona?

"What are you looking at me that way for? Aren't I pretty enough?"

"You know you are," he said, though he hardly recognized his own voice.

"You used to think I was beautiful," she said. She smiled widely and picked up her glass. "Here's to me. Here's to the one of a kind Sally Ell—Sally Springs." She raised her glass high, reached up, and withdrew the straw comically. Then she drank what she could, tipping the glass back and spilling ice over the front of her dress. "Oh, my."

Raleigh reached over and took the glass from her. "Let's get you out of here," he said.

"Now you're talking—and I'm going to make it worth your while, soldier."

He stood beside her and helped her up. "I'm sure of that."

She giggled, took his arm, and leaned against him to make their way across the room. When Raleigh stopped beside his sister, Sally looked up at him with eyes dulled by alcohol and doubt.

Lauren took a deep breath and sighed. She tapped Doug on the arm as though she knew what to expect.

"She needs to get home," Raleigh told his sister. "Will you take her?"

"What?" said Sally, stepping away unsteadily.

"I would be eternally grateful," Raleigh said.

"What are you doing?" shrieked Sally.

A wide circle of people turned to see what was going on. Raleigh's eyes met Wheels's. Wheels winked and turned away.

"Listen, Sally," Raleigh began, drawing her close again. He spoke into her ear. "I could say you've got me all wrong, but that'd be a lie. I think you know me—better, at least, than I ever thought you did. I like you. I've always liked you, and that's why..." He turned back to Lauren and Doug. "I need you to do this for me."

Lauren looked up at Doug, who frowned and then shrugged. "I guess," he said.

"I hate you, Raleigh," Sally said as Lauren and Doug led her toward the exit.

"You don't hate Raleigh," said Lauren congenially.

Sally laughed drunkenly. "I know it."

CHAPTER TWENTY-THREE

1947

"THAT'S PERFECT, SUSAN!" Mona shouted over the blare of the Woody Herman orchestra. She scanned the width of the warm, sunlit room. "Keep your heads up! There you go! Okay, everybody, turn on three! One-two-three!"

The woman in the wall-length mirror—was it really her? In the last several weeks Mona had been startled to see features of her mother's face—what she could remember of them—staring back at her. She concentrated on her round eyes alone until that became too uncomfortable, and then she watched the wind-tossed branches of the red-leafed thundercloud plum beyond the barred windows.

It's April 5th. My last class. I'll be twenty-one in a few days...out of here and living in my own place.

The residents behind her in the mirror; none over nineteen, most of them much younger, their hair short, their teenage faces rounder and more innocent. "Okay, back around in three! One-two-three!"

Mona's body was one with the music as always—her legs and arms floating easily over the worn, blonde wood. She sensed the girls in the class struggling to keep up, never mind that the 78's persistent scratch was, for once, helping to keep the beat.

"You're doing great! Keep going...! One, two, three, four! One, two, three, four!"

She glanced at the mongoloid girl at the end of the first row. She returned the girl's broad grin, then noticed a handful of other dancers with their eyes fixed on her, smiling. She knew they were not smiling from the joy of dancing. They didn't care if they were doing it perfectly, or not. Not now, as the clock above the mirror approached eleven o'clock. Time to say good-bye. Other girls among the thirty-three began to smile at Mona, as well.

She remembered the day three years earlier that she awoke from a fitful afternoon nap to find the air raid curtains drawn and the sleeping room encased in semidarkness. The power had been knocked out by a thunderstorm that still rumbled in the distance. Dorothy sat on the edge of her bunk staring at her with a bored look, evidently waiting for Mona to wake up. Her best friend didn't answer Mona's groggy questions—"What is it? What's happened?"—but sat upright at the first sign of life out of Mona.

"I have an idea for something that will perk you up. I spoke with Mrs. Trout, told her about the dance contest and everything, and she said it could work."

It had been six months since Mona's sterilization. Six months of uncontrolled mood swings—of raging at sticking doors and written words she could not hope to read, of weeping in delight at the onset of hot water in the shower after a week without it—hardly knowing from one minute to the next what to think, not knowing what was left of life—of anything. None of the other girls had been sterilized after the procedure was ruled unconstitutional by the court in Olympia in 1942. Talk of sterilizations, once common in the girls' dormitories, had stopped. But she had been singled out, and many of the older girls knew it. It was though she were a prisoner now. Worst of all, not a single letter from Raleigh. Perhaps they weren't stealing them after all; perhaps he'd quit writing. What a fool she'd been! And now: sterilized. Not worthy of any man, of being married at all, ever, no matter what.

She relived over and over again the moment she had regained consciousness from the anesthesia, the painful pull and strange tightness of the stitches, the nausea, her desperate questions, the two frowning nurses—could she ever forget their faces?—passing back and forth in the hallway without looking at her. It always came as a single, jarring body memory, momentarily paralyzing her; and it was only by pushing it away—pushing it out of her mind entirely—that she could regain her emotional balance. Banishing it this time, she'd become aware of Dorothy's hand on top of hers as she lay in her bunk.

"What could work?" she'd said to Dorothy without interest.

"You can teach dance. They have a singing class, why not a dance class? A jitterbug class?"

Part of the smile that Mona returned to the girls dancing in front of her now was for that moment, three years earlier—for the look of mischievous delight that had crept into Dorothy's eyes when she realized that Mona had no answer, no defense, no rebuttal. Her depression had met something of a match. Dance had a way of drawing Mona out of her moods.

Mona spun away from the class and sniffed back tears. How many dozens of girls had swayed forward and back in this room in front of her, giggled at themselves, paired-up and jumped to their favorite music? On top of everything else, teaching had built Mona's confidence, helped her find the road back after the surgery, after Raleigh's disappearance.

When the eleven o'clock bell rang, the girls rushed forward to hug Mona and say good-bye. Most of them were shorter than she was. Although Mona's shirt was damp from dancing, she could feel their warm tears through the fabric. "I'm going to miss you, too," she said again and again.

The second bell rang. "You better go now," she said. A group of older girls remained, circling Mona, gazing at her as though star-struck. She turned and made eye contact with each of them. "You don't want to be late."

"We're never going to be able to dance like you," said a flat-faced, sandy-haired girl.

"Oh, of course you are!" said Mona. "It takes time, is all." Again, she looked at each girl. "You will. I promise."

A familiar dual tone rang out up and down the hall, followed by: "Mona Garrison to the visitors' room. Mona Garrison to the visitors' room."

* * *

Mona, still breathing heavily from dancing, made a point of not looking at Mrs. Ballard, merely flashed her eyes in the guardian's direction upon entering the visitors' room. It wasn't clear why Mrs. Ballard, the only person in the room, stood up when she came in, only to settle herself back in the armchair.

Mrs. Ballard held up an envelope. "They've given me this. I'll put it in your guardianship account and apply it to your rent."

"What is it?" said Mona from the far corner of the couch. She'd thought of not sitting at all, of staying as far away from Mrs. Ballard as possible. On top of that, the room was stuffy and had a slight medicinal smell that Mona always hated. The foul odor seemed to linger in the small room as though it oozed from the ceiling and was trapped by the vertical green and gold bands of the wallpaper.

"It's fifty dollars. The staff decided to pay you for teaching the dance classes."

Mona opened her eyes wide. Fifty dollars! With the seventy-five she'd saved from the dance contest, that was…well, never mind. It was a lot. It would pay the rent for… It would pay for a long time, at least until she could find work. Dorothy would turn twenty-one in a couple of months and would join her, and then the room rent would be cut in half.

Mona watched out of the corner of her eye as the white envelope disappeared into Mrs. Ballard's purse. Would she ever see that money again?

"Where's this young man with the rental agreement?" said Mrs. Ballard, checking her gold watch.

Mona consulted the clock above the door. "He's not late yet. It's only twenty after." She pictured Dorothy's older brother Tony racing down dirt and gravel roads to arrive by eleven-thirty. He had to come from Tacoma and make a stop in Puyallup to have Dorothy's guardian sign the agreement.

"Let's review the plan for Tuesday," said Mrs. Ballard. "I called your Uncle Simon last night and gave him the address of the boarding house. Most of your things are boxed up and ready to go. He'll drive up and meet us in Tacoma at eleven o'clock. That is…"

"What?" said Mona.

"If you still want to go. Your uncle asked me to tell you…he made me promise to tell you that you are welcome to return home. He could arrange for you to work for Mrs. Moore again, and she would happily take you back."

Mona stared at a framed black and white photograph of Mount Rainier on the opposite wall, and chewed her fingernail. *I could go back.*

She'd thought about it vaguely over the last several months, but not for long, and not seriously. She was an adult, and besides, she and Dorothy wanted to live together. They had been talking about it—had hatched all sorts of schemes and what-ifs—for the last year and a half. She couldn't change her mind now. But… Would they let Dorothy come, too? What would it be like to move back into her old room? *That's what he means, isn't it? The room facing the road? Yes, I'm sure it is.*

She looked at Mrs. Ballard and was reminded of Aunt Grace's stern face. *This is Uncle Simon's idea. They've never mentioned it on their visits. Oh, but how wonderful it would be to be close to Raleigh again.*

Mona had never spoken to her aunt and uncle, or even Mrs. Ballard, about Raleigh. Once sterilized, why would he have wanted her? She could have written to Lauren. Mr. Horowitz would have helped. But what would she have said? That she was no longer able to give a man a child? That she was doomed?

But something was different now. She would be twenty-one in a few days, and once she left the custodial school, Raleigh would have no way to find her even if he wanted to. Would he want to—someday? Her aunt had made it clear that he was not to contact them. At least, while she was at the school, he knew where she was.

How will he ever find me?

"Do you know if Raleigh Starr came back to Yelm after the war?" Her voice trembled a little.

Mrs. Ballard's face darkened. "What does that matter? I assure you I have no idea."

"It doesn't matter, I guess. I was just wondering."

"Well, I would stop wondering if I were you. It's late in the game to be thinking of… What about your friend Dorothy? Isn't she counting on you?"

"Yes."

"Let's stay on track then." Mrs. Ballard produced a folded piece of paper from her purse and handed it to Mona. "Here's the name of the landlord. Can you read it?"

Mona sounded out the letters slowly. "Ju-dy Har-ris."

"Good. Now, listen. Part of living alone is being able to use a phone book. I've cleared this with the office. When we're done here,

I'm going to see another client. While I'm doing that, I want you to go to the office and ask to use their telephone and the phone book—do you understand?"

"Yes, but..." She remembered the last time she had asked to use the telephone. It was to call Mrs. Ballard to force them to give her Raleigh's letters. Would she have to face Mr. Ashworth again?

"They're expecting you. Since you're leaving, they've authorized you to use the phone at my request. I want you to call Mrs. Harris and tell her we will be arriving with your things on Tuesday, between eleven and twelve. You'll have to find her number in the phone book. Can you do that?"

Mona nodded.

Mrs. Ballard looked up. "There's our young man."

"Hi there. Hope I'm not late."

Mona regarded Tony Lambert partly through Mrs. Ballard's eyes. Twenty-five, an apple-shaped body, protruding brows and a dimpled chin. His short black hair sported a single, perpetual wave that threw back a dull sheen. His blue eyes were kind and eager. He held a document in his left hand.

Mrs. Ballard stood up. Tony took a step toward her. "Have you been waiting long?" he asked. He reached across Mona to shake Mrs. Ballard's hand. "I'm Tony Lambert, Dorothy Lambert's brother."

Mona could smell his pungent body odor. Its mixture with the medicinal smell in the room was nauseating. *I used to like the way Raleigh smelled when we practiced on hot days, or rode in the truck with the windows rolled up. Poor Tony. He's been cooped up in his car all morning.*

"Not long," said Mrs. Ballard. "May I have a look at that?"

Tony handed her the document, then sat down next to Mona. "Hi, Mona. How are you today?"

Mona knew that Mrs. Ballard was studying Tony, document or no document. "Fine," she said, not making eye contact with either of them. She remembered the look in Dorothy's eyes when she told Mona, "My brother's got a crush on you. You know that, don't you?"

"What? No."

"Just don't hurt him."

"Of course I wouldn't hurt him."

"I know you wouldn't. Just let him down easily. Know what I mean? He's going to be coming around more. I just know it."

She was not attracted to Tony, not at first and not ever; but there'd been ample proof that Dorothy was right. She liked Tony fine. Couldn't they be friends? How could the brother of her best friend not be her friend? He was always offering to help. He'd insisted on doing the legwork to get the rental agreement from Mrs. Harris so that Mrs. Ballard could sign it. He'd already taken off the following Tuesday to help Uncle Simon with the move.

"Are you getting excited?" said Tony, playfully tapping Mona on the arm. "It's almost time."

Mona smiled at him and nodded. She felt some heat come into her face. "Thank you for helping, Tony. Has Dorothy's guardian signed it?"

"Yup."

Mrs. Ballard examined the document front and back. "I'm sure this is going to be fine, but I'll want to read it over." She looked at Tony. "If you'll excuse us now, I've got work for Mona to do."

No sooner had Tony left than Mrs. Ballard made her way to the door. "I want you to go to the office and make that phone call."

"All right." Mona stood up. "Excuse me!" Mrs. Ballard turned in the hallway. "Are you... Does the lease become final today? I mean, is there time to think about something?"

"About what?" asked Mrs. Ballard.

She didn't know what. Not exactly, anyway, but what if she *did* want to move back with Uncle Simon and Aunt Grace, at least until Dorothy was released?

"I . . . I don't know. I would like to think about what my uncle said."

"Well, think about it, but don't be too long," said Mrs. Ballard. "I'll come find you when I'm done with my next appointment."

Mona did not think about it for too long. Left alone in the visitor's room, Mona realized that moving back to Yelm was not an option. It wouldn't be fair to Dorothy for one thing. And why would she want to go back, to be surrounded by so many memories of Raleigh? Mona moved to the window and separated the chiffon curtains with her fingertips. She looked out at a half-full parking lot. No, just to have

Raleigh know where she was, that's all she wanted. In case he ever wanted to reach her.

I'll call Lauren. I'll give her the new address—2340 Evergreen Way, Tacoma.

A few minutes later, Mona stood behind the glass at the counter in the receptionist's office. The receptionist had brought a black telephone over and placed it on the counter for her convenience, then pointed to a series of phone books on a shelf beneath the counter.

"Can you tell me which one is for Yelm?" Mona asked. Mona had already spotted the large Tacoma phone book, taken it out and set it next to the phone.

"Thurston County," the receptionist mumbled, sliding her finger along the spines of the remaining phone books. "Here it is."

"Thank you." Mona called Miss Harris in Tacoma without difficulty and gave her the message. After quietly hanging up, she thumbed the pages of the Thurston County book in search of last names beginning with S. When she found those, she began looking for S-T. Before she knew it, she was staring at *two* listings for "Starr"—STARR, GEORGE C., ROUTE 2, THOMPSON ROAD, YELM and STARR, RALEIGH A., 420 MOSMAN AVE. SW, YELM. Her heart leapt into her throat. *Raleigh?*

She glanced over her shoulder. The receptionist was busy typing on a large, black typewriter, paper and carbon paper drooping past the carriage. *Do I dare call him? No, I should stick to the plan. Just call Lauren. But wait! What if Lauren doesn't live with her father anymore? What if Mr. Starr answers?*

As she thought these things, the desire to hear Raleigh's voice swept through her. It flooded her heart. What harm could come from calling him, from telling him that she was leaving the custodial school, and giving him her new address?

But what if Mrs. Ballard catches me? She could be here any second.

With trembling fingers she dialed. The ring—first one and then another—seemed to bar her from thinking, from doing what she knew she should be doing—rehearsing what to say. Then a voice: "Hello?"

Why was a woman answering Raleigh's phone? Mona hesitated, and then turned her back on the receptionist. "Is Raleigh Starr there?" she whispered.

"No, he's at work. May I ask who's calling?"

Mona looked up at her own wide eyes staring back at her in the glass partition. Over the line she heard a baby crying. She snapped her eyes shut.

"This is his wife. Can I help you?"

CHAPTER TWENTY-FOUR

1951

"HE OPENS HIS LUNCH PAIL, and it's the same thing all over again: 'Goddammit, another fucking peanut-butter-and-pickle sandwich.'" Sitting on the stool with one leg up at the back of the garage, Wheels was doing his theatrical best. He spit out the words with the weight of his subject's anger visible on his brow. "So he slams the pail shut—right?—and says, 'I swear to God, I'd rather starve to death than eat another one of these pieces of shit.' He sits there on the iron beam with his legs dangling—right?—looking like he's about to cry."

Raleigh had heard this one before. He looked up from the disemboweled carburetor into the face of Jim Martin, the new mechanic-in-training. The seventeen-year-old, a carrot top with freckles and perpetually blushing cheeks, had stopped working. An uncertain half-smile revealed two widely separated front teeth.

"The young fellow next to him says, 'Hey, it's all right, John. You can have half of my cheese sandwich. I'm not that hungry anyway.' So John thinks about it a minute, opens his lunch pail back up and takes out his peanut-butter-and-pickle sandwich and says, 'No, that's all right. I'll eat this turd.' So the same thing happens every day for the next four days—right? John keeps pulling out peanut-butter-and-pickle sandwiches and saying the same thing all over again: 'Another fucking peanut-butter-and-pickle sandwich,' and all the rest. Finally the young fella says, 'Why don't you ask your wife to make you something else?' and John turns to him and says, 'Oh, I make my own lunches.'"

It's funnier than hell every time. Raleigh took the cigarette out of his mouth and laughed as much at the doubled-over redhead as with him.

The phone rang in the office.

"Hey, Jim, get that, will you?" said Raleigh, turning his attention back to the carburetor. "If it's for me, take a message. I gotta get this done."

Wheels watched the teenager disappear through the office door. "He seems like a nice kid."

"He's all right," Raleigh agreed. "Learns pretty quick."

"Speaking of that, how's your class going?"

"It's going."

Raleigh remembered his first conversation with Wheels about the jet engine repair and maintenance class offered by St. Martin's College in Lacey. "Barbara insists I take it," he'd told Wheels. "She wants me to catch on at Boeing."

"Is that what you want?" Wheels had asked, staring at the open hamburger that had been thrust in front of him at the Green Lantern Café.

"Not really. She wants to move back north. Her folks live in Seattle, remember. That's what this is all about."

Wheels had smiled around a long french fry evidently too hot for his lips. "Well, nuts to that." He'd quickly taken a sip of ice water and repeated himself as though he hadn't been heard the first time, "Nuts to that."

Raleigh reached both hands under the carburetor to keep from dropping a small bolt. Wheels rose from the stool and sauntered over to watch him work under the hood of the green Hudson Hornet. Both men seemed content to listen for a while to the sounds of cars passing the shop and a flight of honking geese skirting the rooftops. The imperfect silence seemed to Raleigh to point to something.

Wheels said, "I've been thinking about what you told me last weekend, about Steve Salter selling the Chevy dealership."

"Oh yeah? That's on the QT, remember? He said he *might* sell it. He wasn't sure—"

"I know. But let's say he wants to. What would be keeping you and me from buying it—going in as partners?"

Raleigh didn't think the idea was meant to be serious and didn't look up. "Oh, ten or fifteen thousand dollars, I suppose." He leaned closer to the float valve, removed his cigarette and blew on the valve, then scraped a greasy finger over the aperture. When Wheels didn't respond, Raleigh added, "Five thousand down and another five thousand sleepless nights."

"How about three thousand down—fifteen hundred a piece—and a thousand a month in the bank?"

Raleigh sensed that Wheels was scheming again, trying something on to get a reaction. "You planning on selling pies out of there?"

"What do you mean?" Wheels countered. "I'm serious. This is right up your alley. I could handle sales, and you could manage service. Shit, it's about time we struck out and did something together. I thought about this last night. This makes a hell of a lot more sense than you moving to Renton or Seattle or wherever."

Raleigh pointed to a box wrench resting on top of the grill. Wheels handed it to him.

He's serious.

Raleigh's pulse quickened.

A dealership. Wheels and me? Partners? Henderson Chevrolet. Henderson and Starr Chevrolet.

Raleigh waved a fly away from his face. "What makes you think I could come up with fifteen hundred dollars? Or that Barbara would agree?" His mind was only half on his work now.

Man, talk about fun. Wheels and me managing a business together.

"I'll stake you the money," Wheels answered. "Pay me back when you want."

Wheels had inherited money from his grandmother in the last year. On top of that, Wheels's wife, Cindy, would support anything having to do with her husband's friendship with Raleigh. She seemed to like Raleigh almost as much as Wheels did. That the two men would end up in a business together would strike Cindy as self-evident. He could picture her with her childlike smile saying, "I see you two finally figured it out."

Still, Raleigh wouldn't dream of borrowing from Wheels. That was hardly a partnership. If he couldn't scrape it together, he would borrow it from his dad. More than once since the war, his father had said there were "family funds" available should Raleigh and Barbara need them. It had been a point of pride to say, "Thanks, Dad, but we're doing fine." Maybe this time it would be different.

Raleigh backed out from under the hood and began to wipe his hands on a soiled gray rag. "Your money's no good with me. But I could probably swing it, if you're serious."

Wheels grinned. "You're damn right I'm serious. Why don't we get together next Saturday and talk about it?"

"Can't. It's Sandra's first birthday party. Say, what about your house painting business?"

"I'd keep it, unless it got in the way. Cy can run it. I'd offer him part ownership, let him manage it."

Raleigh smiled, looking at his hands. "Chevrolets, huh?"

Wheels began to sing, "See the USA in your Chevrolet…"

It was the first time Raleigh had ever heard his best friend's singing voice. "Dinah Shore's got nothing on you," he said.

Wheels laughed. "That's what I said—sales."

* * *

Robert Talbot sat up in the lumpy double bed with his back and broad shoulders pressed against the headboard. God he was cute. Barbara watched him take a puff of his Lucky Strike and squint as smoke coiled past his slightly crooked nose and wide forehead. "I love Wednesdays," he said. "I don't think I could live without them."

Barbara was glad for the sound of his voice. It dispelled a random, roaming thought about Raleigh. "I know I can't," she whispered. She lay on her side with her left arm slung over Talbot's taut stomach. Her blonde hair, a mash of curls, framed blue eyes that stared fixedly at the lank beige curtains of the Rest-A-While Motel.

Talbot pushed his fingers through Barbara's locks until he reached the nape of her neck. He traced gentle circles with his fingertips. "How's Michael?" he asked.

"He's fine. He didn't get Sandra's cold." She licked dry lips. "He likes spending Wednesdays with Lauren's kids. Gets to ride Karen's bicycle with training wheels." She left the subject for several seconds, then returned to it. "Do you think about him?" Her eyes were open.

"How can I not?" he answered, tapping ash from his cigarette into the round glass ashtray on the nightstand. He drew in another puff. "Although I shouldn't. He's Raleigh's son now, isn't he?"

Barbara reached to caress the hairs in the valley of his chest. She took her time answering. "You wouldn't marry me. You know I wanted that more than anything."

"Yeah. I—"

"You know that."

"I do." She could tell from the working of his stomach muscles that Talbot was looking down at her. "I wasn't ready. I was going to play baseball. You—it seems so absurd now, doesn't it?"

"You didn't love me," Barbara said flatly. "Let's say it like it was."

"But I did. I just didn't know—"

"Nope."

"What do you mean, nope?"

Barbara snickered softly. "I've loved you since ninth grade. You didn't look at me until we were juniors, and then it was my body you were interested in, not me." She glanced up as if to say "and don't bother denying it." She pulled a pillow closer. The *thunk* she heard next was Talbot's head striking the hollow plaster wall above the headboard. "It's all right—I've gotten over it," Barbara added. "It killed me at first, but I knew you weren't ready."

"I love you now."

"I know." She leaned over and kissed his side.

"And I'm serious," said Talbot. "I don't know what I'd do if you didn't drive up to Seattle. When Sandy got sick last week and you called from Yelm, I thought it would be okay, but it wasn't. I've had a miserable week. Made me want to quit in fact."

"Absence makes the heart grow fonder," she said. She looked up at him and smiled. "Even the heart of a car insurance salesman."

"And you're sure Raleigh doesn't know?"

Her voice turned brittle. "Of course I am. He thinks I'm with Mom all day."

"But she isn't sick any more. What does he—?"

"That she's depressed again. That's what I've told him. She has no friends. She needs to see me every week. He doesn't question it, and neither does Lauren. Besides, he knows I need to be in Seattle. I hate living in the sticks. It's so boring there." She felt a surge of anger at the complication of it all. But she would not be made to feel guilty. She hugged Talbot close. *This is what I want, this is the man I want.*

Talbot had never made it easy—had caused her to suffer for her feelings, in fact, all these years.

She closed her eyes and thought of Raleigh, away every Wednesday night at his class, learning about the repair and maintenance of jet engines; thought of him walking in at eleven fifteen, through the kitchen, exhausted, uninspired, road-weary, unaware that his wife had spent two hours in the arms of another man. *Oh, but you never loved me either, Raleigh. You married me, and I'll always be thankful. I couldn't have supported Michael on my own.*

She looked up at Talbot. "Sometimes I think my life's like an episode of *The Guiding Light*."

CHAPTER TWENTY-FIVE

THE SLAM OF THE SCREEN DOOR reverberated throughout his father's house, followed by the drum of small feet on the wooden stairs. Raleigh could remember when he ran up those steps in much the same way.

"You boys come on down," said Lauren. "Time to sing *Happy Birthday*."

"Cake!" shouted Lauren's oldest, leading his four-year-old cousin Michael down the stairs and around the balustrade.

Barbara cut off her son at a full run as he dashed under the arch leading to the kitchen almost slamming into the red vinyl high chair with the broken leg. "Slow down, Buster," she said, lifting him by the armpits and swinging him over to Raleigh. "Here, take him, will you?" She straightened her apron and went back to attend to the birthday girl.

"Looks like she's ready for anything," said Raleigh's father, who sat at the end of the kitchen table, eyeing the chubby, bibbed Sandra over his raised coffee cup.

"She's always ready," said Barbara. "Look at her."

"This isn't like your birthday party last year, George," said Doug, as he lit the single candle with a cigarette lighter. "I shouldn't have to refill the lighter halfway through."

The company, including George, erupted in bright laughter, scaring the baby. Her lower lip protruded and began to tremble.

Barbara rushed to console her, shooting a recriminatory glance at Doug. "Just light the damn candle, will you?"

Raleigh felt a sting of embarrassment. Where had that come from? Barbara was usually reserved around Doug, and especially around Raleigh and Lauren's father.

Raleigh swayed back and forth for Michael's sake while the others sang *Happy Birthday*. He remembered the argument he'd had with Barbara on the drive out to his father's place that morning.

"You're his only son. It stands to reason you'd get the farm."

"But I don't want the farm," he'd said. "And Lauren and Doug do. Besides, it's a moot point. Dad's not ready to move into town. I don't even know why he brought it up last week."

"Because he's tired of farming," Barbara answered. "He wants to know if you want it, or whether he should sell."

"He can sell it, for all I care," Raleigh had replied, blowing cigarette smoke toward the open wing window of the rattling gray 1948 Ford Coupe.

Barbara held Sandra on her lap while Mike played with army men in the back seat. "And spend all the money?" she asked derisively. "Spend every dime, and we get nothing?"

"Wait a minute." Raleigh snatched glimpses of his wife while managing to navigate the rain-filled potholes on Thompson Road. "What are you talking about? The farm belongs to Dad. He's worked it damn near his whole life. He knows I'm not interested in farming. He's the one who told me to go into business. Years ago. Now that I have the chance, you say no."

"I told you I didn't want to talk about that any more. I'm not going to live here for the rest of my life, Raleigh. I hate it here. The sooner you finish your class, the sooner we can move."

"Then stop talking about Dad's property. It doesn't add up if—"

"But why can't *we* sell it?" Barbara interrupted. "He doesn't need the money. He's made that clear. Lauren and Doug sure as hell don't."

"You think—"

"I don't give a hoot about the farm, but with that money we could buy a house in Seattle. We deserve the—*you* deserve the money. Why shouldn't you have it? Think of the children."

"I've already discussed this with Lauren. She and Doug want to keep horses, want their kids to have the life she and I had growing up."

"What?" Barbara shrieked. "What do you mean you and Lauren have discussed this? Without talking to me?"

"It's not mine, Barbara. If Lauren wants it... Dad's not ready to move. I don't care what he said. Let's drop it, okay?"

"Maybe we can discuss when you intend to get off your... You said six months ago you'd get a better job. Instead, you come home with some cockamamie idea of spending all our money on an auto dealership with Wheels. When are you going to keep your promise to me?"

"What do you mean, my promise?"

"Are you going to repair cars the rest of your life? How long do we have to live in that stupid apartment? I'm too embarrassed to invite my friends over, and they're all seventy miles away, anyway. When am I going to be able to live where I want, where I can invite my friends over?"

As he watched Sandra's chubby fingers dig into the piece of cake cut especially for her, Raleigh felt a searing pain like a white hot coal settling at the bottom of his stomach. *It's never going to happen. I'll never be able to go into business with Wheels.*

* * *

Mona put the dog's supper on the kitchen floor and scratched the back of the animal's neck as it nosed in over the bowl. "There you go, pooch," she whispered. Had the visitor heard? She straightened and took a deep breath, bracing herself before returning to the living room. The meeting had already stretched an hour-and-a-half longer than expected.

All this technical talk. Psychology this, psychology that; legal this, legal that. She warned us, I guess.

Mona took her seat at the opposite end of the coffee table from Dorothy. The two friends glanced at each other for the hundredth time that afternoon.

The attorney looked up from the jumble of papers cluttering the coffee table. Her brown eyes softened momentarily. "I was just telling Dorothy, we want to be able to portray your lives as being as normal as possible. You both work. You shop. You go out, I assume. You keep this nice apartment. You have a dog." The attorney smiled. She picked up her pen. "What's the dog's name, by the way?"

"Lucky," said Dorothy.

"Lucky. Judges love this kind of thing—human interest. I'll ask one of you the dog's name at the hearing tomorrow."

Dorothy rolled her eyes. "We can bring the dog if you like." The attorney rocked back with laughter.

Something in Dorothy's deadpan expression reminded Mona of the night Dorothy's parents first told them about the research being done at the University of Washington on the subject of "learning handicaps." It hadn't occurred to Mona that this could have any bearing on her life, certainly not on her guardianship. For as long as she could remember she'd been told that she was feebleminded, that she needed help, and always would. How could these professors' work change any of that? She was twenty-five now. Maybe if she had been younger when this research starting coming out...

The attorney continued. "Undoing two guardianships at once, that's unchartered territory. I think we can do it, but the judge is going to have questions. The bottom line is, you two are not legally incapacitated. You can make decisions for yourself."

Dorothy looked at Mona while tamping an unopened pack of cigarettes against her palm. "Like naming a dog, for instance."

Mona was used to Dorothy's wit and loved it, but her mind was elsewhere: she was recalling the moment, seven weeks earlier, that Dorothy had shocked her parents—and Mona and Tony, too—while eating at Steve's Gay '90s Restaurant on South Tacoma Way. Wasn't it enough that the Lamberts included Mona at family meals out? Or that they bought her birthday and Christmas presents? Apparently not.

"I'm not doing this lawsuit unless Mona gets her guardianship erased, too."

Mr. Lambert had raised his eyes above his menu and looked around as though his daughter had uttered something nonsensical for the benefit of a neighboring table. Seeing nothing to support that supposition, he said, "What did you—?"

"I mean it, Dad. I'm not doing this. I'm not testifying unless Mona gets to have her guardianship lifted, too. We both have the same thing, a learning handicap or whatever they call it. We're not feebleminded—the way they always said. The attorney can help both of us...and if it's not both of us, it's neither of us."

Mona smiled. It didn't help to remember the uncomfortable hemming and hawing that followed, and what did it matter? A week later, Dorothy and Mona had dashed from the No. 6 bus in a downpour and tripped, giggling, through the doors of the Puget Sound National Bank Building. They stood in the foyer studying the building directory an overlong time, but there it was: BRIAN AND GOODLOE, ATTORNEYS AT LAW, FIFTH FLOOR.

"Are you seeing anyone, Mona?"

Mona heard only her name. In the background, the dog was loudly chewing its food. The neighbors upstairs were playing "Your Hit Parade" on the radio. She looked at the attorney. "I'm sorry?"

"Do you go out with anyone? I mean, that's part of getting along...or it could be, I guess. Do you have dinners out or go to movies? The judge will want to know if you're able to socialize, get yourself around safely, that sort of thing."

Mona could feel herself coloring. *I have lunches with Tony...but that's not what she means. We're just friends.* She pictured the two men she'd dated in the last four years. Neither relationship lasted more than a few months. She'd broken it off both times. They were nice men, but she knew within a few weeks that she was wasting their time, and hers. She could never love them. She could barely stand to kiss them.

I don't want to talk about that, not to a judge—not anyone.

"I get around on the bus," she said at last. "Sometimes I take a taxi, but..." She saw that the attorney was waiting her out. "I'm not dating anyone right now, if that's what you mean."

"My brother's in love with her," said Dorothy casually.

Mona made a face. "No, he's not! He's in love with Blanche."

"Well, he used to be, then. Half the men in this apartment building drool over you, so it's not like you don't have choices."

"Very funny," said Mona.

The attorney smiled broadly. "How about family? Do you have family nearby, Mona?"

"My uncle, Simon Garrison. He lives outside of Yelm."

"Anyone else?"

"My Aunt Grace died about two years ago."

"Okay. Let's switch gears. What would you guys do if there was a fire in the building?"

Dorothy raised her hand. "Ooo! Ooo! I've got this one! Run like hell."

The attorney grinned and turned to Mona. "Believe it or not, this is the kind of thing the judge wants to know. What would *you* do if there was a fire?"

"I'd grab my dog and run down the fire escape."

"What do you mean *your* dog?" said Dorothy, with an unlit cigarette in her mouth.

"You left it in the fire," said Mona. "It's my dog now."

CHAPTER TWENTY-SIX

1953

ACROSS THE STREET from Yelm's Rainier Auto Repair, a man in a gray double-breasted suit sat behind the wheel of the parked car with the driver's side door open. He was lit by the autumn sun from his belt buckle to the knot of his burgundy tie. His visor-shaded eyes scanned a file he'd pulled from his briefcase ten minutes earlier. As soon as the blue bay doors opened at Rainier Auto Repair, he set the file aside and reached into the back of the car for his fedora.

Jim Martin, a mechanic, was rolling a tire toward the southernmost bay when he noticed the man walking toward him, his long, generously cut trousers whipping in the breeze as he crossed the street. Martin stood and let the tire lean against his leg.

"I'm Steve Clark," the man said, thrusting his hand out. Martin wiped his hands on his dungarees and took the man's wide hand in his own. Clark was middle-aged with narrow, horizontal eyes and a puffy face. His neck was creased under the grip of a white collar. "I work for an attorney in Olympia," he said. "I'm looking for a Raleigh Starr. Is he around?"

Martin hesitated. "He's not here."

"I was told he works here," said Clark, frowning.

"Archie!" shouted Martin over his shoulder. He turned back. "Archie's the owner. He can fill you in."

A portly man in his late forties wearing grease-stained gray overalls, stroking down a wisp of black hair above the midpoint of his forehead, strode stiff-legged between two black sedans on lifts. He leaned back on his heels as he walked to compensate for an enormous round belly, and each step sent a tiny tremor though his billowy jowls. He took the hand offered by Clark. "How do you do? Archie Green."

When Clark restated his business, Archie nodded. "Sure, he works here, but he's running late this morning, see? Babysitter hasn't shown up." Archie seemed to read a question in the visitor's eyes. "Wife left him and the kids. Cleaned out the bank account. You know the drill." With the back of one fat wrist, he wiped spittle from the left side of his mouth but let the right side go. "What'd you say you wanted with him?"

Clark rubbed the back of his neck. "Just a bit of legal business," he said. "I have some questions for him. You have his phone number?"

"He hasn't been answering the phone," offered Martin.

Archie's face registered surprise and the redheaded Martin, full of decisive knowledge, said, "You remember last week? I called to see if he could come in on Saturday and help us with that DeSoto, but he never picked up. I had to go over and talk to him. He said he wasn't answering because he figured it might be Barbara."

"By golly, that's right," said Archie. He made a feature of his lower lip. "Going to have to go over there yourself, mister. He lives over on Mosman, about—"

"Boss!" interrupted Martin, his cheeks aflame. He lowered his voice. "You sure he'd want you saying where he lives and all? I don't know, but..."

Archie looked down, evidently reexamining the facts. He scratched the side of his face. "Who'd you say you work for?"

"Tom Richardson, an attorney in Olympia. He represents the estate of Simon Garrison. Mr. Garrison used to live up there on—"

"Oh yeah, sure, on Thompson Road," exclaimed Archie, letting a relieved smile show. "So you got nothing to do with Barbara Starr. That's Raleigh's wife—or ex, or whatever she is. You're not serving divorce papers or nothing like that?"

Clark chuckled and shook his head. "No. I've got nothing to do with that."

"Raleigh'd have me for lunch if I sent you over there with divorce papers." Archie looked at Martin. "I don't see a problem then. His babysitter got a flat on the way over this morning, so who knows when he'll get here. Just tell him to take his time, we got it covered around here."

"I'll do that," said Clark, drawing a pen and a small spiral notebook out of the inside breast pocket of his suit jacket. Mumbling to himself, he flipped to a blank page. "Fire away."

* * *

On the way to answer the knock on the door, Raleigh told six-year-old Michael—for the time being answering to "Peanut Butter Breath"—to get to the bathroom and brush his teeth.

From the sound of heavy steps on the wooden porch, this wasn't the babysitter. Who else would it be at 9:17 in the morning?

In the midst of the third round of knocks, Raleigh, dressed in his grease-stained overalls, opened the door to find a man in a gray business suit and dark gray fedora.

"Mr. Starr?"

"Yes. What do you need?"

This had better not be what I think it is. If she's changed her mind and wants the kids, she's in for one hell of a fight.

"Sorry to bother you. My name's Clark, Steve Clark." Clark pulled a business card from the pocket of his white shirt and handed it to Raleigh. "I work for Tom Richardson, an attorney in Olympia."

Shit, I knew it. You can have your goddam divorce, but you're not getting the kids.

His anger flared, then sank beneath the weight of something more immediate: his responsibility to Michael and Sandra now. Sandra was right behind him, playing with a Betsy McCall doll on the living room rug. Michael would want help with his teeth brushing.

Clark tilted his head. "Do you know Mr. Richardson?"

"I don't think so. Should I?"

"It was the way you reacted. I thought maybe you—"

"No. But I guess I was halfway expecting you. I guess she wasn't kidding." Raleigh frowned and held his hand out to receive the papers he was sure Clark had for him.

Clark hesitated. "I'm not here to serve you, Mr. Starr. I was hoping to ask a few questions."

Questions? What's this about? "Do you represent Barbara Starr?"

"No, sir. Mr. Richardson is a probate attorney. I'm here to ask you about a Mona Garrison."

Raleigh's eyes shot open. "What?"

Mona? Oh my God, is she dead? Did he say probate? Mona is...dead? On top of everything? Can this be happening?

"Do you know her, Mr. Starr? Or did you know her?"

Raleigh stared through Clark, unseeing. His heart was torn in two.

So she is... I can't bear... Not this, too. Jesus God. Is the whole world falling apart?

"You all right, mister?"

Raleigh's eyes focused at the sound of the stranger's voice. "How?" he mumbled.

"How what?"

"How'd she die?"

"Who?"

"Mona."

"Is she dead? Did you think I said she was dead?" Clark's square face twisted with confusion. "No, I said I'm trying to find her. We represent—Mr. Richardson represents—the estate of Simon Garrison."

Clark's words crawled into a mind clouded with grief and braced for bad news. Raleigh's adjustment was slow and theatrical, but a smile eventually dawned. He took hold of the square, padded shoulders of Clark's jacket. "So she's not dead." He laughed. "She's not dead after all."

"No, not that I'm aware of," said Clark uncertainly. "I'm just trying to locate her."

Raleigh continued to smile at the stranger. He pounded on the man's shoulders as though he were wearing shoulder pads. "That's great. Ha! That's great." Without thinking, he stepped further onto the porch, partially closed the door, straightened, and drew an audible breath.

Mona Garrison.

Raleigh looked directly into Clark's pinched blue eyes and shook his head. "Mona," he said, surprised and pleased to roll the sound around his mouth, to recall the sturdiness and fullness of her name spoken aloud. He resisted the temptation to repeat it. He pictured her as he had seen her last, with her grateful, speculative eyes looking into his as he sat on his motorcycle. He felt a sudden freedom unlike anything he had felt in weeks, a crumbling of walls.

Clark said, "We weren't able to find an address for her in Mr. Garrison's papers. I've been asking around." Raleigh had to concentrate on the man's mouth; so sudden and overpowering was the memory of the living Mona. Her smell, the warmth of her embrace, her lips on his cheek. Her gentle spirit. The way she sometimes tilted her head when she spoke to him. Her kindness.

God, I haven't felt this way in so long. I'm happy—right now, this warmth I feel is happiness.

"People around here don't seem to know much about her," Clark continued, "but yesterday, I spoke to someone in Spokane who said he knew of her in high school. Dale Hood. Do you know him? He said I should talk to you—that you'd know if anybody does."

"Dale Hood," Raleigh intoned, just able to keep the man and the memory of Mona separate. He was called back to the shocked look on Hood's face when he discovered him with Mona in the contestant line at the 1941 Western Washington State Fair. "Watch." Isn't that what Raleigh had said to Hood, pointing over the top of Mona's head?

A Ford coupe with loud pipes rumbled down Mosman Avenue. Raleigh followed it with his eyes.

Mona Garrison. Where is she? What's she up to? Does she look the same? Would she remember me?

"So?" said Clark. "You know where I can find her?"

"Huh?" Raleigh hesitated. All right, this man didn't represent Barbara, but he was tied to a lawyer just the same. Raleigh gave him a wary glance. "Tell me what you want with her again?"

"She's his beneficiary," said Clark. "The Mona Garrison Trust. He set it up for her—left her everything: the farm, his investments, his war bonds, the vehicles, everything."

Raleigh's head rocked back. "You're kidding."

"Nope. I read the file this morning. Mona Garrison lived with him and his wife in the thirties, up until about '41 or '42. His wife, Grace Garrison, died about four years ago. She'd sent Mona off to the custodial school in Buckley at age fifteen after she got involved with some neighborhood fella. Apparently, they thought she was retarded or something. Anyway, there's a note in the file that Mr. Garrison felt bad about this—didn't agree with it from the outset or something."

Raleigh stroked the corners of his mouth with his forefinger and thumb. He tasted the first acid drops of apprehension at the back of his throat.

"It went from bad to worse," continued Clark, with a storyteller's composure. "Turns out they sterilized her up there under the—"

The skin contracted between Raleigh's shoulder blades. "Wait a minute! What?"

"Yeah. Under the old eugenics program for the feebleminded."

The strength went out of Raleigh's legs. "You— Wait a minute. They couldn't have!"

"Against her will, too—at least, that's what one of the nurses tells me."

"Oh my God!"

"That was '43—September or October, something like that—a year after the Supreme Court struck down the law. Mona was the last one they ever sterilized up there."

The image of Mona being held down on a surgical table, struggling to free herself, raced through Raleigh's mind. He reached for the handrail.

"Are you all right?" asked the visitor. "Mr. Starr? Hey, you okay? You want to sit down?"

"Are you sure?" Raleigh heard himself say.

"What? Yeah. Hey, you don't look good."

"But..." Raleigh sank slowly to the landing. "How could they do this?" he mumbled. He looked up into Clark's eyes beseechingly.

Clark pointed toward the door. "Can I get you some water or something?"

Raleigh didn't answer. He was half aware of the man opening the apartment door, and the loud hiss of the kitchen faucet. When he felt the cool, wet glass in his hands, Raleigh looked up and nodded. For several minutes, he couldn't speak. His thoughts flew uncontrollably to the image of Mona lying with her abdomen cut open, of lines of blood coursing over her hips, of a doctor's gloved hands probing inside her. When he felt the slow upwelling of tears, he lowered his head and closed his eyes to try to banish the image. Looking up again, he couldn't make eye contact with Clark.

Clark shifted his weight on the steps. "So if you—"

Raleigh shook his head forlornly. "I don't know where she is," he muttered. "I have no idea." He sniffed and cleared his throat. A wave of anger rose inside him.

I've got to hold it together for the kids. At least until the babysitter gets here.

Clark nodded, reached for his small spiral notebook. "Do you know who might know? Can you give me any leads?"

"Her mom lived in Oregon," Raleigh answered. He brought his voice under control. "The Medford area, I think. Her mom lived in a group home of some kind." He disgorged this information in a monotone while staring at the parking strip. An idea struck him. He looked up at the shaking notebook. "She had a guardian. Someone named Ballard."

That's who must have done this.

"Not anymore," said Clark. "That was the first place I looked."

"What do you mean?"

"Mona was named in a lawsuit a couple years back. Brought by the parents of a gal she lived with when she turned twenty-one. This was after they'd been discharged from the custodial school. They both had guardians, but the parents were able to prove that that they weren't incapacitated after all. Both of them, it turns out, have IQs over 120. They have learning handicaps. Some new angle, I guess, on feeblemindedness. Anyway, they went to court to terminate their guardianships. There was quite a write-up in the *Seattle P-I.* They had psychiatrists, psychologists—the whole gamut—from all over hell and back testifying, and sure enough, they won. The guardianships were terminated, and the two gals were held to be competent. All of their rights were restored."

Raleigh looked up at Clark with his mouth open. *And that bitch was supposed to protect her.*

"I've contacted their lawyer, but she doesn't have a current address for Mona or her friend, Dorothy Lambert. Anyway, I guess Old Man Garrison was right. His niece did get a raw deal."

Clark seemed to wait for Raleigh to pick up the signal that he was ready to leave. Raleigh reached up to the handrail and lifted himself, not knowing where the strength was coming from.

I can't believe this.

"Well, I appreciate your time, Mr. Starr," said Clark, touching his fedora. "If you think of anything else, you have my card."

Raleigh didn't answer. *How could this…? Anyone who talked to Mona would know that she wasn't… But they were supposed to protect her. That was the whole deal.* He walked mechanically back into his apartment, closing the door behind him.

CHAPTER TWENTY-SEVEN

RALEIGH EMERGED with Lauren, George, and Wheels through the double doors of the dark outbuilding behind George Starr's house, relief painted on their faces. "That wasn't so bad," said Wheels, removing leather gloves.

It had been four months since Barbara left Raleigh, two and a half months since Clark's visit. Raleigh, bearded, strode to the back of his father's pickup, slammed the tailgate shut, and set the chain hooks. Lauren patted him on the shoulder. "This is the right thing to do, Raleigh. You're going to be happier here, and so will the kids."

"And so will I," said George, rubbing the back of his neck as he walked past them and made his way toward the house.

Lauren and Raleigh watched their father wade through the tall grass. After a few seconds, Raleigh said in a low tone, "I know you and Doug want to live out here. I don't want you to think I'm moving out here permanently."

"Of course you're not," said Lauren. "I know that." They watched their father climb the back steps, open the screen door, and disappear inside the house. "He can handle Michael and Sandra with help. I've got Mrs. Callahan coming on Mondays, Wednesdays, and Fridays, and I'll bring the kids over and help on Tuesdays and Thursdays. When you come home from work, that'll be his time to putter."

Raleigh scratched an ear. "They can be a handful."

"He knows that. He's been through it." Lauren raised arched brows toward her brother. "And you need to start doing better. You're not the first person to ever get a divorce. These kids depend on you. You fought for them, and now you have them, so for heaven's sake—" Lauren cut herself off when Wheels stepped closer. "You two behave," said Lauren, tapping the quarter panel of the Chevy truck and following her father's footsteps through the dew-laden grass.

"I got ten dollars says I won't," Wheels called after her, laughing. Lauren didn't turn. Wheels made a face. "She never did like me, did she?"

Raleigh smiled in spite of himself. "She likes you fine."

The two men retreated to the separate doors of the outbuilding and swung them closed. Raleigh produced a padlock from his back pocket and jammed it through the latch.

"I know—she wants me," Wheels declared facetiously. "She wants me, and she knows she can't have me, and that's tearing her apart."

"Yeah, that's it," said Raleigh, snapping the lock closed.

Wheels rolled down his sleeves and buttoned them. "Hey, so what are we going to do? Let's go by the dealership. Let me show you the new hydraulic hoists."

Raleigh stroked his beard and mustache. "No, I better stick around. Your wife will be bringing the kids by."

Wheels checked his watch. "I told Cindy noon. It's not even ten. C'mon, old man."

Raleigh walked toward the driver's door of the pickup. He remembered the state of the apartment, mold in the refrigerator, spaghetti sauce stains on the stovetop and down the side of the stove, Ry-Krisp crumbs on the draining board, toys strewn across the floor of the living room—a paddleball, dozens of scattered army men, a silver cowboy pistol in a silver-studded holster, at least three of Sandra's dolls. "Then I've got time to clean the apartment. Let me take you to your car."

"You said you were going to clean it tomorrow," Wheels insisted, sliding in on the passenger side. Raleigh didn't answer. He drove over the bumpy field toward the open gate. When they were through, with the truck idling on the gravel surface of Thompson Road, Wheels got out and closed the gate. "Let me at least buy you a piece of pie and a cup of joe," he said, getting in and slamming the door twice to get it to catch. "In fact, you can buy. I carried the heavy end of that steamer trunk, and you know it."

Half of Raleigh's mustache and beard twitched with a reluctant smile. "That can be arranged."

Raleigh drove the next seven miles without speaking. Wheels sat back for the first few minutes. Then he began to fidget. He opened and closed the glove box for no reason and switched on the radio after wondering out loud if the Washington-Stanford game had started. Through papery static, Keith Jackson's familiar voice was announcing the lineups when Wheels said, "You know, you and I should go up and see the USC game this year. It's going to be a dandy. Bunch of my old fraternity brothers are going." When Raleigh didn't answer, Wheels added, "Cindy's sister can watch the kids. Cindy and I'll go, and maybe you could invite Sally. I'll bet she'd go in a heartbeat."

Raleigh's brow puckered. "Ellington?" he said. "Isn't she seeing a dentist from Olympia or something?" He reached for a pack of Chesterfields on the dashboard and pushed in the lighter.

Wheels rolled down his window. "I've got it on good authority she's about to break up with him. Giving him the heave-ho."

Raleigh took the unlit cigarette out of his mouth. "No, thanks. Not after what I've been through."

Wheels turned in his seat. "Wait, I'm not done. Cindy says Sally's yours for the taking—says she's had it bad for you ever since..." Raleigh listened to his friend paint himself into a corner. "Ever since... Plymouth Rock."

"Doesn't matter," said Raleigh, studying the potholes and puddles ahead, but becoming animated. "I can't go to any football games, and I'd just as soon not talk about it."

"What do you mean you can't go to any—"

"I've got to work and raise these kids."

"But you can't work every goddamn day."

"No, but with all these people helping me..." he said, cast low by the ardency in Wheels's voice.

Wheels hesitated and emboldened himself further. "I think we should go to a game this season, even if it's just the two of us. You gotta give yourself a break, old man. I know it's been tough going back to the single life, but you got to start living again."

Raleigh's fist came down on the steering wheel with a loud thud. "Jesus, leave it alone, will you, Wheels?" Stunned by his outburst, Raleigh felt done in. Both men sat stone-faced in the gray light shining through the mud-streaked windshield, a ragged wall of silence between them. Raleigh eased the butt of his cigarette out the wing window. He shifted down as they approached East Fairview. After clearing the intersection he sped up and let the engine do the talking.

At the next stop, he looked past Wheels to check for traffic. He couldn't avoid seeing the hurt expression on his friend's face. Raleigh pulled onto East Fairview and within a few hundred yards edged the pickup onto a turnout next to an empty, paint-starved fruit stand. He shut off the engine and sat back.

"I gotta make this good; that's what I'm talkin' about," Raleigh said, staring straight ahead, his hands still on the wheel. The airy whine of a train in the distance filled the cab. "You think you're doing what has to be done, but then you find out different." Raleigh rolled down the window to spit out into the gravel. "All that time I thought Barb was going up to Seattle because she needed a break from the kids. I knew her mom was sick. She never did want to live down here. But, of course, then she had somebody else."

"Sure."

"I was…" Raleigh probed his teeth with his tongue, and his eyes grew wide with the effort to contain an unwanted emotion.

"Hang in there," said Wheels.

"It just pissed me off like you wouldn't believe. I didn't love her, not the way you're supposed to love a wife. But that's not the worst of it," said Raleigh, his voice distant and hollow. "I thought it was, but… You remember Mona Garrison?"

"Sure."

"You hear what they did to her up at that school?"

It was twenty minutes before Raleigh had ended the story, before the truck lurched forward again, before its worn rear tires spun in the loose gravel. Bouncing onto the paved surface of East Fairview, the engine roared mightily, two long throaty crescendos interrupted by the shifting of gears.

Wheels countered: "I know what you mean, they thought she was feebleminded, man. That's what they did back then. They thought it was for their own good, you know—for their own benefit."

Raleigh slung his left elbow out the window, felt the wind against the side of his face. "It was that bitch of a guardian." Moments later he was studying the road up ahead again. "Do you remember when we were at the lake and the Garrisons brought Mona up there to swim? I went over and talked them into letting me take her to the fair." Raleigh's knuckles were white on the steering wheel. "All to get Sally's attention."

"I saw Mona with my own eyes, Raleigh. Okay, it turned to shit, but you saw something special. You still hear it around here: 'Nobody dances like Mona Garrison.' You gave her that."

Raleigh fumbled with a pack of cigarettes and worked an "it's not about dancing anymore" into the next half mile. He was about to add "and she didn't deserve to be hurt" when Wheels changed the subject.

"So those new hydraulic hoists—we oughta go by and take a look. If I'm any kind of salesman, I'll have you working there someday anyway. That partnership deal is still on the table."

Raleigh shook his head. His eyebrows fierce, he said, "I'm hand to mouth. Don't you know that? I had to borrow from Dad to pay the lawyer."

"Yeah, I figured. But I told you before, it doesn't matter. Right?"

Raleigh stared at the passing houses. "It matters to me."

"Let's go by and take a look anyway."

Raleigh avoided eye contact. He turned on Mosman Avenue. "Another time, maybe."

* * *

"Don't forget what I told you about keeping the tip of the pole up," Raleigh said as he paddled the skiff to deeper water. Michael lifted the tip out of the water where it stayed for ten seconds or so. Raleigh shivered in the early morning breeze.

He's trying.

Raleigh smiled inwardly at the memory of his own fumbling attempts to learn to fish—on this small lake less than a mile from his father's farm, in this skiff, wearing the same stiff, adult-sized canvas life preserver stored in the rafters of his father's garage. Michael's head and thin arms jutted dwarf-like from the oversized life preserver. It was all the six-year-old could do to keep both hands on the pole. "You're doing great," Raleigh said, distracted by a lone male mallard whistling overhead.

"When will I catch a fish?" Michael asked impatiently.

"You have to wait till we stop the boat. Fish know better than to bite a worm moving through the water. They're down there scratching their heads, saying, 'Would you look at that worm? He's swimming! Worms don't swim. I've never eaten a swimming worm, have you, Harry?' And Harry says, 'No, and I'm not about to start, either.' And all the other fish are saying, 'Me neither, me neither.'"

"Worms don't swim," repeated a smiling Michael. The tip of his pole dragged in the water again, but this time Raleigh let it go.

* * *

"Wait till Mom sees the fish I caught," Michael said two hours later, his voice bursting with pride. Raleigh signaled, waited for traffic to clear, and turned onto Thompson Road.

He looked at his son, surprised. "I thought we were going to eat that fish for dinner."

"After I show Mom," Michael said matter-of-factly.

Raleigh pictured the scrawny, five-inch perch wrapped in a plastic bag and frozen like a severed finger in his father's freezer.

When Barbara comes, she can figure out what to do with it.

"She's going to be so proud of you," he said. "You're a good fisherman, you know that?"

Michael nodded.

They drove in silence, the truck rattling over the washboard surface. Twice, Michael turned to watch the tips of the fishing poles waggling over the tailgate. When they reached the edge of the woods south of the Garrison place, Raleigh slowed, and something in his manner caught his son's attention. "What is it, Dad?" asked the little boy.

Raleigh sat up. Two trucks were parked in the Garrisons' drive. Ladders rested against the north side of the house, and men in white coveralls were applying a fresh light yellow over the stripped wood.

Raleigh's breath caught. A sense of anticipation and uncertainty gave way to a feeling of dread.

Did they find Mona? Why are they painting it? Should I stop and ask? No. What if she's there?

He drove by slowly, looking over his shoulder.

Maybe they couldn't find her and they're fixing it up to sell.

Though the house was soon out of sight, Raleigh continued to replay the image of the two workmen on ladders and the fresh, shiny yellow streaks appearing beneath their brushes, the rest of the way home.

* * *

A few minutes later, Raleigh pulled into the weed-infested gravel drive. His father sat on the concrete front porch's top step watching Sandra play in the grass. No sooner had the truck come to a squeaky stop than Michael was out the door. "Grandpa! Grandpa! I caught a fish!"

"You did, huh?" The older man slapped his knee. "Well, how about that."

"Yup."

"What type of fish did you catch?"

"Dad said it was a whopper."

"A whopper?" Raleigh's father howled. "That's the best kind." He held out his hand. "Here, put her in the vise. Congratulations, son. That's terrific."

The handshake was a daily routine. George Starr was adamant that any grandson of his would develop a firm handshake.

"You go on and wash your hands," said Raleigh, carrying the poles and the creel from the back of the truck. Michael complied, and Raleigh sat on the porch next to his father, laying the poles beside him.

"I see you shaved off that godforsaken beard," said his father.

Raleigh had forgotten about it. He rubbed his chin. "Oh, yeah. I guess I did."

"So, what did the boy catch?"

Raleigh grinned. "Five-inch perch. Got it right in here." He lifted the creel off the ground. "He wants to show it to his mom."

"Figures."

"I'll stick it in the freezer, and we'll give her a surprise when she comes next week to pick up the kids."

His father blew a laugh through his nose.

"Say, Dad, I noticed some painters working down at the Garrisons' place. What's going on there?"

"No idea. When did that start?"

"They weren't there when we went out this morning—or if they were, I didn't see them. They're working on the north side of the house."

A logging truck slowed, the driver downshifting to thunderous effect and trundling past at a relative crawl to keep the dust down. Raleigh and his father waved their thanks and received a wave in return.

"Simon left all that property to Mona Garrison, you know," said Raleigh, watching the truck disappear in the distance. "In trust."

"That's what I hear," his father agreed. "Pretty odd altogether. They keep her cooped up in that school all those years. How's she supposed to take care of a farm?"

"That's what the trust is for."

"Still doesn't make a lot of sense to me. I wonder if that means they found her." Raleigh looked at his father, surprised. "He came by here, too—the fellow from the lawyer's office. He said he met with you." His father seemed to take a sudden interest in the toe of his right boot. "I've been meaning to talk to you, son."

Talk to me? About what? Don't tell me we've worn out our welcome already?

His father picked a long, seed-topped grass stem growing close to the porch where the mower couldn't reach. "You've had a lot going on this last little bit, and I haven't known what to say. Not much *to* say, I guess. But, uh, I hope—I think any father'd hope his son will take what's his and leave what's not. People have all sorts of things happen to them. Look at your mom, for example. Nothing I could have done about that, although I thought at the time I'd done something wrong."

Raleigh was surprised to hear his father talking about his mother, but something in his tone surprised him more. Whatever it was, his father had been thinking about this and rehearsing it for some time.

His father examined the long stem of grass and began to split it down the middle. "You just go on. And if you look around, so does everyone else. People are tough, son. This gal Mona is tough. She's going to be okay. I'm tempted to call anybody who survives this world, who marches on to old age, a hero. But you know—those who aren't heroes, they go on too. Most of 'em. Things happen—things they didn't want or don't like. But a day later, or a month later, or a year later, you look around and there they are, marching across that field right beside you. Sometimes you hate them for it, but unless you're set in your ways, that won't last."

Raleigh thought he understood, had a sense of his father's gist. "Take Barbara," his father continued. "I know what she did to you. But one day you'll look over your shoulder and she'll be marching across that field, going the same direction you're going—that we're all going. You're going to admire her for that—maybe pity her, too. We're all in Pickett's Charge, you see. You and Barbara. And Mona, too. This isn't a battle we win—none of us... That deal with Mona, that wasn't your doing. You know that, don't you?"

Raleigh nodded. His breathing slowed.

"You'd have done anything for her. I suspect she knew that."

Raleigh sat staring at Sandra, with a ball and miniature bat beside her, waving a toy army tank in her small hand. He looked up to the tall brown grass that choked the ditch hemming Thompson Road. Then his head fell forward and he shook it against the recurring image of Mona lying unconscious on the surgery table.

George patted his son's knee. "Find a way to let it go—that's what I'm saying. Mona's moving on. She's marching. Believe me, she is."

CHAPTER TWENTY-EIGHT

EIGHT HOURS LATER, Lake Lawrence stretched in front of Raleigh in the pitch-black night, appearing shoreless, without end. He stood with his arms and legs crossed, leaning back against the hood of his car, watching dim spears of light appear and disappear on the lake's inky surface. Bright afternoon memories of summer gatherings and swimming parties seemed to tremble just beneath his feet. And the fires they'd lit? He could have smelled the pine smoke, maybe even the stale odor of beer, he was sure, if he'd troubled himself to breathe deeply enough.

A lightheartedness came and went as though the wheel of all possibilities had turned. *But if lightheartedness is possible*—and he broke off to look down the beach toward the place where she had been, in that ancient black bathing suit, wading over the slippery rocks.

What does it mean that I can't see it? That I can't make out the cedar that stretches into the water? The spot where I lied, where I looked Mrs. Garrison in the eye and told her she and her husband were welcome to join us at the fair?

He began to think of something else, of the war years, of all that had been lost and sacrificed. Steve Lockhart, the Ohioan, and the other men sprawled so hideously in that foxhole. Ted Ellington over Sicily. Ronald Zandt in France. The dozens of men he'd seen carried out of shot-up bombers and fighters in Guam. And then there was Sally. And Mona. One casualty after another.

"Let it go. Find a way to let it go," his father had said.

Can I? Will this night swallow it all? Can there just be me, here, now? Raleigh shivered. No regrets?

He could hear his father's voice again. "Look over your shoulder. You'll see her marching forward. Life goes on."

It's not just me. They did this. That damn guardian and whoever the doctor was… But Mona. She's marching.

A shudder of utter delight came out of nowhere and raced up Raleigh's spine. He could not—no one, he thought, could—expect it to last. But had it come, this hope, heralding the end of a nightmare? He smiled involuntarily into the darkness. To make it real, he had to be closer to her. He'd been avoiding her all this time, not looking at the house as he passed—when he could help it—hoping against hope that he wouldn't run into her in town. That was all the press of regret. But if regret could be let go…?

You will see her marching forward.

Sprung by a sudden hope that she was there, right in that house, he rushed around the end of the car. He had to see her. He had to see the house that held her, at least.

He fishtailed from the lake road onto Thompson Road. The car seemed to float; the potholes were as trifles. Fifteen minutes later, he took an unlikely pleasure in the dust cloud that swept over the sedan as he rolled to a stop 200 yards south of Mona's house. The cloud vanished when he killed the lights. In the distance, there it sat: four gold-lit windows, all on the ground floor, and the rest of the house visible in outline—what he'd known his whole life as "the Garrison place."

You're marching beside me. He imagined Mona somewhere inside. Beyond the house, he could make out the ghostlike image of the barn, its sliding door and hayloft door both open. But how much smaller this was than the old barn. Oh, how he'd wanted out of that horror of black smoke and stench. Where was the mama cat? That's what she'd wanted to know. That's what that look had been for.

It's funny—I put her teenage face in that memory. But no, her features were small and narrow. Her cheeks were concave, and her legs were like spikes. She ran clumsily. And I'm doing the same thing now. I'm imagining she hasn't changed since '42. Of course she has. That was eleven years ago. I have no idea how she looks.

He put his elbow on the window frame and rested his head on his fist. No sign of life, no movement beyond the blinds.

He found it fitting that the window above the porch roof was unlit. *Let it stay that way. If it's hidden in the dark, I can let it go.* Her undulating hips, the pull and release of her nightgown over the contours of her lithe teenage body, strands of hair stuck to the moistness of her face. The driving rhythm pouring through the open window. His abandonment of the road for pleasure—not least that.

His heart leapt to her. He imagined something like the dance corrupted by unwanted hands, reaching adult hands of orderlies and nurses, encircling hands dragging her backwards from the window and down. Her fight as true as her dance, around her blue eyes the whites showing, but one last fugitive glance, too—a question thrown down to him.

Raleigh closed his eyes. It was no good.

He sat up, fingered the key in the ignition. The hint of a shadow moved across one of the windows. He leaned back again. Was it her? It must have been.

"Let it go," his father had said. "Find a way."

But it was all for Sally. God, what they did to you…

It was not then but ten minutes earlier, when he'd raced over the singing gravel of Thompson Road, that an image had flashed before his eyes. It seemed to depart as soon as it had come, but it had set its stamp on the night. It was the memory of sand grains and flecks, the world reduced to a patch of bulletless, deathless ground at the base of a palm tree. With the roar of an approaching Zero in his ears, he had asked, "Could this be the world?" And, in truth, it was world enough for him.

Now, in his abstracted mind, he said: And she—whatever her condition—she is world enough. *A life where the limits can be seen. No chasing—or being chased—beyond boundaries. No fear of a breach.*

"Let me have what I can see," he whispered to himself on the way home.

* * *

Four days later, Raleigh knocked-off at four-twenty, leaving parts of an ornery Pontiac transmission strewn over the length and width of a soiled canvas tarp. He groused about it in the office. "Hope this place doesn't blow up overnight. Hate to lose the chance to spend another five hours on what should have been a two-hour job." Archie's laughter was little comfort, although Raleigh, after grabbing his lunch pail, winked at the shop owner and surrendered a crooked smile on the way out. He turned the key and sat back, pumping the accelerator, letting the stress of the day slowly slough off. He remembered his plan to stop at Wolf's grocery store on the way home.

"What? You do the shopping, too?" Raleigh recognized Joe Zandt's voice across the grocery store parking lot and wasn't surprised to find his old high school classmate leaning against the open door of his Plymouth. Zandt evidently realized his mistake and blushed profusely. "Oh, God, Raleigh. Sorry about that. I forgot."

"That's all right. How you doing, Joe?" Raleigh nodded a greeting to Joe's wife through the window of their car, but her look of commiseration left him cold.

Zandt let a station wagon entering the parking lot pass between them before answering. "Great, I guess. Hey, I see you shaved. Are you back among the living now?"

"Maybe."

"You coming to the class picnic on Saturday? It's at Eldon's place this year."

No was the answer, but Raleigh said: "I wasn't planning on it. What time?"

"You oughta come. Noon, I think."

Raleigh had started for the grocery store's entrance, walking backwards. "We'll see." He waved good-bye and turned around.

"I think Sally's going to be there, if you're interested."

Lord, if you would all just quit dangling her in front of me.

He waved back over his shoulder carelessly. Seconds later, he was swallowed by the relative darkness of the store.

He picked up a shopping basket and swerved to the left, toward the vegetables.

As if I have time for a picnic.

Faint smells—strawberries, floor wax, freshly baked bread—filled his nostrils, overcoming the odor of grease and oil from his overalls.

I'll get corn and green beans for tonight and beets for tomorrow.

He would be managing the kids on Saturday, and the last thing he had at his disposal were any chits for babysitting. He weaved through the two lines at the checkout, exchanging hellos with several people he knew. He waited under a murky light for a tangle of grocery carts to clear. Growing impatient, he detoured around them and arrived at a large, round table—new since his last visit. It was a clearance toy display: red, yellow, blue, and white beach balls; jigsaw puzzles; pink and orange plastic tea sets; tennis rackets. He picked up a paddleball game to replace one Michael had broken. He examined it before stuffing the crinkling, plastic-wrapped toy back into its jam-packed cardboard display box.

The elastic band will last about a day. Let's get our groceries and get out.

He veered toward mounds of colorful vegetables. A subtle but unmistakable improvement in the quality of the air coincided with a slight revival of his spirits. It had been a long day. That transmission had given him fits, but tomorrow was another day.

A sale announcement over the loudspeaker was followed by something orchestral. A syrupy cover of a Frank Sinatra song. He rested his basket on the shimmering edge of the display case. The string beans looked good. So did the summer squash. He'd go with both.

While waiting his turn for a paper bag, his eyes wandered to the nearest dry goods shelves twenty feet away. Beyond loaves of Wonder Bread, in the narrow space open to the next aisle, he caught sight of a face at once strange and familiar.

It looks like her, but—oh my God, is it her?

The woman stood with eyes downcast, a scowl on her face, reading—or attempting to read—a label on the back of a jar. She raised the jar up to the light. Her eyes seemed immense to him.

They were never that big, were they? And her hair. It's so much longer. And wavier. And she has no bangs. Her hair's parted down the middle. Didn't Mona used to part her hair on the side? No, maybe that's not her.

He couldn't see the woman's mouth.

The nose is right, but this woman has a harder look. No, it can't be…

And then she did it: she pulled her hair back over her left ear, and the move was so characteristic of Mona that he could not have forgotten it in a million years. She lifted her chin and her upper lip came into view for a split second. Her gracefully arched upper lip.

Raleigh's heart leapt into his throat.

Oh, God. Mona!

Where seconds before he'd found ample reasons for doubt, every angle of her forehead, the roundness and flush of her cheeks, the folds and shape of her ear—everything—was *her*. He stumbled back against another shopper. "Oh, excuse me," he said, disoriented, turning one way and another. The women around him—they were all women—stared.

"Are you all right, young man?" said a gray-haired woman wearing a silver and garnet barrette, her bulbous blue eyes magnified by black butterfly frame glasses.

Raleigh stared as though he were hearing English uttered for the first time, then turned back to the vision beyond the Wonder Bread.

Mona? Oh God, it is her.

She hadn't moved, and appeared to be struggling to read the same label. Her concentration was fixed somewhere between the object and her dark blue eyes.

Raleigh lost track of time. He next became aware of himself sidestepping behind the crowd gathered at the summer toy table. He dashed behind a life-size cardboard cutout of William Boyd as Hopalong Cassidy. He had no vegetables, no groceries.

Oh God, I'm an idiot.

He peeked over the head of the Western film hero. He'd left his shopping basket balanced on a pile of yellow summer squash. He gave an awkward smile to the women still staring at him from the vegetable section, then turned and measured the distance to the door with his eyes.

From this vantage point, he could see Mona completely. His heart filled with an intensity of emotion that threatened to immobilize him. Was it remorse? Fear? Desire? It had elements of all of these, but…

Jeez, she's beautiful. Her face is so much older—but, of course, she's older.

Mona looked up and turned her head toward him. He dipped down again. When he peered out at last—this time, absurdly, to the side of Hopalong's head—she had returned to the task at hand. Raleigh ran on tiptoes the last five steps to the double doors and out into the warm afternoon air. With his mind reeling, he made his way to his car and got in as though he were being chased.

He found a tolerable rhythm to his breathing again. "I can't believe it," he said, putting his hand on his chest. He felt droplets of moisture collecting and spilling down inside his shirt.

It's really her!

He swallowed with difficulty.

What did I expect? Of course, I was going to see her. When she comes out, I'll talk to her. I'll say hello. Maybe I should go back in and talk to her. I've got to go back for groceries anyway.

The thought terrified him. "I'm an idiot. Even getting shot at I wasn't this scared."

How's she going to react? No, I'll wait.

Five minutes later, he was still talking to himself, rubbing his hands one way and the other over the steering wheel.

She looks so good.

He glanced into the rearview mirror at the incipient crow's-feet on his face, moved his mouth back and forth to look for frown lines. He was glad he'd shaved his beard.

Something in the look of his eyes unsettled him. The heaviness in his chest had returned.

If this isn't misery, what is? I should drive out of here as fast as I can. With my luck I'd pass the doors just as she comes out. She'd see me. No, I better stay put. As if you want to leave, you fraud. The Borax mule team couldn't drag you away.

Sweat began to roll from his armpits. He opened the side window and lit a cigarette, hoping, perversely, that she wouldn't come out.

Wouldn't it be great if she went out the back door? Escaped through the alley?

He would have laughed had he been in a better mood. He watched shoppers emerge from the darkened double doors: an assortment of older women, young women, couples, all but two pushing noisy grocery carts over the asphalt parking lot, some putting on sunglasses but most squinting under the bright afternoon overcast. The hems of the women's colorful rayon dresses flapped in the breeze.

When Mona appeared in the doorway at last, Raleigh exhaled a second long, slow, nervous breath into his fist. She pushed a cart with three bulging bags of groceries and her purse. She forced the cart over the lip of the threshold, stopped to put on a large pair of sunglasses, and eased the cart down the ramp.

Raleigh's heart went to full stop. His mouth fell open involuntarily.

She angled the cart toward the line of cars parked across from him, and as she drew closer, he sunk down by inches.

Could I be any more ridiculous? What in the world is wrong with me?

Mona was in front of his car, no more than twenty feet away. She looked straight ahead. As she passed, Raleigh sat up again, unable to take his eyes off her.

I've got to go out there. What about the restraining order? That was more than ten years ago. She was a kid. I…I have to acknowledge her. I can't avoid her. Let me at least say hello, and I'm glad to see you.

As he pulled the door handle and felt the latch release, he spotted someone else. A large man in his early thirties was approaching Mona—clean-shaven but with a permanent five o'clock shadow, his dark hair home to a single wave over the top of his scalp. He wore a wrinkled white shirt that stretched and smoothed itself over a large belly, and a thin blue tie, loose at the neck.

What's this? Where'd he come from? Is he going to talk to her?

As the man drew closer to Mona, she stepped away from the cart, and he took over and began to push it while Mona continued to walk at his side. He said something to her, and she responded with a gentle smile and a few words, but otherwise the two didn't look at each other. They stopped at the back of a tan 1952 Chrysler New Yorker. The man fished in his pants pocket for his keys and opened the trunk.

Raleigh sat back, groaning softly.

Oh my God, don't tell me she's married.

He tried to think of other possibilities, but nothing came to him.

Oh shit! Of course she is. Why wouldn't she be? Why the hell didn't I think of this? A beautiful woman would… Mona Garrison, married. And you—idiot—thinking you could love her forever. That you've loved her all these years.

Raleigh opened and shut his door again as quietly as possible, then smiled in spite of himself when the dark-haired man, but not Mona, glanced in his direction.

It figures—you would look and not her.

Less than a minute later, Raleigh watched in disbelief as Mona got into the Chrysler. The two drove away without talking, making a slow, cautious, settled-into-marriage turn on to Jefferson.

CHAPTER TWENTY-NINE

LAUREN LOOKED ONCE, twice at the woman kneeling beside the weed-infested flower bed in front of the Garrison place, her back to the road. "Is that Mona?" *That is her.* She brought her car to a stop, leaned over, and opened the passenger-side window. It was sweltering inside the car. "Mona?" she called out. "Is that you?"

The woman twisted around and shaded her eyes.

"Yes?" said Mona haltingly, standing up.

Lauren smiled and waved enthusiastically. "It's me, Lauren." *My, she's all grown up. Her face is thinner. She's changed her hair color.*

Mona's wary expression softened into a smile. She dropped a handful of weeds and walked toward the car, stopping at the edge of the rough lawn. Squinting one moment, shading her eyes the next, she said, "Wonderful to see you."

"I'll say!" *Such a good-looking woman! I wonder if she's okay.* "I heard you were back. The rumors were true, huh?"

Mona chuckled. "I guess so." She gazed into the back seat at the children. Her smile widened. She looked back at Lauren. "Do you have time for coffee?"

Lauren thought for a second, then held up a small brown paper sack. "If you have time for a cookie. I made these this morning for Dad. The kids have been pestering me since we left the house to have one. Truth is, I wouldn't mind one myself."

Mona laughed. "Sure. And I have milk for the kids."

I wonder if he's been by to see her.

Mona brought two steaming cups of coffee rattling on saucers from the kitchen. Lauren, who'd been eyeing the boxes stacked at the bottom of the stairs, reached out to take one. They chatted for a quarter of an hour and finally Lauren thought to ask, "How'd you meet this Dr. Wells and her husband?"

Mona moved the sugar bowl closer and said, "She's a friend of Dr. Snodgrass. He spoke at the trial—the trial with Dorothy and me. He called and said he had a friend in Federal Way looking for a live-in housekeeper, and would I like to meet her."

"And you lived there how long?"

"A year and a half."

"I bet they were sorry to see you go."

Mona sipped her coffee. "They've invited Dorothy and me for Thanksgiving. That's wonderful, isn't it?"

Lauren chuckled. "Do you have to clean the house when you go back?" *She's just as sweet and unassuming as ever. What are you going to do, Raleigh? But maybe she has someone.*

Mona smiled. "I don't think so. They've hired another girl."

Lauren glanced at her children eating quietly at the dining room table, then let her eyes travel half the circumference of the living room. "So this is your place now." She turned to find Mona staring down at the ripples in her coffee.

"Yes," Mona said at last. "I don't know how I got so lucky."

"Can you manage all this?" When Mona didn't answer, Lauren said, "Of course you can. There's a trustee, isn't there? The lawyer."

"Mr. Richardson," said Mona, looking up.

"He'll help you. And I'm here if you need anything. And so is Dad...and so is Raleigh."

"Thank you, but I've got friends helping me right now."

Lauren waited for more, watched Mona reach for a cookie, examine it, and take a bite. *She didn't react to Raleigh's name. I need to protect him if she's moved on. It would be better if I told him.*

"These are delicious," Mona said.

"Do you have someone in your life, Mona? A husband? A boyfriend?"

Mona swallowed and licked her lips. "No."

Lauren set her cup down and turned it, examining its floral design. "What are your plans now that you're here?"

"Work. I want to work, clean houses. Mr. Richardson says there's money from the sale of Uncle Simon's war bonds and such, but I should save it. Do you know anybody in Yelm who needs a housecleaner?"

"Aunt Edith has Mrs. Sprague now; otherwise, I know she'd love to have you back. I'll tell you what: I'll keep my ear to the ground."

"Mr. Richardson's helping me get a business license. He's coming tomorrow night to go over the paperwork."

"Mommy," said Lauren's son. "Can I have another cookie?"

"No, those are for Grandpa. You and Karen finish up so we can deliver them." Lauren smiled at Mona.

"Would the kids like more milk?" Mona asked, putting her cup on the coffee table.

"No, they're fine. We need to run. We'll let you get back to your weeding."

Mona stood up after Lauren. "I hope you'll drop by again," she said.

"Oh, we will, we will. Come along, you two. Put your glasses in the kitchen."

Mona slid a lock of hair behind her left ear. "Is Raleigh all right? I haven't seen him."

Lauren's brows shot up. *Doesn't she know about the restraining order?* "You haven't? He hasn't stopped by at all?"

Mona shook her head. Five-year-old Karen ran crashing into Mona's legs and hugged her. Mona smiled and squeezed her back. "Thank you so much for coming. Will you come visit me again?" Karen nodded.

Would they arrest him for saying hello? After ten years? "I'll tell him to get his rear end down here to say hello," said Lauren.

Peter was next to hug Mona, adding, "Thank you."

"You're welcome, sweetheart," said Mona. "No, don't tell him. I know I'll see him when the time is right." She followed her company down the porch steps and chatted with Lauren about inconsequential things, about her need to acquire a truck and learn to drive, and the advantages of a pickup over a car for someone in the housecleaning business.

* * *

The moment he heard steps approaching the door, Raleigh thought of Mr. Garrison. It would hardly have surprised him if the thick-chested old man had opened the door, greeted him, and stepped back to let him in. He could imagine the half-smile of his former neighbor's thin lips—the red suspenders over a sturdy plaid shirt. Things were not so different now. The freshly painted house was gray in the moonlight—no different than it had ever been. The small, concrete porch was the same. The cool night air tinged with the scent of the cottonwoods and earthy, dew-laden grass was the same. The house reverberating with footsteps—as always. Only the light from the window of the front room was brighter than it had been before, and this night it lit—even revealed the colors of—the Cadillac and the Chrysler New Yorker parked in front.

Raleigh felt a tremor in his chest remembering that Mr. Garrison was dead and that the home, which all his life had been "the Garrison place," was now Mona's and her husband's. He couldn't imagine whose Cadillac this was or who was about to open the door. What would he have said to Mr. Garrison? "I can't tell you how sorry I am about what they did to Mona up there at the custodial school. Those bastards should be strung up. I'm sure, had you known—"

Had you known, it never would have happened. None of this.

The porch light went on. The door opened. Beyond the screen stood the apple-shaped man Raleigh had seen several days earlier in the parking lot at Wolf's grocery store. "Yes? Can I help you?"

Mona's husband was shorter than Mr. Garrison had been, filled much less of the doorway. He'd seemed taller in the parking lot. The fact that he had a strong, protruding brow and dimples that pulsed in and out when he talked was news to Raleigh. *Fine. He's a decent-looking fellow. Good. I'm happy for her.*

"Hello," Raleigh said, opening the screen door and extending his hand toward the man. "I'm Raleigh Starr. I'm a neighbor from up the way."

"Tony Lambert," said the man uncertainly, taking Raleigh's hand.

"Is Mona home?" Raleigh leaned over to look past Tony. Mona sat at the dining room table wearing a long-sleeved white blouse and a red skirt. Beside her was a man of fifty-five or sixty in a gray suit with a thin black tie. He held a sheet of paper in his hand and sat frozen, leaning slightly toward Mona, as though he'd been explaining something to her. Mona held a pen in her hand. Both of them were looking up. A strange feeling began to overtake Raleigh.

"Raleigh?" she said uncertainly.

Tony stepped back to let Raleigh in. "I'm a friend of your wife's," Raleigh explained, slapping Tony's shoulder good-naturedly as he passed and moved toward the living room.

Tony took a further step back, taken by surprise. "I think there must be..." His voice trailed off as he walked into the living room a step behind Raleigh. "I'm sorry. Who did you say you were?"

"Raleigh Starr. I've known your wife for more years than I can count." Raleigh stared at Mona, tried to smile, tried to pretend everything was all right, but he felt the muscles in his face beginning to ache and lose function, and the blood draining from his face. *Oh my God, can I do this? Yes, I have to.* His unfocused eyes shifted to the man sitting to Mona's left.

Something doesn't seem right, but I don't know what.

He thought of the door behind him, remembering how he'd flailed to find the ladder in the loft of the burning barn. Was this any different? Wasn't his heart beating just as fast now?

Breathe. Breathe!

The middle-aged man was on his feet, buttoning his coat. His lips moved around his name, but Raleigh didn't hear it. Thomas Something-or-other. "I'm Mona's attorney. We're just going over some paper—"

Don't run. Not again. Say what you're here to say, then go.

"I just want to get this out," Raleigh said. He ignored the man's hand but gave him a compensating nod. "Please excuse me. All of you." He let his eyes blur over Mona's surprised, open face. There was a sound coming from the kitchen of dishes being stacked. *All right, someone else is here. It doesn't matter. It's Mona and her husband I need to talk to.*

Mona started to stand up. "No," said Raleigh preemptively. She sat again. "Please, Mona, just let me... This is my fault. None of this would have happened if I had just—if I had left you alone. I lied to your aunt and uncle, and I took you to the Osprey Club like an idiot. It was childish of me." Richardson, the attorney, looked at Mona, confused. "And then—" Raleigh, without taking his eyes off Mona, took a half-step back so that her husband could hear. "And then, I fell in love with you." He glanced at Tony. "That's right. And I went out there to the custodial school during the war to see her."

Raleigh was almost shouting now, a kind of low-volume shout. An attractive blonde woman in her mid-twenties appeared in the kitchen door, wiping a plate with a white dish towel. She settled against the doorframe to listen. "So, you see, it's all my fault. What they did to her." He looked back at Mona. "What they did to you, Mona. I did that."

Mona shook her head slightly, a tender light in her eyes.

"I need you to forgive me—both of you."

Tony began, "I think you may have—" but Raleigh cut him off by throwing his hand up.

"No. Please. I… I know what you're going to say." But Raleigh didn't know, and against a growing sense that something was wrong—he couldn't put his finger on it—he pushed on. "With the restraining order and all, I shouldn't even be here. I know that." Raleigh faced Mona again.

That's probably it. Her husband knows about the restraining order. He wants me to leave.

"But I had to come. I was an idiot, Mona. I took advantage of you. However long it takes, I'll wait the rest of my life for you to forgive me. Now, I really have to—"

Raleigh wanted three things as he dashed toward the door: to hear Mona's sweet voice one more time, to not hear anything from anyone—which was contradictory—and then to be gone. To be miles away. He had managed to reach the bottom step of the porch when another idea struck him. He swore under his breath, then tore back through the screen door and entered the home to find everyone exactly where he'd left them, with the same surprised and nonplussed expressions on their faces—except for the blonde woman in the kitchen door, who was smiling and bent over on the verge of laughter. Raleigh waited until Tony turned to him. He felt the blood rise to his face. "I'm sorry—Tony is it?—there's one more thing. Take her to Glacier Park, will you? She wants to go. Don't ask me how I know that, just do it. It's her dream." He spun around and headed for the door.

Less than a minute later, as he sped down Mona's drive he was cursing himself roundly. His car dipped into a steep pothole then jumped up onto the surface of Thompson Road.

CHAPTER THIRTY

THE NEXT DAY, a little after one in the afternoon, George Starr stood frozen at the sight of the guest at his front door. Mona had stopped just off the mat carrying a bundle wrapped in a blue- checked dish towel. A shy, self-conscious smile played across her mouth. "Good afternoon, Mr. Starr." She colored slightly behind her handful of remaining freckles. "I don't know if—I'm Mona," she said. "I—"

"Of course," George said, stepping back and opening the door wider. "Come in, won't you?" He looked at the bundle.

Mona inched closer but didn't cross the threshold. She pushed the bundle forward. "I made this," she said.

George took it with an embarrassed smile. The aroma of the warm apple pie wafted back into her nostrils from the foyer. "That's wonderful, Mona. Thank you."

"It's for Raleigh...and for his children, and you," Mona intoned, as though calling on reserves of concentration. "And Lauren and Doug and Karen and Peter."

George looked over Mona's shoulder toward the driveway. "How'd you get here?"

Mona blinked self-consciously. "Oh. I...I had a friend drop me. I hope that's okay."

George seemed to grapple with an idea as he nodded. He moved to the foot of the stairs. "Michael! Sandra! You kids come down here. We're going to go get a soda."

"A soda?" came a young voice. "Honest?"

Screams of delight and the sounds of scampering feet filled the house. Michael ran down the stairs, followed by Sandra. They stopped at the sight of the strange woman standing at the door.

"Michael, Sandra, this is a friend of ours, a friend of your dad's. This is Miss Garrison. Can you say hello?"

Michael lowered his eyes then stepped forward and reached out a small hand. Mona shook it, squeezing her lips together and furrowing her brow in response to the six-year-old's exaggerated solemnity. Behind him, Sandra curtseyed.

"Hello," said Mona, curtseying in response. Michael stretched to see what the blue and white dishcloth held. "I've brought you some apple pie. Do you like apple pie, Michael?" When Michael nodded enthusiastically, Mona knelt down to talk to Sandra face-to-face. "How about you, sweetheart? Do you like apple pie, too? You do? Me too. It's one of my favorites."

She looked up at George with eyes sparkling. "Oh, they're so precious! What beautiful grandchildren you have!"

George mumbled his agreement but seemed more interested in moving the kids along. "All right, let's get in the car. Here, let me put this in the kitchen." Mona stood up. "Can you keep an eye on them?" said George.

"Of course," said Mona. She watched the children scamper past her and pile into the indigo-blue Pontiac in the drive.

"And now, Miss Garrison," said George when he returned, taking a tattered, grease-stained baseball cap from a hook on the wall and placing it on his head. He raised his brows expectantly. "If you'll excuse us." He stepped out on the porch. "You'll find Raleigh in the small shed out back. You can go around that way."

"Thank you."

George spoke over his shoulder as he descended the steps. "Tell Raleigh we'll be back in an hour, will you?"

"Sure."

* * *

Mona tiptoed to within six feet of Raleigh, who was bent over the engine of his father's Model A pickup. "Hello again," she said.

"Oh!" Raleigh jumped back, nearly tripping over his toolbox. "You scared me." Raleigh's mouth fell open next. "Oh." Mona stood in the calf-high grass beyond the threshold. Her smile widened in two stages in the face of Raleigh's changing expressions.

"It's you," he whispered.

Mona nodded. "I didn't mean to..."

"It's all right. I didn't expect you, is all." He tried to smile.

"I brought a pie," said Mona. "Your dad put it in the kitchen."

Oh, my God. She is so beautiful.

"It's an apple pie," she added.

That look. She's not angry. She's marching...like you said, Dad.

Mona's shoulders dropped as though she'd been holding onto something but had to let it go. "I'm so glad you remembered that we danced at the fair, Raleigh. I've always wondered if you did."

"Are you kidding? I'll never forget." The relief shining in Mona's eyes transformed Raleigh's mood. "And I'll always remember it...the way you looked that night." It was not what he meant to say. He meant to say: "and I will always remember you, Mona," but something prevented him from saying this at the last moment. Mona looked down and smiled. "I'm afraid that's just how it is."

He realized two things: that he was on the verge of speaking before thinking—without thinking—to a married woman, just like he'd done the night before, and that what seemed to stretch out before him, in thought, was a serene sea of the substance of truth such as he had never known. Yes, she was married, but no one would ever take these feelings away from him. A whole expanse, silvery, sunlit, and doubtless. He caught himself and raised his eyes above the shimmering surface to the textured sky.

"I remember that night, too," Mona said. She colored slightly as the seconds passed without a response from Raleigh. "I made the pie this morning...for you."

Did she hear what I said? Maybe she's trying to ignore it. She's married, after all... Wait! Did she say she made a pie for me?

"For me?" he asked.

"Yes. But I know you'll share it with Michael and Sandra, and your father, and Lauren and her family, too." She blushed. "And I will have to make you another one, I promise."

Raleigh chuckled. "You're too kind. You don't have—"

"No, please." She hesitated and seemed to weigh some initiative in her mind. "I'm sorry your wife left you."

Raleigh's smile vanished. "How do you know about that? And how do you know Michael and Sandra's names?"

"Your father introduced me," she said, pointing back toward the house. "I met them. They're wonderful."

"And Barbara—you know about her?"

"Is she your wife?"

Raleigh nodded. "She was. Not anymore."

"Lauren told me she left you. I'm so sorry, Raleigh."

Behind him, his frustration and regret: like a black basalt cliff a thousand feet high, capable of crumbling. Before him, that sea as flat as a mirror.

Married, but unable to have… I wish you hadn't come. I know that sea is you.

Raleigh picked up a rag from on top of the radiator and began to wipe his hands. He glanced up at Mona then walked around to the other side of the Model A and lifted the hood panel. "This thing has about had it," he said to distract himself. "Do you remember this old beast?"

Mona stepped closer and looked past his shoulder. "If anyone can fix it, you can."

Her scent reached his nostrils. It was the same sweet, slight jasmine smell he remembered.

She's not giving me a chance.

She stood with a hand on one hip. "I have a favor to ask you."

Oh Jesus, I love her smell. Of all the women in the world… A favor?

He looked up while his hand tested a hose clamp. "Oh, yeah?"

"In exchange for the pie."

She was being funny. *You have to know Mona to know when she's being funny. I know her. I know Mona Garrison.*

"What's the favor?"

"I want you to teach me to drive a Chevrolet—a red 1953 Chevrolet pickup," she said. Raleigh straightened. "Uncle Simon's trust is buying it. All I have to do is learn to drive and get a license." Mona seemed amused by Raleigh's expression.

Wow! What confidence. She's changed.

"What's wrong with the Garrisons' old Buick?" he asked.

"The attorney says I can get a pickup. A reliable one. I told him I wanted a pickup for my cleaning supplies. The way you used to do it."

"You told him that?"

Mona pushed a wedge of hair behind her left ear. "Yes. He's my trustee. There's money, but I need to work. And I want to. Will you do it? Lauren told me you would."

Raleigh's brow puckered. "Lauren?"

"When she stopped by with the cookies. She said she was going to talk to you, but I said I would talk to you myself."

Raleigh felt the skin at the back of his neck tingle. *You don't know about the restraining order, do you? But Lauren does. What was she thinking?*

"What about your husband? Can't he teach you to drive?"

Mona erupted in laughter.

"What?" said Raleigh, swiping the bottom of his nose with the back of his wrist.

"My husband?"

"Tony, or whatever his name is."

Mona's expression brimmed with amusement.

"The one last night—the one who helped you with the groceries last week, and drove off with you." Raleigh's voice was tinged with righteousness, but he had a sinking feeling all the same.

"Tony? He's not my husband." She looked at her hands. "He's a friend. Tony Lambert. He and Dorothy—she's my best friend—are helping me get set up." Mona's eyes went to a new idea, and her mouth opened wide. "That was *you*!"

"What do you mean?"

"At the grocery store. A woman came... She told me a crazy-looking man had stared at me from behind a cowboy—Hopalong Cassidy—and I should be careful. He was hiding, but he ran away."

Raleigh's shame was complete. "You... I didn't know if..."

Mona tilted her head and offered a smile that Raleigh found agonizingly attractive. He tried to focus on that and not relive the embarrassing episode. "So he's not your husband," he heard himself say. A strange flutter began in his chest. Doors and shutters that he thought were closed forever were flying open in quick succession. "Or your boyfriend or anything like that?" Mona shook her head.

But last night, I told him to take you to Glacier Park. Why didn't you...? Why didn't anybody...? Because I ran out of the house before anyone could say a word, that's why.

"But he could still teach you to drive," Raleigh said to fill the silence, regretting the words almost the second they'd left his lips. He didn't know what he was doing.

You mean you're really not married? You have no—?

"No. Oh, maybe, but Lauren said you'd do it. And Wheels did, too."

"Wheels?"

Do what? Oh, teach you to drive you mean. I would, but what about—?

"He said you'd have time. He said you've been hankering to come in and see the shop. I think he thinks you want to work there, but you don't know it yet, or something like that. That's what he said. He called you his silent partner."

Raleigh shook his head wearily.

"He said you were the most silent of all silent partners in the world." Mona laughed. "Like a mummy in Egypt."

"He did, huh?" Raleigh smiled with one side of his mouth. "And let me guess. Wheels wants to sell you this new pickup?"

"Sure. He's your friend. I was going to ask you to go with me, but since you hadn't stopped by to say hello—until last night, that is—I thought maybe you were mad at me or something." Mona's face grew serious. Her eyes held questions that went back years.

"I'm not mad," Raleigh said, running a hand through his hair. "It's just that—well, I'm not supposed to come near you." His stomach churned at the thought that anything could still come between them.

"Wheels said you should drive the pickup to make sure of something or other. He said you'd know what to look for."

"Did you hear what I said? The court ordered me to—" Mona's nodding stopped him.

"I know about that," she said.

"You do?"

"My lawyer explained it last night. But I talked to him on the telephone this morning. He's going to squish it, or squash it, or something." She smiled slyly. "It can't be that important if he can just squish it."

There was the anticipatory smile Raleigh found so intoxicating. Did she enjoy shocking him?

She lowered her head and said, "So, will you?"

Raleigh was speechless, full of emotion.

"Wheels said you would," she repeated.

Raleigh swallowed. "I… I guess I will, but because you asked me, not him."

They stood looking at each other in the half-light of the shed until Raleigh glanced past the open doors. Mona seemed to take this as a signal. "I'm glad," she said. She dipped her chin and turned away.

Raleigh started to speak just as Mona turned and said, "Your dad told me to tell you he'll be home with the kids in an hour. They went for sodas."

Raleigh's eyebrows shot up. "They did? That's not like him."

Mona shrugged. More silence stretched the distance between them. Raleigh felt trapped in the shed.

She's in silhouette with me standing here. I'm so tired of this distance. What do I do? Run up and kiss her?

"I better go," Mona said at last.

It hadn't occurred to him how she'd arrived, or that she might not have a car waiting for her in the driveway. He rubbed his hands on the front of his shirt and started toward her. "Let me walk you out."

They were no more than three steps along when Mona said, "So the answer is yes?"

Oh my God, the answer has always been yes.

"You will teach me to drive?"

Raleigh chuckled to himself. His momentary lapse gave him an excuse to turn to her, to take in the curve of her cheek, the exquisite shape and strength of her nose, her bearing as she walked carefully over the rough ground, holding her skirt. She smiled, awaiting his answer.

"I don't have much choice if you've brought me an apple pie, do I?"

Her smile widened. "I'm going to make you another one, too." Her eyes flashed to his to clear the way for an explanation. "I got so nervous when your dad came to the door that I told him the pie was for him." She began to giggle. "And Michael and Sandra should have some, too—along with you, of course."

"Well, that's fine," said Raleigh.

"But then I said Lauren and Doug should have some, too, and Karen and Peter, too." She snorted, as though realizing for the first time what she had done.

When Raleigh guffawed and said, "Oh my God, you gave away my entire pie!" She clung to his arm—still walking—and doubled over with laughter.

A few moments later, Mona stopped. She seemed to be thinking of something else, something she'd been holding onto. "Is it too far to walk—to my house, I mean?"

Raleigh chuckled. "It's six miles."

Mona winced playfully. "Too far?"

"Maybe. Two or three hours. Something like that."

They began to walk again. When they arrived at the corner of the house, Mona looked at Raleigh. "That's too far, isn't it? I was going to ask you if you wanted to walk me home. I thought your dad could pick you up, or Tony could take you home, or something." Mona stopped, and Raleigh stopped with her. "If not, it's okay. I can call Tony and he'll pick me up. He said to just call whenever I—"

Raleigh's grin seemed to stop her. "We could walk until Dad and the kids come by, then we'll drop them off and I'll take you home."

"That would be wonderful."

Mona walked close to Raleigh to the edge of the drive. A red-tailed hawk screeched in the distance. She stopped and shaded her eyes to see it. "I used to think that was the loneliest sound in the world," she said.

Raleigh soaked in the sight of her as though he were admiring a work of art. He smiled in case the artwork looked back. *You're perfect. No one could be more perfect.*

Together, Raleigh and Mona crossed the drive and stepped onto Thompson Road. He reached for her hand and felt her fingers reach for his.

SHARING 'THE ROAD'

With the advent of eBooks and self-publishing, nearly 6,000 titles are released or re-released each week in the United States. To get a book noticed in this environment is extremely challenging.

I'm determined to do what I can where THOMPSON ROAD *is concerned, and I'm asking you for your help. First, if you enjoyed* THOMPSON ROAD, *would you be so kind as to tell five friends about it? I would take five friends over "five stars" any day. Secondly, I'm happy to appear at book clubs anywhere in the world (via Skype) to discuss the book and answer questions. Finally, I'd like to stay in touch. I reply to all reader emails (although it may take me a day or two to get back to you). Reach me at scottwyattauthor@gmail.com.*

SCOTT WYATT
SAMMAMISH, WA (USA)
SEPTEMBER 1, 2015

ABOUT THE AUTHOR

Scott has written three novels: BEYOND THE SAND CREEK BRIDGE (2012); DIMENSION M (2013); and THOMPSON ROAD (2015). He is a graduate of Stanford University and the University of Washington Law School, and founder of the Companion Flag Project, an international nonprofit designed to increase public awareness of all that human beings have in common in spite of their differences, diversity, and separation. He has four children and six grandchildren, and lives with his wife Rochelle in Washington State.

ACKNOWLEDGMENTS

I take sole credit for the protagonists' names, Raleigh Starr and Mona Garrison. Almost everything else, it seems, was a team effort. My heartfelt thanks go to a great many people, including: Lauren Basson, Gary Bloxham, Brita Butler-Wall, Nicole Caldwell, Barbara Carole, Stephen Cote, Peter Curtis, Mo Diehl, Cheryl Hauser, Scott Jarol, Larry Kirshbaum, Lynn Knight, Doug Margeson, Lise McCleerey, Tom Mooney, Sandy Nygaard, Lisa Poisso, Les Ramsden, and Frank Winningham.

Much of the credit, but none of the blame, for THOMPSON ROAD goes to my creative team at Booktrope Publishing: Erin Curlett, Laura Hidalgo, Stephanie Konat, and Vicki Sly; and to my wonderful beta readers. Thank you!

My family's encouragement and support have once again proven invaluable to me. Thank you to my mother, Betty Wyatt, my sister, Christine Wyatt, and to my children, to whom this book is dedicated.

The largest thanks goes to my wife Rochelle, for her constant love, good humor, and support.

A READER BONUS:

CHAPTER ONE OF

BEYOND THE SAND CREEK BRIDGE

KWANGCHOW, CHINA

1882

MEI-YIN STOOD SHIVERING beneath an umbrella of bamboo and oiled paper. The rain-soaked blanket that she clutched in front of her neck sagged over her narrow shoulders and threw its excess to the ground in deep muddy folds. Her aunt, Lai-Ping, stepped out from the cover of the umbrella holding a candle that burned feebly in the bottom of a tin cup. She knocked on the door of the dark house then stepped back. Neither woman moved. The stench of night soil—human waste left in buckets on doorsteps up and down the crowded alley, to be collected before dawn and taken to fertilize the fields outside Kwangchow—was unusually strong. There was no wind to temper it.

Her aunt did not turn, nor utter a word. Despite the near silence in the deserted alley—all she could hear was a chorus of drips from the eaves all around them—and the more perfect silence of the house, her aunt seemed certain her three reserved and evenly spaced taps upon the brightly painted door were adequate. Mei-Yin wasn't so sure. Two minutes passed. The rain began to fall heavily again, and as the women listened they could hear a great downpour approaching, dancing raucously over the tiled rooftops. Mei Yin reminded herself to breathe. She watched as Lai-Ping's robe grew black with rain, and by the time the door opened, spears of wet hair were clinging to her aunt's throat and broad forehead.

A plump, gray-haired woman with one eye closed sidled into the doorway. Her face was puffy, marked by sleep. She wore a white mourning robe, loosely tied over a heavily embroidered sleeping gown, and carried in her right hand a white candle, its flame flickering furiously as she pushed it forward. "Who goes there?" she croaked. Mei-Yin, who had been awake for hours, was startled by her harsh tone. "Lai-Ping, is that you?" The woman's teeth were as black as the shadows in the room behind her.

"It is I, Jong Suk-Wah."

"What are you doing here?" Suk-Wah thrust the candle in Mei-Yin's direction. "And who is this?"

Mei-Yin felt her heart sink. She willed it to rise up and beat again, her breath to return. "I am Mei-Yin," she tried to say, but Lai-Ping stopped her with a sidelong glance and a tilt of her head, as if to say, "Remember what I said."

"This is Mei-Yin," her aunt said. "She is the firstborn of my youngest sister. I have told you about her. She is the beautiful one."

The householder made a halfhearted attempt to examine the girl. Mei-Yin shrank back then caught herself and inched forward into the circle of light, her eyes lowered respectfully. "The firstborn of your youngest sister," the householder mumbled. "I do not know this girl." She seemed about to ask Lai-Ping for more information when she remembered herself. "It's raining. Forgive me, Lai-Ping. Come in, come in. Both of you. You're soaking!"

She led them into a small room ringed by faint, quivering shadows. In the corner, near an arched passageway, a brazier burned low. Mei-Yin removed the blanket from her shoulders. The householder took it and pointed them toward two large plaited mats covering the floor of pressed earth. She placed her white candle on a table beside the doorway. Three low wooden stools were brought out from a back room. "I am a poor hostess," Suk-Wah moaned, shaking her head. She set another white candle on the table and lit it with the flame of the first. She took the tin cup from Lai-Ping and blew out its candle. "I will make tea."

Mei-Yin sat quickly on the stool placed to the left of the two remaining, as etiquette required, and began to look around. *So this is Suk-Wah's home,* she thought. *How odd that I haven't been here before.*

Suk-Wah and Lai-Ping had been friends for more than forty years. Mei-Yin had heard her aunt speak of the widow Jong Suk-Wah countless times. Seeing the old woman now, and sitting in her home, it was all just as she'd imagined. She felt as though she, too, had known Suk-Wah for years.

In the undulating candlelight, Mei-Yin spotted a painting of the God of Wealth hanging near the doorway. It was identical to the one that hung in her father's house—last year's standard. In the opposite corner of the room, on a low, round rattan table, were the stunted remnants of four white candles, a wilted chrysanthemum, a bowl of fruit, and two incense trays, meticulously arranged around a framed portrait of a young man. *Suk-Wah's son, Gok-Wing, was quite handsome,* thought Mei-Yin. *This is as Lai-Ping has told me. I'm sure this shrine does not go unnoticed in heaven.* She looked away the moment Suk-Wah entered the room.

"Your grief and kindness are well met," whispered Lai-Ping, receiving with both hands a porcelain bowl of steaming tea from her friend. Lai-Ping set the bowl on the grass mat in front of her, placed her hands in her sleeves, and did not speak again until Suk-Wah had served Mei-Yin and was settled on her stool. Lai-Ping bowed her head. She took up her tea, sipped it, and said, "This is the rose bud and orange spice tea I brought to you last week."

"Yes," replied Suk-Wah slowly. "There is none more delicious."

A soft hissing arose as embers in the brazier shifted. Mei-Yin felt the weight of each passing second. She was sure these two older women were prone to sit in long, companionable silences. *Can there be any doubt that my father has discovered me gone by now? Hurry, Lai-Ping! Please! Ask her!*

Lai-Ping glanced at her niece and turned to face Suk-Wah. She drew a long breath. "I seem to remember that your son Gok-Wing was under contract with the House of Huang before he died, to return to America, the land we call Gold Mountain."

Mei-Yin shuddered. She stared through the ornamental grate of the brazier at the languid glowing flame. The House of Huang was among the leading trading houses in Kwangchow, but it had acquired most of its reputation and wealth serving as middleman for foreign shippers in the coolie trade, or as agent for British companies importing

Indian opium through the southern treaty ports after China's defeat in the Opium Wars. Following gold discoveries in California, the House of Huang had turned its attention to the demand for cheap foreign labor to work the placer mines, and, years later, to build the great American railroads. It contracted with American companies and labor purveyors, promising to fill their quotas—and the holds of their ships—with Chinese men, men who thought of themselves not as "Chinese" but as "sons of Han," or "Tang people."

Once under contract, a son of Han was no longer his own man, but the "stock in trade" of the House of Huang. Mei-Yin had heard stories of cruelty and mistreatment visited on men who failed to honor their agreements with the House of Huang.

Suk-Wah's shock at the mention of her son's name within a week of his death was not lost in the dim light. The shape of her eyes made it plain she was no longer half-asleep. "Yes." She glanced at Mei-Yin, then back. "Why do you ask this, Lai-Ping?"

"And the ship that was to transport him? Was it the *China Sea,* the American vessel that lies at the quay as we speak?"

"Yes, I think so. The *China Sea*. How did you . . . ? He was to depart tomor—No, it's after midnight, isn't it? He was to leave today. Today was the—"

"Today then," snapped Lai-Ping. Suk-Wah froze. Mei-Yin was sure she was preparing to cry over such talk of her son when Lai-Ping changed her tone and spoke quickly and preemptively. "What time today, Suk-Wah?"

"I don't know these things. Why do you ask me such things?" She turned to face Mei-Yin again, her eyes pleading. "My son is only just dead."

Mei-Yin bowed her head and nodded. She imagined Gok-Wing's limp body being pulled from the Pearl River. He'd been fishing with a friend. Their boat overturned. He couldn't make it to shore.

Mei-Yin pushed the dreadful image out of her mind. *Stop it! You weren't there. You don't know anything about it.* She pressed her lips together.

A silence descended upon the room. *The ship will be leaving any minute,* Mei-Yin realized, looking up quickly. *Oh, Lai-Ping. Perhaps it's left already. Perhaps it's too late for this plan of yours.* She moved her hand toward her aunt but did not touch her. Lai-Ping seemed determined to ignore her. The gray-haired woman had fixed her gaze on Suk-Wah. Lai-Ping seemed to be bearing down on her, so unmercifully, in fact, that Mei-Yin found herself glancing across at the old woman to see what effect this was having. She watched Suk-Wah raise a trembling cup of tea to her lips. Mei-Yin bowed her head again, swallowing back some of her impatience. *On the other hand, it's still dark. Perhaps, if Suk-Wah will agree, there is time.*

"There is a favor I must ask of you," said Lai-Ping. Her voice was firm and unfriendly. Mei-Yin could not help thinking how terrible it was to be making so little room for the other's grief. But then she considered their long friendship, all they had been through, the grief they had known together in these difficult times, and realized that Lai-Ping's way was direct, not inconsistent with compassion. "It concerns the girl. She is a virgin and is promised to a sojourner. What is his name, child?"

Mei-Yin started. "Hok-L—"

"Promised?" interrupted Suk-Wah. "I assume you mean their fathers have arranged a marriage?"

"No," answered Lai-Ping flatly. "Not in the traditional sense. His name, dear?"

"Hok-Ling."

"Yes. Hok-Ling. His father was the fish vendor who for many years sold live eel and carp near the Flowery Pagoda. Do you remember him, Suk-Wah? He was dark and wiry, with a dirty pigtail, but his barrels were always clean and freshly painted yellow, black, and red." Suk-Wah shook her head vacantly.

Lai-Ping waved her hand in the air. "Well, never mind about him. He's old now, and wealthy in his years. But his third-born son, Hok-Ling, is away to the Gold Mountain, just as your son might have been had Heaven not unexpectedly thrown open its doors to him. It's been more than the three years, and the man-child has not returned to Kwangchow. Mei-Yin's father has received no word concerning him."

"*Her* father?" asked Suk-Wah, trying to catch up. "Do you mean *his* father?"

"No. Let me explain, though we have little time. Hok-Ling and Mei-Yin have known each other since childhood. He attended school near her father's house and in their youth there were not hairs enough on a pig to count the half-truths they told or the artifices they employed to ensure meeting at one place or another. After his eighth year of education he was chosen for the civil service examinations, but the famine hit that spring, and his mother was taken ill. He was forced by circumstance to forgo the examinations.

"When Mei-Yin was old enough to bear sons, Yeung Men-Hoi, the husband of my sister, who, as I've told you before, is a man of evil destiny, threatened to sell his daughter on the street. Many, many times he threatened, for he recognized a price in gold for one so beautiful. Twice he brought home drunken men from the teahouses, men who reached through their robes to pull up their girdles and put on important faces and called out, "We are here to see this treasure your husband brags about!" But each time my sister refused to let them see her, and railed openly against her husband. For this, while the men watched dumbly, she received his hand. Twice she has picked up teeth in the door yard, but, as you see, Mei-Yin is here. She has not been sold as a concubine.

"Four autumns ago, the man-child Hok-Ling brought baskets of oranges and eggs, and two handsome carp, and he presented them with a sincere blessing to Mei-Yin's father. After he made the proper apologies for the absence of his own father, who was ill, he begged permission to step into the street and speak frankly to Men-Hoi on a matter of great importance." Lai-Ping leaned forward a little. "It may be supposed," she added confidentially, "that Mei-Yin's father did not see Hok-Ling make eye contact with the blushing girl as they passed out of the house. But my sister? Do you think she is capable of missing such a thing?"

Mei-Yin remembered a kiss stolen in the twilight of a summer's eve near the home of Hok-Ling's father. Hok-Ling was sixteen then. He kissed her and then, holding her shoulders, stared intently into her eyes and said, "I wish to be with you always, Mei-Yin. I will never be satisfied with anyone else." And it was exactly so for her then, although she did not say it. Would she feel the same now? Would he?

"It was then Hok-Ling persuaded Men-Hoi to enter into a solemn agreement. In exchange for the promise of his daughter, Hok-Ling would contract with the House of Huang to sojourn three years on the Gold Mountain, there to work on the American railroads. He would receive the customary daily wage of one silver dollar, and, as the men lived in camps along the route and could live cheaply, he would be able to return a large portion, perhaps as much as two-thirds of this amount, to Kwangchow. It was agreed that one-half would be paid directly to Men-Hoi."

Lai-Ping stopped. She picked up her tea and sipped it, while her eyes, still and dark, held the balance of her story above the steaming liquid. She swallowed, licked her lips, and her brows shot up, involuntarily signaling once again her approval of the drink.

It was all Mei-Yin could do to hold her tongue. Was it not in her nature to speak freely on matters of importance? And here, after all, was the picture of her life being drawn in words. Slow words. Unnecessary words. Wasn't *she* the one to do this? But she bit her lip, remembering her aunt's stern warning: "When we arrive, you will remain still. Do not interrupt. Leave everything in my hands."

"You see," Lai-Ping finally continued, scrutinizing the dark specks at the bottom of her bowl, "half the money was to be Men-Hoi's, to do with as he pleased. This was his requital. The other half, however, he was to hold in safekeeping until Hok-Ling returned. This would be held as a dowry, for it was agreed that when Hok-Ling returned to take the girl from Men-Hoi, not a penny more would change hands between them. Such was their agreement.

"But," Lai-Ping added, looking into Suk-Wah's eyes, "Yeung Men-Hoi is not an honorable man. You know this, Suk-Wah. His words are—how should I say?—empty and vile." She lowered the bowl to the ground. "And now, dear, I must speak very quickly.

"The man-child has not returned from the Gold Mountain, although the three years of his contract ended many months ago. There is still some money paid out on his account at the House of Huang, but it is a fraction of what it was before. It can be assumed he is alive. Perhaps he is ill or injured, or in some extremity. We do not know. No one has heard from him or about him. Since this is all in the hands of the gods, it is not something to worry about. But, unfortunately, there is more. You see, my sister's husband, Men-Hoi, arrived home only a few hours ago this very night and announced to my sister that he had just lost Mei-Yin at the mahjong table."

Suk-Wah gasped. She covered her mouth and looked at Mei-Yin across the new distance created by her pity. Mei-Yin felt the sting of tears. Suk-Wah turned back to her friend, disbelieving.

Lai-Ping nodded. "He has instructed my sister to collect Mei-Yin's things and make ready to deliver her over to a water carrier at the hour of sunrise. When Men-Hoi went into the street to relieve himself, Mei-Yin fled the house at once and came straightaway to my door. My sister could not come, you see, for her feet were poorly bound all those years ago, and she suffers greatly. It is for this reason that she refused to have any of her daughters' feet bound. But never mind . . . we have come here, for the gods have instructed me to ask a favor of you."

Mei-Yin's frightened eyes swung to Suk-Wah.

"I don't understand. What favor could I do?"

"It is this, gracious lady. Give my luckless niece the papers that Gok-Wing received from the House of Huang, those that authorize him to board the *China Sea* and return to America. Also, bring out a suit of his clothing and his hat. Mei-Yin must go in his place. We must leave at once—do you see? For the ship will sail with the first tide." Lai-Ping paused. "Why do you look at me this way, Suk-Wah? There is no other way."

Suk-Wah's mouth had fallen open. Then her lips began to move around words that she had no breath to utter.

Mei-Yin shifted forward and went to her knees. She extended her arm, preparing to appeal to Suk-Wah, but Lai-Ping once again checked her, lifting a finger and shaking her head sternly. She cleared her throat again as if to remind Mei-Yin of her earlier warning.

"What you ask is impossible!" cried Suk-Wah. "It's out of the question!"

"We will bind her bosom, of course." Lai-Ping said, giving no sign of having heard Suk-Wah. "I have given her a small amount of money, one and a half *tael*. It will not be easy for her. How could it be? But I believe she will manage. When she arrives in San Francisco, she will go to the home of Cheng Tien, the son of Cheng Xio Ping, the barber. He is a friend of mine. He will help her find Hok-Ling."

Suk-Wah wailed softly, "What in the world are you talking about? Do you even know what you're asking?"

"She is my niece. I told you that."

"Yes, what about—"

Suddenly, Lai-Ping lunged forward and took hold of Suk-Wah's shoulders. *"Shhh! What's that?"* With her finger pressed to her lips, she turned toward the door. Mei-Yin had heard it, too, and her heart sank momentarily, then rose up again, flailing in her chest. *It's him! He's found us!*

The noise grew louder. They could make out the pounding of horses—two or three—galloping over the muddy road, splashing through puddles. The sounds grew louder still, and the sharp jangling and squeaking of bridles and saddles rose up in a sharp crescendo. At the point of its most jarring effect inside the small room, the noise began to fade as quickly as it had arisen. A few moments later, it was a distant rumble and thrum in the night. Lai-Ping sat back. "It's nothing," she sighed. "Forgive me, Suk-Wah, but, you see, Mei-Yin is in great danger. We must go quickly."

Suk-Wah looked at both women, frightened. "But if the House of Huang were to find out—"

"If you are asked, Gok-Wing's papers were stolen. Mei-Yin is prepared to confess that she acquired them from a thief. It is she who will be punished, not you."

Yes, thought Mei-Yin, her heart racing. *I will. But I can't stay here. I must get to the Gold Mountain. I must try to find him. I don't care what happens. I have at least to try.* When Suk-Wah saw the determination and courage in Mei-Yin's eyes she turned away at once.

"What about the man, Lai-Ping? The husband of your sister? What you ask me to do, I cannot, for it would bring shame to him. I cannot cause a man, even such a one as Yeung Men-Hoi, to lose face."

"You won't," replied Lai-Ping. "Surely you can see that he has brought dishonor upon his own name, and that of his family and ancestors. He has suffered the loss of face already, and those who dwell in the house of his ancestors will no doubt suffer by the same token. He is beset by *gui,* evil spirits." It went without saying Men-Hoi was in danger of never gaining complete redemption, for the solemn agreement that he had made with the man-child Hok-Ling, and his failure to keep it, were facts widely known. The sojourner's money had been squandered. "He has spent the money on prostitutes and opium," Lai-Ping went on.

"We have talked about this before, Suk-Wah. There are so many good and reasonable, hard-working men. But he is not one of them."

Lai-Ping turned and stared blankly at Mei-Yin, as though some new thought were just forming in her mind. "She *must* go in Gok-Wing's place. You have heard of the Chinese Exclusion Act, the law passed by the American government? For the next ten years, all Tang people are forbidden from immigrating to the Gold Mountain to work. A single exception has been made for laborers like Gok-Wing, who have already been there, and who were there before the eleventh month of their year 1880. His documents are proof of this. Were this not the case, I would not have come."

Suk-Wah frowned. "Still, Lai-Ping, I could never . . . I must consult a fortune-teller before considering this."

"Forgive me, gracious lady," interrupted Mei-Yin, unable to hold back any longer. "There is also the matter of the advance."

"Mei-Yin!" snapped Lai-Ping.

"The *what*?" cried Suk-Wah. "What are you talking about? What advance?" The old woman turned to her friend. "What is she talking about, Lai-Ping?"

Mei-Yin didn't wait. She leaned toward Suk-Wah and fixed her eyes on the collar of the white mourning robe. "Surely, my lady, you are aware that your son received fifteen silver dollars when he contracted with the House of Huang? It is called 'the advance.' It is the same amount paid by all of the great houses of the Crown Colony, when men are hired for the demon companies in America."

"Oh, *that*," croaked Suk-Wah, letting a little relieved smile bend her eyes. "Yes, yes. We received that. But that was—"

"Why, don't you know? You must repay—"

Mei-Yin stopped. *Has it really come to this? Look at her. The poor, dear woman. What must she think of me? How selfish I am! How unwomanly, and in the hour of her grieving.*

Washing over these thoughts, however, she began to hear the echo of her mother's voice, the choked words that had come to her through the darkness of shattered sleep only hours before. "Daughter, listen! I have tried to protect you, but there is no more I can do. Do you understand? You are old enough to bear sons, and your father has spoken. He is a man . . . my husband . . . and I must obey him. If you are to find safety, you must act for yourself."

And she remembered Lai-Ping's words, spoken to her two hours later as she sat, exhausted and wet, at Lai-Ping's table. "Your mother and I have lived all these years in fear of only one thing, Mei-Yin, that one day you would be harmed by a man. That a man—I presumed it would be your father—would dominate you and control you and break your unusual spirit. I cannot stand the thought of this. I cannot stand the power that men have when it is used in disregard of a woman's life, of her well-being. A mahjong game. I hate this man! Go to the Gold Mountain, child. There, at least, a woman is not a man's property. There, you can find safety and comfort. Be free, child, and you will find your own happiness. This is your destiny. I'm sure of it."

Mei-Yin turned partway toward this powerful, independent woman who had been her favorite aunt for as long as she could remember. Lai-Ping sat with eyes closed. *And to think I have questioned the source of my spirit and independence. Who is here with me? Who is trying to save me now, when my father has spoken?*

It would be months before Mei-Yin, reliving this anguished night, would realize that neither her mother nor Lai-Ping had mentioned Hok-Ling. "Be free. Find your happiness," is what they said, the two women who loved her most.

Mei-Yin turned and began to search the dimly lit face of Suk-Wah. "Kind lady, you must refund this money if Jong Gok-Wing does not board the ship this morning. If his name is not crossed off. It is an advance against wages, you see? It is paid initially by the House of Huang, in addition to the cost of passage to Gold Mountain. The House of Huang is reimbursed by the American labor agents for each man who reports to the ship, as promised. Later, the money is deducted from each man's wages on Gold Mountain. In this way, both the House of Huang and the demon company are reimbursed in full. Only the man's wages are advanced. Hok-Ling called it a 'credit-ticket system' or something like that. In any event, if Gok-Wing does not board the ship, the House of Huang will demand repayment."

"How can this be?" cried Suk-Wah. "Are you absolutely sure of this, child?"

Mei-Yin nodded. Not only did Hok-Ling explain this arrangement to her but she had heard the same from girlfriends whose fathers and brothers had gone off to work on Gold Mountain. Suk-Wah lowered her eyes, and when she looked up again, turning first to Mei-Yin and then to Lai-Ping, her mouth formed a terrible smile. "I cannot repay this." She pressed her right hand to her forehead and began to rock gently back and forth. "I cannot repay this," she sobbed. "I cannot. I cannot."

Mei-Yin and Lai-Ping sat with Suk-Wah without speaking. After several minutes had passed, Mei-Yin watched her aunt extend her hands to take up her tea again.

Suk-Wah cried into the night, "I have spent this money for a monument . . . a beautiful monument to be placed near the wall of the city in honor of my son. Don't you see? It's gone!"

Urgently, Mei-Yin reached for the woman's hand. "Let me go then, gracious lady! Let me go! I will board the ship and see that your son's name is crossed off the list!"

MORE GREAT READS FROM BOOKTROPE

***Earth* by Caroline Allen** (Literary Fiction) In rural Missouri in the 1970s, thirteen-year-old Pearl Swinton has just had her first mystical vision. There is no place for Pearl's "gift" in the bloody reality of subsistence farming and rural poverty, so Pearl must find her own way. Told with fierce lyricism, Earth is a story about the importance of finding one's sense of self in dire circumstances and against the odds.

***Our Orbit* by Anesa Miller** (Literary Fiction) Four children from the poor side of town are separated after their mother's untimely death and their father's arrest for anti-government activity. The youngest girl quickly comes to love her foster family, but tensions escalate over conflicting religious views.

***The Damnable Legacy* by G. Elizabeth Kretchmer** (Literary Fiction) A gripping novel about love, survival, and attachment. Set largely in Alaska and narrated from the afterlife, it asks how far we should go to achieve our goals-- and at what cost.

***The Garden of Unfortunate Souls* by Eddie Mark** (Literary Fiction) In 1980s Buffalo, New York, two African American families are altered forever after the mayor's son crashes into the home of an eccentric single mother in one of the city's most notorious neighborhoods.

***The To-Do List* by JC Miller** (Literary Fiction) Ginny Cooper's secret online obsession sets in motion a darkly comic misadventure.

***To The Promised Land* by Michael Boylan** (Literary Fiction) *To The Promised Land* addresses the question: are there limits to forgiveness (personal, business, political)?